Lust at First Bite
Sexy Vampire Short Stories

Look out for other Black Lace short fiction collections

Already Published: *Wicked Words 1–10, Sex in the Office, Sex on Holiday, Sex and the Sportsclub, Sex on the Move, Sex in Uniform, Sex in the Kitchen, Sex and Music, Sex and Shopping, Sex in Public, Sex with Strangers, Love on the Dark Side (Paranormal Erotica).*

Paranormal erotic romance novella collections:
Lust Bites
Possession
Magic and Desire
Enchanted

Lust at First Bite
Sexy Vampire Short Stories
Edited by Lindsay Gordon

BL

This book is a work of fiction. In real life, make sure
you practise safe, sane and consensual sex.

Published by Black Lace 2008

2 4 6 8 10 9 7 5 3 1

First published in Great Britain in 2008 by Black Lace, Virgin Books, Random House,
20 Vauxhall Bridge Road, London SW1V 2SA
www.black-lace-books.com/www.virginbooks.com/www.rbooks.co.uk

Addresses for companies within The Random House Group Limited can be found at:
www.randomhouse.co.uk/offices.htm

The Random House Group Limited Reg. No. 954009

Distributed in the USA by Macmillan, 175 Fifth Avenue, New York, NY 10010, USA

A CIP catalogue record for this book is available from the British Library

ISBN 9780352345066

The Random House Group Limited supports The Forest Stewardship Council [FSC], the leading
international forest certification organisation. All our titles that are printed on Greenpeace-
approved FSC-certified paper carry the FSC logo. Our paper procurement policy can be found at
www.rbooks.co.uk/environment

Printed and bound in Great Britain by CPI Bookmarque

Contents

Playing
Charlotte Stein

He says in that purring pleasing chocolate voice: 'Let's play that game.'

And of course I feign ignorance. It's no fun if you don't feign ignorance. I frown and snort and bat at him, and ask what game. As though we never play and he's just a fool who should stop wasting my time really.

We wrestle, briefly: him over me, trying to get past the props and cages I make of my arms. He snaps – clack, clack, clack – at my throat, but he's miles away. He also knows to rein himself in when I bare my own teeth, silently, hardly threatening. But baring my teeth in that way is only an illusion of hardly threatening. He knows what it means really.

Be so very careful of my deadly smile, my dear.

'You know which game, tease,' he says, finally. His eyes are that flat pale vampire no-colour, but I can read him anyway. It's in the snapping and the exposing of his throat and the flush to his skin.

He's showing his blood to me, directly and indirectly, and it's almost as arousing as his warm solid body rocking against mine.

'You've been thinking of it since last time,' I tell him, but without accusation. My sex is molten and my nipples are pinpricks and accusations don't lead to where both parts of my body want to go.

I flick my tongue over his mouth when it gets too close and he responds unthinking and instinctive: he licks at me back. Our tongues occasionally meet, or flutter over the curl of a lip or the curve of a jaw, but mostly it's just an excuse to urge ourselves closer together, get more into that wet brief contact.

He loves licking. He adores tasting. The more he can get into his mouth, the better he likes it – oh, how often I am pleased that the man I chose has such an oral fixation! He was made to be a vampire really. He likes me completely exposed and all in his mouth at once, my pussy spread for the enjoyment of his taste buds.

One of the reasons I love being a vampire, he once said to me, is because everything tastes more alive.

And arousing.

I never loved a cock in my mouth before; I love it now. I love the soft hard feel of it, the taste of it, like salt sweet candy. I love that first little hint of how aroused I'm making him, and his words ('Oh baby, you're so good at this!') as evidence of such leaks into my hungry mouth.

The sounds he makes when he tastes me: all those low vibrating moans. All the things he's learned to make me juicier, wetter, make me cream myself for his delectation. He knows that if he just barely circles the tip of my clit with his little pointed tongue, I'll grow gradually slicker and slicker until I come in a flood.

It's making my clit ache now just thinking about it, so I cheat and slip my hand into my panties.

Of course it gives him the upper hand. But really it only adds to the pleasure I'm bringing myself to have him pin my other hand to the bed.

'Let's just fuck real fast and dirty,' I say. 'I'm gonna come in about a second anyway.'

'Little sluts don't get their own way. I want to play the game,' he replies, but his voice is hoarse. 'You can keep fucking yourself while we play though – God yeah. That would be perrr-fect.'

He leans into me and I sigh into his mouth as I gather his meaning. I have to slide my fingers into my pussy and away from my clit to stave off orgasm.

'So I'm the helpless *masturbating* victim, is that it? You're the big bad dirty vampire who catches me exploring my tight little virgin slit, right?'

'I am a very very dirty vampire.'

'I know, love.'

'So we can, then? Play, I mean.'

'I want you to find me just as I'm coming. I want you to plunder me, and seek out my secret desires, and so forth.'

'Tell you I'm your bonded soul mate . . .'

'. . . and so must fuck me to within an inch of my life.'

'Not to mention all the other perverted sex acts life-soul-bonded mates need to perform.'

'It just wouldn't be destiny – oh God that's so good – without perverted sex acts.'

And then he's gone, whisper quick. It still turns me on, after all these years. Who wouldn't be turned on by such speed and strength and agility? Let's face it, the allure of the vampire is at least partially built around the idea of their power, and what that power might be like . . . in the bedroom. All that darkness, all that mouthing and sucking and stamina.

It was me who turned him into what he is now, but the idea is still like a siren's song. He was beautiful in life; he is something sort of painful to look at in death.

Though technically, it's not really death.

All the blood swelling my clit, the same making that ridge inside his jeans, the sound of our hearts pounding in each other's ears ... we are definitely alive. It wouldn't be half so sweet if we weren't. Though the other half is sweet because of what we are.

I remember the first time we had sex after I had turned him. At first he was tender and sore and almost bitter, because of course he hadn't realised how hard turning could be. But then things settled, and his bruises and tenderness melted away and left behind what it always does: rampant, torturous desire.

For both blood and sex.

At first he hadn't been able to cope with it. I'd come home and find him stretching his tether to the bathtub, him inside, shaking and freaking out in icy water. Because he was so hot, so very hot, God please help me, Jin.

So I did help him. I helped him with everything: first with feeding, and then with that bright burning lust.

However, I didn't let him fuck me for a long long time. You can't, you see. If you let a newbie fuck you he or she is likely to tear you apart. You have to start slow and I did. I told him to masturbate for me to begin with and, oh, he raged at me. How dare I keep him tied up like this and deny him my mouth, my hands, my sex? What a bitch I was, how he hated me.

But he took his cock in his hand and jerked himself off anyway.

It disturbed him brutally when his eyes changed and his teeth emerged just as he climaxed. Even more so that he then tried to eat the pillow. But it at least made things clear to him: that's what happens when you come. The urge is to bite, immediately.

And so we progressed, slowly. I'd stand over him; at first half dressed, then the next time almost naked, then naked. Over time he began to control himself better; he'd fuck himself slower and ease into the transformation, holding himself on

4

the edge of orgasm with those little pointed fangs drawn – so lovely.

Once he learned not to bite the pillow or himself, I let him progress to oils. I would allow him to slick oil all over his glorious body, and all over his cock, and then would wait to see if he could control himself with a slippery fist like my slippery pussy. We feel every new layer of sensation so acutely that just the difference between slick and not slick can mean we bite or don't.

But he passed, that time. He passed quivering like a plucked wire and gasping that he wanted to be inside me. So badly, oh God, so badly.

Sometimes he would beg me from his room. I would hear him in there, doing himself, gasping for me to let him taste my pussy. Oh, the poetry that came out of his mouth in honour of my pussy! How he could smell it blooming and luscious, how he could imagine the taste of my honey, how he knew I ached for him too because he could almost hear my pussy ripening for him.

He had said to me: *You loved that first fuck we had – it's why you decided to turn me, right? It wasn't me begging before you got my pants around my thighs, it was that fuck.*

He's partly right. Mostly it was because he had gasped: *This is the hottest thing that's ever happened to me*, with my teeth still in his neck. So I suppose it's linked to sex. It was the way he put his hand in my hair and urged me on as though I was actually giving him head, and his other hand pressing at his groin as though he just couldn't help himself.

I remember his wondering words, frightened but thrilled through with desire: *Are you going to kill me? Are you? Jesus. I'm gonna be killed by a vampire. Unless you make me what you are, oh please make me what you are, oh man, this is so hot . . .*

And we all know how that ended.

I give up thrusting my fingers into myself, and find my clit. It's as stiff as anything and responds immediately to my stroking fingers, but even more so when I push the strap of my nightie down and expose one breast, then gently pinch and rub my nipple.

I make a series of high short cries of pleasure – thinking of my pretend innocence – while at the same time I remember the rough feel of his rudely pushed down jeans against my inner thighs, his thick cock surging inside me, surging because my pointed teeth and my roughness had made him so hot.

What a little trickster he was. What a wicked boy.

But he wasn't – and isn't – a boy. He has always been a man, a 35-year-old man. It's just that thirty-five seems like a boy to me. My boy who I gave into not because he had come to the point where he didn't need any more training, but because I wanted him inside me again, desperately, like that time in the parking lot.

The feel of him that first time after I turned him! The low desperate groan he had made as I sank down on his cock, and those eyes, pale and hooded. I remember him murmuring *Yes, take me*, and I had loved him and wanted him so hard for it. It turned that switch in me, the hot little switch of arousal and lust.

He submitted so totally to me. There is always that thin line between training a newbie and sex, because they have to be tied, and they have to submit to your will and do everything you ask. But he enjoyed all of it in a sexual way too.

He liked opening himself to me and obeying, even when he pretended he didn't. As I rode his cock he had turned his face to one side, exposing his throat. And all the while he had whimpered with pleasure, and muttered about how it felt to have me fucking him, and then finally: *Come on, baby, I can't keep it off much longer.*

Oh, I love my blue-eyed vampire boy.

Even when in such agonies of ecstasy, he had thought of me. His big rough thumb had searched out my clit, but I didn't really need it. I was already on the edge and, seeing him biting his lip before twisting and moaning that it was going to be too much, way too much, I should get off him, only made me come harder.

He hadn't bitten me, but he had held his body rigid, and pressed his lips together, and closed his eyes tight against it all. It seemed to go on forever, too, him quivering beneath me, and then finally he had let out a whooshing breath and a series of gasps, and gone limp.

Later, I had let him feed on me. And after, we made love again.

We usually make love again. And again. And again.

Sometimes I want to tell him: *Oh, it's as good for me as it is for you. I wanted you so much, I want you so much, you don't know how long I went without sex.* I envy him a trainer and a companion who gave in to him so soon and continues to do so, because I never had anything like that.

Mine made me work so hard. He made me work for every little scrap until I was sure the blood rage would have been better. He gave me nothing, even though I begged and pleaded, and he made me understand that we can never have anything, because this is how it is for us.

We must control ourselves, at all times.

And so it was a long time between the last sex I had as a human and sex with him.

It won't be long now. Now he's going to come and ravish me. I don't mind which way around we are – him dominating, me dominating, neither of us bothering to be on top – as long as we're bringing each other pleasure. Oh, his first delicious surprise when I had played the victim!

No please, I had whimpered. *Please don't hurt me, Alex*.

And his eyes had flashed bright and hard and, when coming inside me with his teeth in my shoulder, he had jerked all over as though electrocuted. He had petted me afterwards, and soaped my back in the tub, and washed my hair.

Because I am so good to him, my vampire boy. He cooed that to me: *So, so good, to open up to me like that, Jin. My beautiful vampire girl*.

When I suck two fingers into my mouth and transfer the slickness to the taut bud of my nipple, my body arches up off the bed of its own accord.

My clit jumps beneath my messily working fingers and the hot surges of pleasure crystallise into one long bloom of sensation that rolls in waves over me. I moan aloud, 'Oh I'm coming, I'm coming,' because I know it will excite him and then, in the ebbing descent of my orgasm, I pretend I see him in the doorway for the first time.

How shocked I am! How ashamed and frightened! Here I am, this innocent virgin girl, being spied on by a filthy great man! And he's ... He's not quite as he should be. His face – half cut by shadow – looks strange and wild, and his eyes are burning bright holes into me.

He steps forwards, out of the darkness by the half-open door, and light exposes his too pale eyes and his curling upper lip.

'What ... What do you want with me?' I say, revelling in the tremulous sound of my own voice. Lust is making my words fracture, but it sounds as though something else is doing the job: my terrible terrible fear at being approached by this monster!

And he is a monster. When he hears my thin pathetic voice he cocks his head to one side – the consummate predator. His mouth moves in a half-mime of a bite, teeth not quite meeting but giving the faintest impression of what they might do. His small steps roll in a way that I am envious of, like his hips are oiled for stalking.

'I'll call the police!' I cry, and he tilts his head to the other side, still sizing me up. What a tasty morsel I am!

My pussy swells and aches in spite of my innocent self. He'll be able to smell the slick scent of my arousal from over there, and the knowledge makes me adore his restraint. Before today he has fucked me on a train, in bathrooms, in alleys, and all because my scent drove him to it. But in honour of the game, he is a picture of self-control.

He prowls right up to the bed without speaking, and the tension draws itself up as taut as those twanging muscles on the backs of his thighs. I almost feel the dread I would if I were really just an innocent human girl, and I leap up to patter my small useless fists against his still clothed chest.

I can't remember ever being as weak as I'm pretending to be, and there's something undeniably electric about it. Not in my submission exactly, but in his strange immoveable calm, his uninterest in my struggles, his predatory composure. There is something completely inhuman about his eyes and his always half-biting mouth and it frightens and thrills me.

Was this what it was like for him? God, how awful I must have seemed, how alien. How lovely, too. Like discovering that we're really not alone on this planet but here, here is another species from dreams and myth, living right alongside us.

I understand what he meant by that, now.

He grabs my flailing fists and then throws me back onto the bed. Of course I am usually far, far faster than him – if I were to do the same thing to him, I would be able to throw him back and leap onto him in the same movement, and before he hit the mattress – but it's so fun to play! The hints of his weaknesses and his errors – I would have most likely had time to squirm away across the bed – just seem to make it even better.

I do squirm back, but I also allow him enough time to smack one hand into the meat of my thigh like a snake striking, and then I squeal as only humans can.

'No, please!' I say, and this time I see his expression sag, just a little. I like what it sags into, too: tenderness towards me, and concern, and bare as brass lust. He licks his lips almost nervously, before ever so slowly dragging me back, back across the bed towards him.

Just the one hand, on my thigh.

Of course I struggle. What self-respecting innocent victim wouldn't? He snarls and it pumps a surge of desire through me hot enough to sort of break character – I urge my hips up at him. However, this can't really be counted as a spoiling of the game, since most humans can rarely contain themselves either.

Sometimes their squirming and squealing too closely resembles desire to be anything but, though they can hardly be blamed. We always smell so good, and lure them in like little silly fishes to our sharp as a razor hook.

'Oh don't, don't,' I say, and now he is delighting in it. His mouth has turned up at the corners, and he's squeezing my plump thigh, and he looks good enough to eat.

He looks good enough to eat me.

I try to sit up again and manage to grab a hold of his shirt. My two selves war briefly, and my intention – to rip the material – wins out against the little innocent ingénue and her desire only to hurt him. Both meet very nicely, however; the shirt tears completely from one of his shoulders, exposing his lovely golden flesh.

He grits his teeth then, in real anger. His favourite shirt! And when he takes hold of the hand that's still clawing at him, he bends the wrist so that there's a flare of pain. My instinct is immediately to hurt him back, but I fight it, and give him a little whimper instead. A little frustrated and frightened 'Aha'.

He likes that very much it seems. He groans in resignation, yanks me to him by that one still jangling wrist and clamps his mouth to my throat.

I've always loved him feeding from me. He feeds as though I sustain him, as though he belongs to me and I am his salvation. It is never about him controlling me or hurting me; I am the one giving him this bliss. Other vampires do not behave in the same way when biting one of their own kind; they claw and inflict pain and assert themselves over each other.

I love him for being different.

When he finally wrenches himself away I am limp and melting away on a sea of sensation: the pricking and pulling of the tender skin at my throat, the blooming fullness between my thighs, the feel of my body flowing into his. I'm utterly boneless in his arms and do nothing while he gasps out the pleasure of his long drink.

His hands roam freely about my body and I mewl to both our delights: 'My father will disown me.'

He laughs low and rich, and looks down at me with his cool eyes and his mouth perversely bloody. 'For only that?' he says. 'But there's so much more I wanted to show you.'

Oh you darling boy!

'After all, I've tasted you. It's only fair that you should taste me. Don't you think?'

I pretend not to know what he means but fizz with the excitement of knowing what he means. 'If I drink your blood, I will be damned for ever!' I say, all wide eyes and trembling lips.

'What makes you think that it's my blood I want you to taste?' he says, and allows a hint of sultry tease to enter his play-roughened voice. At the same time, he unfastens just the top button of his jeans.

I loved this part of the game the last time we played it, because he found it very difficult to keep a straight face. One might think that this would spoil the pretence, but somehow it doesn't. He is my too-eager-to-be-the-serious-one-in-control slut and I adore him for it.

'Whatever can you mean?' I say, and he almost laughs.

'From the looks of what you were doing to yourself in here, you know exactly what I mean. Admit it. You've been waiting for a dark stranger to come here and take over you. That's what you were thinking of while your hand played between your legs. And even now, even after I've shown you what I am and tasted your blood, you long for me.'

'Yessss,' I say, with teeth clenched and body coiling up to his. I have no idea which woman is talking. Later he will be pouty with me for giving in so easily, but I can hardly care.

'You want to be ruined by a monster like me?' His voice is now without laughter. It is tight and vibrating.

'Yes, oh yes.'

'What would your father say if he could see you now, spread out like a slut?'

'I don't care, I don't care.'

'You don't care what I am?'

'No, God help me, no. I burn for you! Make me what you are!'

His eyes flare briefly. 'Spread your legs for me and maybe I will.'

Sensation pulses once between my legs and makes me obey him. I spread them as wide as they will go and crook my knees so that I am completely exposed to him.

'I can smell how wet you are,' he murmurs, and I feel my cheeks heat. I suppose it looks like a blush of shame, and perhaps I am enough into the game that it nearly is. 'And I'm going to have you there. But first you're going to take me in your mouth.'

'Oh, I can't!' I squeal.

'Sluts who spread their legs for strangers can do just about anything,' he replies, and finishes unbuttoning his fly.

By this point I am almost mad to touch myself, or to rub against him, or to drag him down and roll him underneath me, but it's the restraint, you see. The restraint is addictive and I won't deny that it makes the end twice as good.

I can see his hands shaking and his throat working, and he winces when he touches himself, as though just that contact is too much. I realise that I've already had one release of tension so far tonight and it wasn't enough – God knows how he's faring. Badly, if the state of his prick is anything to go by. Free of his jeans it curves almost up to his belly, red and slick at the tip and fat and swollen all the way to the base. He licks at the blood around his mouth and his cock quivers.

The first time he truly breaks character is as he guides my mouth to him, and he whispers to me: 'Go easy.'

Of course I know why. He's going to come at the slightest provocation, and my usual bag of tricks all count as such. He should know that I'm going to be a blundering fool about it, but maybe that will be just as bad.

Either way, I fight the urge to suck him deep into my mouth while licking up every drop of that gleaming fluid at the tip, and instead barely make contact. I take him in, but with just a graze of my lips and my tongue. It's difficult, considering his size, but not impossible.

But then the dark stranger comes back and, oh, I love how he's such a bitch!

He grabs me by the hair, and shakes my head, and growls at me: 'Do it properly. Taste me, little Miss Innocent.'

So I think I will be a bitch, too.

I flick my darkest gaze up at him, and make my mouth a tight little moue, and slide slickly aaa-lll-lll the way down. On the slow pull back up, I let my tongue squirm against his shaft, before dancing over the head. The taste of him sizzles through me immediately, lighting fires, and my teeth try to come out and play for the first time.

Control is easy for me, but not *that* easy.

'Oh God, yes,' he moans, and his head goes back. He's so unable to stop himself that his hand in my hair pushes, urging me to work him.

And I do. It's my pleasure to. I give him long, hard, sucking strokes, just ever so lightly grazing him with my teeth as I do, savouring the flavour and feel of him. I tongue that sweet sensitive spot and his body curls – just before he pushes me away.

When I'm sprawled back on the bed once more, he takes a moment of panting and tugging before launching himself on me.

'So how did it feel?' he asks, with his flickering vampire gaze darting over my face. 'How did it feel to have a cock in your mouth?'

Said cock is sliding against my slippery slit, perfectly. With every bump of his hips, the tip connects with my clit and pleasure shimmies through me.

'Please,' I whimper. 'Please.'

I wiggle my own hips, trying to maintain contact. How I'm not managing it is beyond me, since I am as swollen as he was in my mouth. My clit feels huge and thick, and every time he rubs over it more cream flows from my clenching hungry pussy. How he can resist sliding in I have no idea. His heart is beating like a rabbit's, and his blood is so hot it's burning me through his skin.

'You liked it, didn't you?' he murmurs, tender now. 'You loved it. You want me to take you.'

'Always,' I say. 'Always.'

He has mercy on me then – on both of us. He pushes into me in one smooth stroke, but I hardly get to see his expression, or the lovely arc of his throat, because my back arches of its own accord and I make some inhuman sound. The heat of him flows right through me, igniting every faint nerve ending I have and it's bliss, it's bliss.

As a human, it was never like this: that moment of penetration. But penetration is what we do, it's what we are, and it mingles and messes up to become one long consumption of one another. I eat him up and he pushes his way into me.

I wrap my legs around his waist and pull him even tighter to me – with too much strength for an innocent human, but who could care at this point? I am beyond our game, and tear at his shirt until he is bare to me.

His thrusts are jerky and rapid, but his loss of control makes up for his sloppiness. I love the way he bites his lip, and occasionally bursts out some unintelligible thing, and then his cries, his short breathless cries of pleasure.

'Oh, baby,' he moans. 'Is it that good?'

Because my eyes have changed, and my teeth are sharp. I suppose it is that good, if I'm losing my control.

'Bite me,' he says. 'Bite me, Jin. Give in.'

'I thought I was your innocent girl,' I reply, and he grins as his hips churn, harder now, faster. He knows just the right angle to hit, even when he's reckless and almost lost, and I can feel myself fracturing. I was taught my lessons so well, so brutally, but not enough to withstand this. Not enough for my blue-eyed vampire boy.

'You are,' he says through laughter. 'You are my innocent girl, my badass vampire bitch, my dark stranger, my Jin.'

And then I come, long and shivering right through, and as I do I clasp his throat to my mouth and sink my teeth in. His body immediately goes rigid against mine and his cock jerks inside me once, twice, three times, while all the sounds of his pleasure rush out of him, loud and full of shake and shimmy.

His seed fills my pussy as his blood fills my mouth, and both are ecstasy. He is ecstasy. I may have made him, but he has made me too.

He has made me, my blue-eyed vampire boy, because before him life was all work, work, work, and now life is all about the games we play.

The Blood of the Martyrs

Janine Ashbless

The saint looked no more than four feet tall, but I supposed that had more to do with how he was laid out than his original stature. Underneath an oil painting that depicted him preaching to fishermen, he lay scattered with dingy white plastic roses. The glass panes of his case were dirty and his linen shroud and cap had turned brown. In the odd, dim light of the church of Santi Angeli Custodi his bare skull seemed to wear an inappropriately jaunty grin.

Coming as I do from a vague weddings-and-baptisms-only Anglican background, I was finding Italian Catholicism quite as much a shock to the senses as any Buddhist or Hindu temple. The fake votive candles that lit up at the deposition of a few coins, the High Renaissance oil paintings that belonged in a museum, the Stations of the Cross sculpted in grisly detail, the statues with their bleeding, glowing hearts – the mixture of stately beauty and chintzy tackiness was exotic and heady. Most of all I couldn't get over the display of bodily relics, from tiny crystal caskets containing holy bloodstains to withered arms framed in gold, to full skeletons like the saint before me. In England we keep dead people in churches too; we just don't put them on display.

'Emily?'

The Professor's voice echoed in the empty church. I straightened up from the glass sarcophagus. 'Good morning, Paolo.'

He strode over, his hands in his pockets. Venice in October seemed pleasantly warm to me, but he wore a hat and a long coat over his jacket. No tie, mind, just an open-necked shirt, and he took the hat off as he approached the saint's last mortal remains and crossed himself. 'Good morning, Emily. Have you had a look at the damage yet?'

'I thought I'd wait for you.'

He smiled, nodding. I was only his postgraduate assistant, and I was new to Venice. My Italian was stumbling so we spoke in English. My knowledge of ecclesiastical architecture was twice as good as it was last week and only half as complete as it would be next week. So it would have been presumptuous of me to step beyond the roped-off pews and go poking around before my mentor arrived.

Materials conservation, that's my discipline. To further it I'd come to a city that was literally crumbling into sea.

'I had a look last week, when the call came through,' he said. Paolo Rossini was dark-eyed and greying, every inch an elegantly groomed academic. Only the rigger boots over his casual trousers hinted at a practical capacity. 'This is a serious case of subsidence and will be expensive to deal with. Come on through.' He lifted the rope so I could step under, and we passed into the gloomy area beyond the saint's altar. There was another large altar – wooden not stone this time – against the back wall and, immediately visible, a major problem. The floor here was on the verge of collapse, the multi-hued marble sagging like a sheet. In the corner was a hole in the wall, low down, through which canal water could be seen lapping. I came to an abrupt halt, not liking the idea of getting too close. 'We're sixty centimetres above average water level here,' he remarked from behind me, putting his hand on my bottom and squeezing gently. 'A high tide and . . .'

My heart began to race. 'The pilings have collapsed?' I asked, trying to sound focused. I'm a cautious type usually. I wouldn't describe myself as the kind to get involved with my professor within days of meeting him, especially when that man was happily married and made no secret of it, when he lived in a country that I was only a visitor to, when he was twice my age. Yet, somehow, it had happened. And just his proximity was enough to drive me crazy with desire. I was trying to think only about Venice's wooden foundations but failing miserably.

Paolo's hand slid up and down the jut of my bum cheeks, over the crack. He had this way when we were having sex of wrapping his arm around my bum and squeezing tight – I've never met anyone else who does it, but something about that pressure kicks me straight onto a plateau of arousal, making me spread and gasp. At this moment he was just teasing, but it was having its effect anyway. I felt a hot wetness bloom between my clenched thighs.

'It seems likely.' He put his other hand on my hip. 'Emily, why have you worn this skirt? Is it appropriate wear for a site visit? Are you trying to distract me?'

I was quite proud of the skirt actually; it was knee-length and elegantly cut, very professional, very Italian. But it *was* leather. A sigh escaped my lips as his fingers smoothed across the soft skin. 'Yes, Professor,' I admitted.

'Then this afternoon in my office I will go through your wardrobe and explain exactly what you should and should not wear.' He patted my bum warningly and I knew what he meant. The Professor had it in his head, despite my attempts to enlighten him, that all English girls liked to have their bottoms smacked. He would put me over his knee and tug that tight skirt up to my hips and paddle my upraised cheeks with his bare hand, and then he'd lay me across his big antique desk to fuck me.

The thing is, just the anticipation of that made my panties sodden.

'In the meantime,' he continued in his reasoned, gentle tones, 'since you have lured my attention from the object of our visit, you must make up for it. Get down on your knees, Emily.'

'In here?' I hissed, turning to scan the church. It seemed we had the place to ourselves on this weekday morning, but I was a bit shocked. Paolo was a good Catholic after all.

His handsome face was rueful. 'Already I will have to confess lusting after your wickedness in the House of God. We had better make it worthwhile.' So saying he drew me to the shadow behind an altar pillar and pressed me to my knees on the cold stone. I went down willingly. This wasn't what anyone would call a serious relationship, but it had me under a spell. There was nothing I wanted more than to touch his cock, any time. So even though we were perfectly visible to anyone who might look round the corner, when he unzipped his fly I took his hot, sticky prick in my mouth, sucking away the last vestiges of softness, tasting his salt and his eager musk. I only wished I could feel his lips on my own pussy at the same time. Paolo put his hands on my bobbed hair as if blessing me.

My Italian might be poor, but I could tell for damn sure that as he stiffened and arched and thrust into my mouth, his face transfigured, it was a Hail Mary he was saying over and over under his breath.

Catholics have all the fun.

Afterwards, my lips burning with sin, he pulled me to my feet and smoothed down my messed hair for me. 'You would make a saint transgress,' he murmured.

'Then why stop?' Dizzy with my own need I pressed against him, but he only patted my bottom and laughed.

'Wait. It will be all the better for anticipation, Emily.'

I was nearly panting, but I bit my lip and didn't argue. He was adamant, I knew. He was the one who called the shots and he liked to make me wait. My frustrated dependence on his whim turned both of us on.

Abandoning me, the Professor walked out onto the sagging flagstones, towards the hole in the wall.

'Is that a good idea?' I asked. Back home they would have closed the church to the public and covered everything in scaffolding for a structural flaw even half as obvious. The Professor cast me a look of amusement.

'Hundreds of tonnes of stone have stood here for more than seven centuries. Do you think my weight will make a difference?' He prodded at inner stones of the wall with a trowel he produced from his coat pocket. Chunks of grout fell away. 'Hm. The mortar is very soft in the lower courses here. Rotten. Come on, Emily. What are the conservation priorities?'

I came closer, stepping gingerly, but the bowed slabs beneath my feet did not shift. 'The altar?' I said. 'If they're going to underpin the foundations all this woodwork will need removing while the work is going on. The altar painting ...'

'School of Bellini,' said Paolo dismissively. 'Not a great piece. The altar itself though has historical interest.'

The oil painting in question was rather dark and depicted the Crucifixion. I'd seen so many paintings of the style by this point, with their elaborate faux-classical costumes and their overweight saints bobbing and gesticulating, that I was a bit numb to them. This one was only remarkable for the oddly pale man in the foreground opposite the Virgin and St John. The altar itself was of dark wood gilded in places, carved with Latin script. It towered over our heads. The shifting of the floor had popped some pegged joints though, and boards had slipped.

'It's going to need restoring,' I said approaching for a better look. 'What's the importance?'

'It's dedicated to Sant'Aronne. There, in the picture.'

'I've not heard of him.' The figure was, oddly, wearing a mixture of furs and pseudo-Eastern garb with a turban, despite being as white as sheet beneath it, and the palm of one outstretched hand was dripping blood. 'Was he a leper?'

'Albino, they say.' Paolo folded his arms over his chest, pleased to be able to lecture me. 'He's a local saint, one of many never officially canonised, and in 1969 the Vatican took him off the official calendar. This church used to be called Sant'Aronne before it became the Holy Guardian Angels.'

'I see.' So yes, the city would regard this as part of its heritage. It might be useful when it came to raising funds.

Paolo gestured with his trowel at the painting. 'Aronne, the story goes, was a foreigner who converted in the twelfth century, and ended his life here in Venice. He's supposed to have received the stigmata – though that is disputed of course because he would have predated Saint Francis – and those who touched his wounds would have visions of God. Wishing to become a living martyr, he asked to be immured in a cell and fed only through a slit in the wall until his death.'

'Lovely.' I suppressed a shudder and stooped to pick up a painted board that had fallen away from the altar table. One side was splintered, so I knelt to check where it had come from, and then discovered that down here in the shadows there was a gaping hole in the woodwork against the back wall, invisible because the old wood was as dark as the gap.

'Paolo?'

'What?' He ambled over, grunted, then fished around in his pocket for a torch. The first pass of the beam showed only blackness beyond the broken wood, a deep space.

'This must go under the Chapel of San Bartolomeo, behind that wall,' I said, casting around as if it would help my mental map. 'That's raised above ground level.' For the first time I properly noticed the damp smell that up till now I'd assumed was due to the canal outside.

Paolo shuffled in closer, put his shoulder to the wood and peered along the torch beam. I couldn't see past his head, but he didn't block my view for long. He jerked back, wide-eyed.

'Mother of God!'

'What?'

'Ah. Ah.' He was visibly donning his professional demeanour. 'Take a look, Emily.' He passed me the torch. With some trepidation, I squinted in.

Behind the altar and below ground level was a small low-ceilinged stone chamber. I'd never heard of anyone digging a cellar in Venice and wasn't surprised that this one was flooded with silt. Against the far wall, up to its hips in dried mud, was a corpse. I nearly dropped the torch.

'Oh good God!'

At least, that's what it must have been. It looked like a naked man, and what else but a body could have been down here that long?

'Incredible, isn't it? Mother of God ... And he's incorrupt!' The Professor crossed himself.

I recognised the traditional sign of saintliness. 'They immured Aronne *here*?' I squeaked.

'They built the church over his cell, I suppose.' Impatient, Paolo pushed his head and shoulders in next to mine. 'This is wonderful. Look at the state of preservation!'

I took another hard look. The body was of a gaunt, muscular man. Every rib and every muscle group was visible. His head had fallen forwards on his chest and long white hair draped his face. Even the fluff in the pits of his arms was the colour of tow. Black cobwebs across his shoulders might have been the remains of clothes, but his skin was white, dead white, like slush. 'Saponification of the tissues?' I said huskily. The damp state of the cellar made it possible; water dripped from the ceiling while we watched. Something else had occurred to me though: 'He's chained up.'

'What?'

'Look.' The corpse's arms were raised, held either side of his head by blackened metal manacles. 'Why's he been chained?' I wondered.

Paolo shook his head. Then he began to pull at the medieval boards, working them loose. I opened my mouth to protest, then shut it again. What my professor wanted to do was rather up to him.

'Should we get a priest?' was my half-hearted suggestion.

'In a minute. Let's have a closer look.'

I winced as he pulled the panelling out piece by piece and laid it aside. 'You're not going in, are you?'

'I want photos in situ.' As soon as the gap was big enough he swivelled around and thrust his feet in. A big wet splat from the roof painted the toe of his boot. 'Pass me my hat, Emily.'

I obeyed. Then he took the torch and wriggled down into the cell. The mud on the floor turned out to be solid enough for him to stand on and he flashed me a grin. Then, crouched on his haunches, he shuffled over to the body. I could hear him muttering to himself in Italian. When he was within a metre or two he slipped his cellphone from his jacket and began to take photographs. The corpse's skin was so pale it seemed to glow from the flash. He moved in closer.

I didn't really understand what happened next.

The corpse jerked its head up. In the torchlight its eyes glowed red. It yanked its arms free from the corroded manacles, which shattered to fragments, and dropped them round his neck. The Professor opened his mouth in shock. The corpse opened its mouth too, lunging for his face in an obscene open-jawed kiss – and its teeth were like snakes' fangs. I screamed, recoiled from the gap, tried to stand, smacked my head hard against the edge of the altar table and blacked out.

I woke in the Ospedale Civile, with a policeman sat next to my bed. My statement, when they found a nurse who could act as interpreter, was of little help to him. I claimed not to remember anything much. It turned out that a priest had found me by the altar to Sant'Aronne, unconscious and alone, next to a hole in the wall leading to an empty chamber. Professor Rossini was nowhere to be found, they said, though his phone was lying within that cellar and part of the floor seemed to have been disturbed.

What could they do? I didn't remember any attacker and signs were that I had simply banged my head. We had both been there on official business. If a crime had taken place it didn't seem clear. The Professor's absence was the only mystery.

Discharged, I went back to my apartment and spent two days in bed. I did not dare phone Paolo's home, though I checked with the university both days.

His wife. The thought made me nauseous. I felt weak with guilt, and with the burden of a horror I couldn't share. My glimpse had been so fleeting that I struggled to work out whether any of it had been real.

Then on the second night I heard the rattle of a pebble on my window, and I looked out into the tiny *campo* to see Paolo standing in the shadows. I recognised his dark hat and coat, the paler boots. He lifted a hand and beckoned me down. I struggled with the window latch, but by the time I had it open he was gone.

I slipped a wrap on over my brushed-cotton pyjamas and hurried down into the square. The Professor stood silhouetted against a corner. He nodded at me and slipped away, even as

I saw him. So I followed. The streets of Venice are badly lit and all but deserted by night, but it is safer to walk round than any other city that I've lived in. I'd never felt the narrow little alleys and the dark silent stretches of canals to be threatening. Still, I would not have followed him like that for long, not without beginning to doubt his silence and his elusiveness.

But he didn't take me far. Only to a church: San Pantalon. My experience was that Venetian churches are kept locked after dark, but the door to this one opened for him and he slipped inside, leaving the way clear and a faint glow of light visible from within. So I entered.

Inside the church was lit only by the low bulbs they have in the side chapels. By day the ceiling of the nave is covered in the most amazing trompe l'oeil painting, but that night the main body of the church was in deep shadow. I could make out lines of pews, and in one of them a dark figure sitting.

'Paolo? What are we doing here?'

'I have come to make confession to you, Emily.'

The moment he spoke I knew it wasn't the Professor. It was Paolo's accent, his inflection on my name, but not his voice. I turned and blundered back towards the door. And in less time than it took for me to take ten paces he was out of the pew and round me and stood blocking my way, and his hand closed on my throat, choking off any scream I might have uttered.

I expected his hand to be cold; it was feverishly hot and dry. I expected him to stink of carrion; he smelled only of brine and earth.

'Emily,' he said softly. His voice was deeper than Paolo's. I hung in his clutch like a captured rabbit, eyes wide and rolling. His pale face glimmered under a white fell of hair; the hat had fallen off. Without warning he loosened his grasp and let me slip. Sobbing for breath, I turned and ran back up the centre aisle, towards the altar. He got there before me, with a flap of his long coat. I scooted between two pews and he intercepted me again, backing me up against the closed grille of a chapel, and then he bent over me, one arm gripping a bar to either side to block my escape, and growled, 'You must not run.'

My legs nearly folded. I saw dimly his face, angular and bleakly handsome, the brows so white even against his pallid skin that it looked naked. His eyes glinted red where they caught the glow of the chapel lights. They weren't wrong about him having been albino. His hair was still long and ragged, but it was thick and glossy now. He'd put on weight. He looked almost healthy.

'Do you know who I am, Emily?'

'Aronne,' I whispered.

He tilted his head in a nod, pleased. His face moved to within an inch of mine.

'This's a church,' I gabbled. 'What're you –? You can't –'

He swept his face from my right ear to my left, and I recoiled to stop him touching me. I saw his nostrils flaring as he breathed the scent of my panic; it was a horribly animalistic gesture. But his next words were a contradiction of this: 'Yes. But I am a good Christian. Redeemed by the blood of the Lamb.'

I lost most of my remaining breath in a sob. The strange thing was, he didn't sound like he was mocking. He sounded like he meant it. But he still sounded like a predator.

'Then let me – Please, let me go.'

He shook his head. 'I came to make confession to you, Emily. Will you hear me?'

I managed a convulsive nod. It was better than him touching me. And anything was better than him revealing again those teeth I'd seen.

'I ask forgiveness, Emily. Out of hunger I've killed a man.'

Everything in my head went suddenly quiet. I stopped

wriggling. For a moment I even stopped breathing. I could hear my own pulse in my ears. 'Paolo?'

'Yes.' Contrition was audible even in that one syllable. 'I woke ravenous. I forgot myself and my soul in the hunger.'

'Where is he?' I breathed.

'At the bottom of the Lagoon.'

'Oh God.'

'I had to break his neck – I had drunk so deep, you see. Otherwise he would have come back to find you and I couldn't let him do that. I've sworn an oath before God to make no more offspring.'

I squirmed in horror at that.

'He died unshriven and that is upon my soul. But with his lifeblood he left me his words, his memories . . . you.' His crimson eyes flickered in the light, burning into me. 'His mistress.'

A squeal died unborn in my throat.

'Strange, isn't it? In my own time you would have been counted a heretic.' His mouth pulled sideways.

'What? No . . .'

'Don't worry. I understand that things have changed. When last I lived, cruelty was no vice, and now I wake in an era where neither courage nor honour is counted a virtue.' He sounded grim. 'But the Church abides. And God has seen fit to punish my pride in thinking that I might die a martyr and so put an end to my long days. He wishes me to live, and so in suffering atone for all my crimes. So I will beg forgiveness of the heretic mistress of the man I slew. And I will atone.'

So saying he lifted one of his hands from the grille, showing me his palm. A black spot appeared in the centre of the white skin, which split, like a tiny mouth opening, and dark liquid welled up from the hole and trickled down to his wrist.

'Drink,' he whispered.

I shrank back against the metal struts, shaking my head. Aronne's lips wrinkled in a snarl; I caught a glimpse of those terrifying teeth before he grabbed the hair at the back of my head with his other hand and pulled my head back to expose my throat.

'Do not refuse the Grace offered you!' There was a bass growl in his voice that was completely inhuman. For a moment his mouth hovered over my throat. I whimpered. Then his clutch eased and his expression grew softer, though no less dark. 'I remember. Paolo knew you well. You are an obedient woman, Emily. It gives you pleasure, doesn't it? Take the blood. This is why God has put me upon the Earth. This is why I still live. Obey me. Drink.'

He pushed my face to his open palm. I shut my eyes as I felt the hot fluid on my lips. It tasted bright and coppery. I thought I might faint.

Then the light broke on me with a roar, and I saw. Vistas opened behind my eyes. I saw Aronne and me pressed together in the nave of the church, lit as if from within, his blood streaming into me like liquid gold. I saw through Aronne's eyes, in a flashing succession of scenes: he was dressed in laminar armour and watching a horde of horsemen gather before his banner; he was leaping from roof to roof in a burning town, hunting the men who fled down the alleys below his feet; he was bathing in a Roman-style bath, but the water was red; he was muffled from the torturing sun and watching a procession of clergy approach him with crosses and icons, to kneel at his feet. Other scenes passed so quickly I could see little but blood. Then he was crouched over a man in a dirty brown robe, teeth in his pumping neck, feeding. The man was a monk. He was dying and Aronne was drinking his memories, his knowledge – his faith.

And then the visions changed. The light grew too strong. The pictures broke into boiling fractal lacework, infinite layers of intermeshed Mandelbrot patterns, a spiralling tunnel of geometric intersections where order became roiling chaos which became order of such complexity that it dazzled the mind, and everything led up and out and toward the dazzling glorious source of the light. The sense of fierce, hot joy was overwhelming, flooding every cell of my body. The sense of recognition and of being recognised, of being infinitely small yet gathered into something immense, made me weep and laugh and stretch my arms out and touch the face of the light.

Then I was back in my own body, and I was pressed against Aronne, my heart hammering, my mouth sticky, my body full of fire and my mind reeling.

'Did you see Him?' he whispered, easing my head back from his throat. His body was all muscle under Paolo's stolen clothes, every inch hot and hard. I'd had my teeth sunk in his neck; I glimpsed bloody half-circles on his pallid skin. 'Did you see the face of God?'

I tried to clear my throat. I could feel his very obvious sexual arousal. The feeding had excited him: my vulnerable body pressed to his, prey to predator, almost asking for death.

'Yes?' he urged, and I nodded. Because I did understand. I understood how his tainted blood, an alchemical mix of psychotropic substances, could convince a medieval believer that they had seen God. What other explanation would they understand?

'I cannot,' he groaned. 'My blood is a gift for mankind, but not for me. You are blessed, Emily.'

I wondered which was worse: lying to a saint or lying to a vampire. The visions had shaken me, moved me, filled me with heat and awe, but they had not convinced me. These days we no longer believe that spiritual enlightenment can be found in hallucinogens.

'Your blood, though . . .' His fingers were gentle on my throat, stroking the pulse, even as the lift of his lips betrayed the tips of his teeth. 'Tithe me a little, Emily. I have starved for nine centuries.'

My eyes widened.

'I will not hurt you.'

Yes, I thought, like an alcoholic will stop at only one glass. But I couldn't resist his need, and not just because he was physically so much stronger. The charged particles of the vision were still pouring through my body. My limbs felt heavy, my heart pounded thick and fast, my skin fizzed with the chemical memory. And he was holding me still, close against him. My unhinged mind could not respond to something so over-whelming, so my body was left to its own instinctive responses: terror and submission. I lifted my chin.

Gratitude lit his eyes, momentarily holding hunger at bay. He shook his head. 'Too much.' He slipped the buttons of my pyjama top instead, one at a time like a lover, until he was able to bare my shoulder. 'Here.'

I nodded, certain he did not need my permission. He stooped to my shoulder. His mouth was hot.

The first wave was sharp, pure pain, the second euphoria. It was like when the Professor laid me over his knee and smacked my bare cheeks as hard as he could, until bottom and hand alike were burning with heat. It was pain, but it was good pain. It made my heart race. It made me soar. It made me open up like a blossom of sensation. I suddenly realised that my panties were sopping wet and had been since I came round from my visionary journey, that my sex was heavy and hot and my breasts tingling with need. I groaned out loud.

Aronne's hands tightened on my hips. I pushed up into him. And again I felt the insistent jut of his erection.

Slowly he withdrew his mouth so he could look me in the

eye. His lips were dark with blood. Holding his gaze, I reached between my breasts and slipped the remaining buttons, opening the pyjama top, revealing my flushed breasts. My nipples were engorged and hard. Paolo had enjoyed putting sprung paper clips on those deceptively fragile points, then playing with them until I begged for release.

'Bite those,' I whispered, shaking.

Aronne's eyes widened. 'I remember this . . .' He shook his head slightly. 'His memories of you are very strong. He was obsessed with you.' His gaze burned. 'Your breasts, still so young and perfect. ' He touched them, just with the very tips of his fingers, and I shook with fear and pleasure. Then he turned me, rolling me to face the ornate bars, and pulled down my pyjama bottoms. I felt the cold church air on my skin. His voice was almost dreamy as he caressed me. 'Your sweet round bottom, that rolls so temptingly as you walk.' His hot hands cupped and stroked my bum cheeks, sending aching messages through to my clit and belly. 'Your hot wet *fica*, hidden from sight yet always there for him to touch,' he growled, finding it with his fingers, delving deep. 'The perfume of your body lingering on his hands and face, tasted secretly while he lectured or wrote notes or attended meetings.'

My pussy was all juice and plump, swollen flesh. He painted me wet up the entire length of my crack, right to my puckered hole, and I gripped the metal until my knuckles went white. But then he turned me back to face him again, his nails light yet threatening on my skin, scoring faint pink trails down my flanks. I knew they were longing to find the blood beneath, that he was barely restraining himself.

'The look in your eyes when he gave you an order and you obeyed so gratefully . . . Oh, he adored that. He needed that.' He shivered, his eyes hooded. 'Whatever he asked of you, Emily, you would do it. You would submit to every one of his deepest and most unthinkable desires. You knelt down in that church, Emily, and sucked his cock like an angel worshipping at the Throne of God. That was his memory.'

I wet my lips and he caught his breath.

'Let me live to remember him,' I whispered. 'Please.' I pressed my hand to his cock through his clothes and Aronne froze. The fabric was straining. I rubbed him up and down, outlining a length that felt almost too hard for flesh, then went for his belt buckle and zip with both hands. Paolo's trousers were familiar to my fingers; I'd last touched them in a different church, but with the same intent.

'Ah.' His breath was hot on my lips. 'This is sin.'

'It will be forgiven,' I whispered.

He stared. We were both trembling now. Ghost pale, his cock sprang out into my grasp. Hot velvet skin moved under my hands as I measured his rigid length. I dared to look down. His prick was big and ruthlessly eager, not sharing his misgivings. A bead of moisture gleamed at the tip: no pearl, but a ruby.

I wanted to take the body and blood in my mouth.

Do this in remembrance of Me.

Stolen clothes. Stolen memories. They were too much for him. This saint had the appetites of a predator, whetted to a razor edge by years of deprivation and darkness. His eyes were scarlet reflective discs of light as he stooped and picked me up, jamming me against the chapel bars. His arm went under my bottom, holding my weight, squeezing me just as Paolo used to. And then he opened my loose pyjama jacket, the last pathetic piece of clothing between me and those jaws, and with immense care bit my breasts, over and over. His teeth were so sharp that the bites hurt comparatively little, but every puncture sent the lightning of Heaven crashing up and down my body. His tongue burned and soothed me simultaneously, lapping at my flesh. I wrapped my legs round his torso and knotted my hands in his white hair and rode the waves of shock and euphoria, surrendering myself to his strength and his need.

Hunters and prey alike, we are creatures of overriding instinct.

His other hand was busy too. I didn't realise until he released my breasts and lowered me onto that cock of his, a length so long and thick it felt like I was being impaled on a stake. He made a noise that sounded like relief. I cried out and grabbed the bars behind my head for support as he began to surge into me. He pressed his mouth to mine and I tasted my own blood; I thought he was going to bite my face but he refrained somehow, staring at me with tortured, ravenous eyes as he thrust savagely into me, over and over again.

I came, shaking and screaming and crying because I was frightened of it coming to an end, because it was the last pleasure I would ever know in my life.

When I was done he lifted me bodily over to the nearest pew and set me down on my knees upon the wood so that he could enter me from behind. I grabbed the seat back and thrust out my bottom, welcoming his frantic re-entry. He tore the pyjama top from my back and bit at my shoulders, groaning, lapping the blood. He spoke in a language I'd never heard – certainly not Italian – as he pumped his cock in and out, gasping and spitting onto my back. It took him enormous effort. When finally he rammed home he nearly collapsed over my shoulders.

I felt like I'd been torn nearly in half. I assumed he would complete the process.

But he rolled away from me. I slithered to the floor, my thighs too weak to support me any longer, drenched in sweat, my back and breasts on fire from his cruel kisses.

'Emily.'

His face flickered out of the shadows. The tear tracks painted from his eyes to his jawline looked black in the dim light, but

I knew that even his tears were blood. He gathered my naked body in his arms and laid my head against his chest and we sat there on the stone floor, in the dark and the chill, cut off by an infinite void from God and humanity.

And he was warm.

Then he left me.

It was our bad luck that we released the vampire. It was Venice's good luck that Paolo was what he was: a university professor, but a traditional Catholic too.

Now I stare out of the aeroplane window at the piscine outline of Venice's islands swimming in the silver lagoon. Taking advantage of a bright morning I have fled, ashamed but determined to save myself. Isn't it what anyone would do?

The vampire was right that ours is not an age that values courage.

If I stayed, what would happen to me then? What will happen, sooner or later? It is only obedience to God that is restraining Aronne's appetites – so what happens if he kills a scientific atheist? What happens if he imbibes their understanding of a world driven by ruthless evolutionary struggle – Nature red in tooth and claw?

Teeth and claws could not be redder than his. But even though I flee, part of me hopes that he will hunt me down.

Janine Ashbless is the author of the Black Lace novels *Divine Torment*, *Burning Bright* and *Wildwood*. She has one single author collection – *Cruel Enchantment* – and her second collection – *Dark Enchantment* – will be published by Black Lace in early 2009. Her paranormal erotic novellas are included in the Black Lace collections *Magic and Desire* and *Enchanted*.

Only the Beginning

Terri Pray

Linda sat bolt upright, her gaze darting around the unfamiliar room, memories flooding back in a rush that left her gasping for breath. Why did it hurt to breathe?

Soft material brushed over her nude form as she twisted on the bed, searching the room for a clue to how she had ended up here.

Nude?

Her clothing! What had happened to all her clothes?

Confusion followed the rush of the memories, images that made no sense. A bar. A few drinks. What day was it? Friday still, or had she slept through the night? There had been a party? Yes, Helen's birthday. They'd all been there. Everyone from work had been there. She frowned, there had been someone else there. Gentle fingers that had moved over her back, cupped her ass cheeks and lifted her up into a kiss that had never ended. His smell, the feel of his body against hers, that smile. She could remember his smile.

Her body clenched, vulva rippling with the vague recollection of his touch. Heat coated her inner walls, the need to feel him again. His lips on her body, the feel of his erection between her thighs, those gasped moments of pleasure beneath him as his teeth had grazed across her neck.

Teeth. Sharp teeth.

Linda's eyes closed, a low moan slipping from her lips before she could prevent it. Her skin tingled at the memory of his touch. The memory was vague, a shadow that she struggled to recall in detail, yet it was still enough to light the fires in her soul.

Her bare feet touched the floor as she pushed out of the bed. She had to try to make sense of the memories. Thick carpet, lush, silken beneath her feet; odd she did not remember carpet feeling like this before. She snagged one of the sheets from the bed and wrapped it tight about her naked form, a deep shiver running through her body at the touch of the sensuous material.

Her breath caught at the back of her throat as she clutched the sheet about her body. A thousand fingers of pleasure caressed a path over her skin, awakening every nerve ending. She grasped the end of the bed, forcing her mind to focus past the delicious delight. Just a sheet, nothing more than a piece of bedding, yet it had brought her body almost to the point of release in a single brush of soft material over her otherwise naked form.

Her neck hurt, a deep ache that felt almost like a bruise. What had she been left with, a love bite? Those damn sharp teeth. He had to have bitten her. No love bite caused the sort of pain she now felt. The sheet slipped a little from her breasts, forcing her to retie it. A shiver of delight brought to life by the soft caress of material. Damn it, where had he put her clothes and just what had he done to her during the night? Her body was sore. Not just the bruises on her neck, but between her thighs, her stomach, breathing still left her ribs with a dull ache.

'You're awake.' A voice akin to liquid velvet wrapped about her body. 'I had begun to wonder how long you would remain asleep, lass.'

Lass? Who in hell's name called women 'lass' any more?

Her breath caught in the back of her throat, stomach tightened as she met his gaze. Eyes the colour of a storm-tossed sea looked back at her across the lush room. Long brown hair spilled over his shoulders, lines of fire, little more than hints of vivid auburn, caught the low light of the room. Her gaze moved over his face, down to his chest. *And what a chest.* Bare to the waist, he could have given a stripper a run for their money in that department, except for the lack of suntan, with smooth toned muscles under his pale skin.

Memories flooded back.

The man from the bar.

'I remember you.'

'I'm sure you do, at least partially. The rest will return in time.' Soft spoken, a gentle voice, yet she could hear it, that dangerous edge of steel under the pleasant packaging.

'What am I doing here?'

'You were sleeping.' He shrugged, turning away from her as he walked across the room and picked up a robe from the side of the door. 'You might feel a little more comfortable wearing this, though I am not going to object if you wish to remain in that sheet. It is quite becoming.'

She snatched the robe from his hand as soon as it was within reach.

'Manners, lass, do please try to remember them.' His gaze narrowed, all traces of sensuality lost from his lips as they tightened into a harsh line. 'I will not stand for such behaviour in my home.'

'That's something I can change. Just give me my clothes and I'll be gone.' *Bastard.* Who did he think he was, trying to correct her behaviour like that?

'Ah, I'm afraid I can't let you leave. Not just yet at least. It would not be safe.'

'For who, you or me? Afraid I'll go running to the cops and

38

report a rape?' she growled, pulling on the robe and tying it tight before she let the sheet fall to the floor.

'It would be difficult to report such. You were quite willing, I assure you of that. Even when I bit you.' He smiled, gesturing to one of the large padded chairs by the fire place. 'I suggest you sit down, we have a lot to discuss.'

Her nipples crinkled, hardening into coral points beneath the silken wrap. The passage of his gaze felt like a dozen fingers over her skin, heat touching her cheeks long before Linda darted to the chair.

'It will all make sense in time. I promise you that much, Linda.'

'Who are you?'

'Donald Burns.' He smiled, a light touching his eyes. 'Not a name I expect you to know, but my family has been here for some time.'

'What am I doing here?' Linda shifted in the chair, curling her feet up under her ass. The robe tugged down over her body as much as possible. The last thing she needed was to leave him a decent view, although she now had no doubt that he had seen his fill of her naked form the night before.

'You seemed to enjoy my touch last night. As I said the memories will return in time.'

'How did you ...?'

'Your face, it's quite easy to read, or at least it is to me.'

Her fingers tightened on the edges of the robe. Such a soft material, silken, it caressed her form with the sensuous delight of a lover. 'How did I end up here? Did I have too much to drink?'

'Not quite like that. You were very careful in what you had to drink. You even refused to let me fetch one for you. Not that I blame you. There are men who are less than gentlemanly in their pursuit of pleasure.' He watched her closely. 'It might be said that you acted with a quite proper form of behaviour in that respect. We sat, talked for a bit, danced and you agreed to come home with me. It was as simple as that,' Donald explained. 'I did not force you, drug you or make you drink endless amounts. You were, in fact, quite sober. However we did enjoy an intimate time together.'

'I don't believe you. I'm not a fool. I don't go home with men I don't know.' Her body heated beneath his gaze, twin points pressed against the robe that barely covered her form and she shivered, forced to try to control her reactions. Whatever had happened, he wasn't going to touch her again.

'You did last night. I can be quite persuasive when I have to be.' His smile reminded her of a cat stalking its prey. 'And I admit you were more stubborn than most I try to tempt. A few words, a smile, a simple kiss, those are normally enough to do the job. But not you. Your mind simply refused to cave in. It's rare to find such a challenge. I'm sure you'll agree that once the glove had been laid down to me it would have been foolish to pass you by.'

'I don't understand. What challenge? Just because I didn't drop at your feet?' Arrogant bastard. Did he think every woman had to do that, or would do that? 'I followed you home though, so I guess I'm not that strong.'

'I had to take time persuading you.'

'Ah, so my crime is being stubborn?'

'More than that. Your mind is strong, Linda. Very strong,' Donald explained, his voice low, calm. That same hint of velvet- or silk-wrapped steel she had heard before now sent a shiver through her body. The hair on the back of her neck stood up, her thighs tightened, the urge to press them together almost overpowering. 'Women can give me something. Pleasure. The substance I need to live, but there are rare ones. There are ones with the strength to resist me that can offer my kind so much more than a night of pleasure between silken sheets. I need a woman like you at my side. Not just for a single night, or a week, or a month, but eternity.'

'You're mad.' She tried shaking off the sensations that plagued her body, clear her mind enough to think straight, but every breath brought a new wave of delight in some form. The tempting smells, the material around her body, his smile, voice, even the feeling from the soft cushions that padded the luxurious chair. Her entire body had awoken with a new lease on life and now embraced every sensation offered.

Alive, in a way she had never known before.

'No, just determined.' Donald shrugged off the insult, his upper lips curling into a deep smile baring the teeth beneath. Teeth that looked far too sharp. 'You have a core of steel. You'll need it if you wish to retain your sanity. Oh, believe me, Linda, the years can be enough to drive you to madness, but that is a dangerous path to walk.'

'Vampire?' Linda blanched.

'Yes.' His lips pulled back from his upper teeth, tongue caressing over the sharp points before they were hidden again under an all too perfect smile. 'What did you think I was with teeth like this?'

Vampire?

Legends. The source of bad fantasy stories, corny horror movies and the occasional romance novel. They did not exist. Could not exist and she had been unfortunate enough to end up in the hands of some poor delusional fool with a set of fake teeth.

'They are quite real, Linda. As I am sure the marks on your neck show.'

She brushed over the bruises. 'What? These are just love bites'

'Oh, they are far more than that, dear Linda.' Donald leaned back in the chair. 'It hurt, when you woke, didn't it? To think, even to breathe. Your body no longer felt as though it belonged to you. You had never known such a pain on waking as you did today.'

'What did you do to me, you bastard?' How had he known just what she had dealt with when she had woken?

'My parents were married when I was born, so kindly refrain from calling me that again, Linda. It's truly not a ladylike thing to say.'

Ladylike? What the fuck? 'I'll call you anything I want, you lying sack of shit. Now I want my clothes and I want to go home.' Fury burned through her body, chasing away the shame that came from sitting in front of a man she did not know dressed in nothing more than a thin robe.

'Keep a civil tongue in your head.'

'Or you'll do what?'

'I'll be forced to teach you a lesson in manners, Linda. One you will not forget in a long time.'

'Threats are a really stupid thing to pull on me. You're already facing problems from keeping me here against my wishes.' Linda's hands gripped the arms of the chair, pushing her out of the soft confines. Yet his threat had other reactions, ones she didn't intend to let him know about. Heat rippled through her womb, coating her lower lips in a silken caress, offering the hint of so much more to come. 'I intend to leave. Now!'

He moved without warning. So quickly that she did not even see him begin to leave the chair before she felt his fingers tightened about her throat. 'I don't think so, my lass. I really don't think so.'

Pressure forced her onto her toes, a low whimper of pain and fear carried into the air. Her nails dug into his hands, trying to pull them away from her throat.

'Fight me all you want. I'm older. Stronger. Far more experienced in this life than you are. And I made you.' His fingers closed on her throat as he lifted her up from the floor. Panic fuelled her kicks. She had to break free of him before he crushed her throat. One hand. That's all it had taken, one hand to lift her up from the floor. His gaze narrowed on her face, eyes intense, small lines tightening about her mouth. 'Learn this well, my lass. Learn or you will end up facing a real punishment.'

Then the pressure was gone, his touch gentle, holding her in place, her pulse fluttering beneath his fingers.

'You hurt me . . .'

'I warned you to behave. Perhaps I do need to give you another lesson, or will you listen to me whilst I explain?' Donald stood in front of her, his voice calm, collected and soft. A far cry from the moment of terror she had just experienced. 'You have a lot to learn, my lass, and it would be better for you if you at least attempted to listen politely instead of making demands or dishing out insults.' He reached out, cupping her cheek. 'This life can offer so much pleasure if you but give yourself the time to adapt to it.'

Without warning he leaned in, his lips brushing over hers, a tender, delicate touch that left her wanting so much more. Her nipples pressed against the robe, her breath catching in the back of her throat as she leaned into his lips.

No! Remember what he's done to you.

'You've been turned, lass.'

'Turned?' She curled back into the chair. She had fallen into the hands of a mad man, someone insane enough to have escaped from the local mental institution.

'Into one of my kind. A vampire. You tasted of me, I tasted of you, your mind merged with mine for a short time. Just enough to let the barriers down and force you from the life you knew into the life you now face.' His voice caressed her senses, tempting her with images of his touch, pleasure, pain shared even as her mind tried to reject them.

'You don't really expect me to believe that, do you?' If he was telling the truth then she had died. Hadn't she?

'Please, try to relax, my lass, it will make the evening far more pleasant for you.' He sighed and shook his head, his gaze never leaving her trembling form. 'No, I do not expect you to accept this immediately. Such things do tend to take a while to sink in. I recall when I was turned. I believe I fought the idea for several days, even when the change took me fully. It wasn't until I tried to ignore the craving to feed that I finally gave in.' Every move he made spoke of an elegance from an earlier age. His manners were almost out of place in this day and age.

Linda brushed the tip of her tongue against her teeth, searching for some sign of fangs. 'I don't really feel that different. And my teeth are the same.'

'They will begin to change in the next few days, lass.'

'I see, so what proof do I have that this is not some sick joke?' With no fangs there was nothing to back up his words. 'Try looking at this from my point of view, Donald.' If that was even his name; she had only his word for all of this.

'Your ribs hurt, breathing was painful when you awoke, as if you were doing something you had not done in a while. Things smell different now and feel odd beneath your feet, your fingers. Why, even that robe covering that delicious body of yours now offers new sensations to you.'

'I'm just a little sensitive today. That's all.' How did he know all this about her? She hadn't said anything about it, and he didn't know her well enough to read her mannerisms. 'You're saying you changed me into a creature of the night, the undead, one of those blood-sucking monsters from the movies?' Even if he believed that nonsense she was not about to. So her skin tingled and her lungs hurt, so what? She'd spent too much time in the club, breathing in the smoke, that's all.

'Yes and no. The film industry does so like to exaggerate our kind.' He shrugged and turned the same devastating smile on her that she recalled from the club. Her memories were returning. That smile, his touch, the way he had moved her across the dance floor. The others in her party had watched, slack-jawed and wide-eyed as she had moved with him to the beat of the music.

'So I'm just going to have to get used to this, the way my body now feels?' Linda fought the urge to test just how sensitive her body had become. How would it react under her own fingers?

A blush claimed her cheeks as Linda slammed that thought back into the wicked little box it had escaped from.

'Not all of that strangeness will be such a bad thing. Your skin is hypersensitive now. Imagine what it would be like to lie on the bed and have a piece of fur brushed over your body.' His voice was little more than a whisper. 'You can almost feel it, can't you?'

'I really don't think this is the time or place for ...' She felt her gaze drawn to his lips, the soft shapes they formed with each word. How would they feel against her skin? Gods. She was doing it again. Her body craved his touch, desired him, wanted to know what he would do to her, how his fingers might feel along her bare skin as she arched beneath him.

'But it is. I brought you over into this life to be my companion. Why would I then ignore the delights your body can offer? It would be ill-mannered of me to hide those sensual pleasures from you.' Donald smiled, leaning back in his chair. 'You would not wish to have all the facts hidden from you?'

'No, I guess not.' She tried to look away from him, to shut

out the thoughts of his body pressed against her own. 'Sorry, I guess I am not being that grateful, or I simply don't understand all this. I don't remember being bitten, or tasting your blood.'

'Ah, lass, sweet lass, it will all come back to you soon enough, have patience.'

'You took my life from me, killed me and you expect me to have patience?' she growled. Her fingers tightened on the arms of the chair. How dare he treat her in such a manner. 'My life is over.'

'No, lass, it's only just begun.'

'Liar,' she snapped.

'Look to your heart, your mind, your body and think of the wonders you will live to experience. The joy, the delight of a thousand kisses, soft touches that will bring you a pleasure no mortal has ever lived through. All of this would have been denied to you if I had not entered your life.' His voice slid through her mind in the same way that the robe slipped over her skin.

'You arrogant son of a bitch. You killed me!' Anger flared into life beyond anything she had known before. A rage that urged her to move across the room, strike him, lash out, see his blood spill onto the floor until he knew the level of pain she now carried in her heart.

No, she had to keep it under control. If she struck out at him, what damage would she cause? So what if she did not have the experience he laid claim to, she could still attack him and cause some serious damage.

Blood dripping down his face, pleas for mercy as she yanked back his head before biting into the soft flesh of his neck . . .

'Do it. If you think you can. Attack me. Fight back. Show me the rage you feel.' He rose from the chair, gaze locked with hers. 'If you think you can do it, then show me. Attack me.

Don't just sit there trying to make yourself believe that you're holding back for my protection.'

'Don't push me around, damn it.'

'Challenging me?' He stalked towards her, closing the gap between them.

'No, I'm not.' She slid from the chair, backing away. 'Please, leave me alone.'

'I think what you really want to say is "please touch me".'

'No.' *Yes.* She backed up, touching a wall behind her, nowhere left to run as he reached out and touched her. His thumb traced across her lips. A simple caress that offered so much more. A low moan followed his touch, her thighs pressed tight, a soft rock pushing through her hips in the need to feel something more at his hands.

'Ah yes, there it is. The hunger.' His hand slid into her hair, fingers tightening in the long, dark length. 'Surrender to it.'

A protest formed on her lips, silenced by his touch.

She groaned, arching towards him, hardening nipples pressed tight to his chest under the pressure of his grip. Her body tingled into life, desire blazing a path through her core into the walls of her vulva. His tongue delved into her mouth, stroking the tender insides. Her mind screamed a denial, urging her to move back, to break the kiss, but her body had other ideas as he teased along her lips before he drew away, his hand still tight in her hair.

Gods.

Kisses did not do things like this to her. Not normally. She could feel him, taste him, every inch of her body responded to him, craving more than just the delight of his kiss. So very much more.

'You can feel it, can't you? A need unlike anything you have ever known before.'

'Yes,' she groaned. Her hands clenched against his trousers, nails scraping deep.

'I don't even have to touch you in order to tease you now,' he whispered against her lips.

'No.' She pressed tighter to him. The robe slipped across her flesh, urging new waves of sensation through her form. Her stomach tightened, goosebumps rose along her back, while each shivering breath only served to arouse her further. 'But I want you to.'

'To what? Say it, lass.'

Don't do it. Don't give in to this. You'll regret it. He stole your life, your family, friends, everything. Don't give him the one thing you have left. Your passion. Fight him. Lash out. Destroy him. You have the power to now. He told you that you were like him. You've seen the strength he has. Use it.

'Touch me.' She no longer cared about the warnings her mind tried to scream at her.

'Where?' His lips brushed down over her neck.

'Everywhere.' The robe parted under his touch, sliding down over her back and pooled about her feet. 'Please, just touch me.'

'I plan to.' With a low growl he wrapped his arms about her naked form, lifting her from the floor as he turned to stalk across the room. He lowered her down onto the bed, tracing a line of long slow nibbling kisses down her neck, over her soft skin. 'You taste so good, my lass. Sweet, innocent, yet filled with a passion you have yet to unleash on the world.'

She groaned, back arching up from the silken sheets, nipples hardening to points that he delighted in capturing between his lips. A soft, wicked tongue stroked over those sensitive buds, urging a low cry of pleasure into life. Her hips rolled towards him, liquid heat coating her inner walls. A craving to feel his body slide against her own grew beyond her understanding. He growled, sucking one ripe nipple into his mouth, then flicking his tongue around the throbbing nub.

'Gods,' she cried out, arching up from the bed, her hands sliding into his hair. 'That feels so good.'

His teeth scraped across the trapped bud, as one hand slid between her thighs, parting them, his finger tapping her soft lower lips apart. She had never let someone just take her to bed. Not like this.

'You like this, don't you, lass?' One finger tapped against the tight aching nub of her clit. Each new touch sent a shudder through her body, as though one caress had turned into a thousand travelling fingers across her form. Impossible, yet it still happened. He shifted across her body, the tip of his tongue leaving a long, shivering path of delight from one breast to the other, circling her untouched nipple before closing on it. She cried out as he sucked the sensitive nub hard into his mouth.

'Yes, gods, yes I do.' Her hips lifted towards him, heels pressing into the bedding. 'Hate it, love it, fear it.'

'Need it,' he growled against her skin. He pressed past her labia, into the damp confines of her sex.

'All and more.' Oh, she wanted so very much more than she had the ability to put into words. A soft shudder racked through her body, hips rocking down onto his finger. She wanted it buried deeper in her wicked form, to feel it press against her rippling walls until she screamed out in need.

'Patience, lass, it's worth the wait.' He glanced up at her over her breasts, sharp teeth catching against her flesh. Not enough to cut, to part the skin, but still a sharp moment of pain. Her eyes widened, fingers tightened into the bedding. A low rock claimed her hips. No, she'd changed so much. Pain had always been an area she had refused to explore before, now her body surged almost from the bed at a soft nip.

'Please.' She tried to press down further onto his finger.

'Not yet.' He nibbled slowly over her stomach, tapping his

probing finger against her tight inner walls. 'You're not ready yet.'

But she was. Her body felt ready. Her hips rolled down against his touch, craving so much more than he seemed willing to offer. Yet still he kept the slow pace of delightful torture that left her body aching.

Soft nibbling kisses worked down her stomach until he eased between her widespread thighs. Oh gods, did he plan on using his tongue there? His breath brushed over her clit, lips closing on the tight pip of flesh, forcing a cry of sheer delight into being. Linda half sat up, reaching for him, her fingers closed on his hair, holding him tight. With each soft touch between her thighs she groaned, her hips pressing tight to his lips. Her body ached with a need that he denied and yet teased to a higher level at the same time.

'Your world has changed around you. This is just the beginning, lass.' His finger tapped at that soft shell-like spot within her core.

Her inner walls rippled, trying to close on his finger. She couldn't hold onto this much longer. Her fingers tightened in his hair, her hips rocked down against his face. Her vulva shuddered in need about his finger, coated with the heated cream of her own desire.

His tongue wrapped about her clit and a low growl vibrated through her body. A second finger joined the first within her heated sex. How could he expect her to keep control of her desires when he was going to do things like this?

'Please, gods, please. I have to ...'

'No, not yet.' He lifted away from her clit, after flicking his tongue over it one last time. 'Hold on to it, lass. Hold on. It's worth the wait.'

With a low growl she sat up and pulled his head back between her thighs. Her hips rolled fully, heat building within her core, the pressure almost too much to bear as she rocked down against his fingers. She had to come.

She pressed down hard on his fingers, against his lips, rocking with each breath that forced through her body. Pleasure ruled her now. Pleasure and need. She would not wait. She set the pace. Her needs. Her body. Her desire.

He growled, pulling away from her grip, his hands closed on her wrists as he pushed her back to the bed. 'I am in charge here, my lass. Not you. It is best you remember that.' He held both her wrists in one hand. His free hand moved to his trousers, opening them before he slid them down from his body. 'You are my lass and will answer to me.'

Protests formed and died on her lips.

'You want this, don't you? The feel of my cock inside you, stretching your walls, filling you.' He leaned close, licking a soft path along her neck, tracing the line of her pulse beneath the skin.

'Yes.' A word, a plea, it didn't matter, it was the only thing she could say.

Without another word he thrust into her body, his rigid cock parting her lower lips. Her walls tightened in delight about his length, a low groan shared between them. Even with the grip he had on her wrists her hands clenched tight. She wanted to hold him, be held tight by him, yet he held her firmly against the bedding.

'So hot, tight, delicious,' he growled against her neck. 'I knew from the moment I laid eyes on you that you would be the one.' Sharp teeth brushed over the vein so close to the surface. 'I need you. Gods, lass I need you.'

'Need you!' Her words were little more than gasps of delight. She arched her neck, offering it up to him. 'Please let me touch you.'

'Do you want me to bite you?' His words vibrated through

her neck, each thrust into her warm, wet and willing walls sending her higher, deeper into that plane of pure delight. 'Do you want to feel what it is like to be a vampire, to know the blending of minds that can occur when our kind feeds from each other?'

'Yes,' Linda whimpered, tipping her chin up further, her eyes closing as she waited for that sharp moment of pain. Would she scream? She did not know enough about his kind, their kind, to guess at how it would feel.

Each breath triggered new waves of delight through her being, her sex rippling on his thick cock. Nipples hard against his chest, her thighs wrapped about his hips, heels locked behind his taut ass to press him deeper into her willing body.

Sweat beaded across her breasts and still she wanted more. Never before had she permitted someone to hold her down, control her during sex, yet now she only had to think about his hand on her wrists and her vulva tried to close on him. His tongue licked a slow path over her throat, teasing her with the idea of the bite, yet she could not withdraw the offer made.

'Ask me to bite you.'

'Bite me,' Linda purred.

'No, ask me. Don't tell me. Don't demand it. Ask me. Better yet, beg.' The tips of his teeth pressed against her throat, a hint of pressure behind them. 'You want it that badly then show me. Tell me. Plead for me to do it to you.'

Such a smooth chest. Firm muscles. Soft skin. His nipples rubbed against her breasts, her arms still pinned above her head, held by one strong hand. Her vulva clenched about his cock, heating built well beyond the point of no return.

'Please, bite me.'

'Why should I?' He nibbled down her throat.

'Because I want it, need it. Please.'

'Are you begging me?' Donald growled softly against the tender skin of her throat.

'Yes,' she hissed, lifting up her chin fully. His breath warmed her skin, a soft tickle from the tip of his tongue traced her pulse. 'Please, bite me. I'm begging you. Bite me, please.'

His hips rolled, pressing his cock against her hidden spot. 'Beg me again, my lass.'

Her thighs tightened fully on his hips. She had never felt anything this intense before. Every nerve ending burned with the need to bring her body to orgasm. She groaned beneath him, her eyes closed, a thousand erotic images flashing through her mind as she spoke. 'Please, bite me. I want your teeth in my body. I need to feel them sliding into my throat, to know you feed from me. I want to be yours. Fully yours. In all ways. Feed from me. Bite me. Taste me. I'm begging you.'

He thrust deeper into her core, his teeth lifting from her throat for a moment before he bit deep into her neck. Pain shot through her, lancing like a white light that forced a scream into life. She could not stop him, did not want to stop him any longer. Her body arched tight beneath him, her thighs closed on his hips and her heels dug into his ass, as each thrust pushed her higher than the one before.

He swallowed hard, drinking her blood, circling his hips as she shuddered beneath him. It should have turned her off. Shut her down. Instead her mind fled, leaving a wanton, needful body behind that pressed to him with each thrust, each beat of her heart. Time ceased to have meaning, pain merged with pleasure, sweat and blood beaded in the hollow of her throat.

Come for me. His voice echoed through her mind. *Come for me and enter your new life.*

With his words the pressure finally fought its way free in a mix of fire and ice that throbbed through her veins. Her back arched, half lifting him upwards and still he fed from her throat. Her thighs tightened, her ass lifted from the bed, liquid heat wrapped about his cock as she screamed her release.

Somewhere in the mix of her blood and heat he roared his own release against her throat. His cock throbbing, shuddering into her sex until he pulled back, licking softly over her throat, closing the wound with a near gentle caress.

Donald rolled them across the bed, then nestled her head against his chest, his grip gone from her wrists. Now he held her tenderly, his fingers brushing through her hair as she eased down from the release he had forced into being. Slowly her vision returned to normal only to meet his storm-tossed gaze.

'I told you, my lass. Death is only the beginning.'

The Funhouse Is Closed Mondays
Kristina Lloyd

'I just don't think it's very ethical, Suze, that's all,' said Simeon. 'I'm a sick fuck, sure. I know that. But even *I* have limits.'

'Aw, that's so sweet, babes,' murmured Suzanne. 'Limits. Really quaint.'

'And I don't want to hang out with vamps who think that's an OK way to feed. It's gross.'

Suzanne didn't reply. In the Hallowe'en half-light, she was busy fixing a cravat around a plastic skeleton's neck.

'Don't you think, Suze?' prompted Simeon.

Suzanne shrugged. 'Blood's blood,' she said, turning to him. 'My main problem is lack of cock.'

'*Plus ça*,' drawled Simeon, sounding ever so slightly bitchy. He was reclining sideways in a dinky electric car, flamboyant and wasted, with his legs hooked over the door, black hair draping his ivory-white face, his violet eyes glinting like evil little jewels.

Coney Island in autumn wasn't the best place for a couple of snow vampires. However, making a home in a derelict ghost train, a dark ride that nobody rode any more, suited Simeon and Suzanne to a tee. During the day they slept under a painted moon in their windowless theatre while outside, leaf fall and litter tumbled through a kitsch wasteland of carousels, Ferris wheels, roller coasters and crumbling sideshow shacks. At night, pale, slim and ghastly, the two of them slipped out of their hatch, creatures from the Haunted House coming alive to stalk New York.

'Christophe's changed,' said Suzanne.

'Everything's changed,' complained Simeon. 'I remember –'

'Yeah, yeah,' said Suzanne. 'The good old days when the streets were paved with syringes. But that's normal, Sim. Places change. But vampires, the ones you love, shouldn't they be a bit more stable?' Arms outstretched, Suzanne balanced along a narrow plank and leaped nimbly over a pit containing a corpse in its coffin, skin and cloth dripping from its bones, eyes popping.

'Christophe's going through one of his Charlie Manson phases,' said Simeon. 'I've seen it before. I keep hoping he'll grow out of it but, you know, he's a vampire. Emotional maturity's kinda tricky.'

'All those women,' whined Suzanne. She perched herself by Simeon's car, feet dangling towards the track. 'It's so unfair.'

'Tell me about it,' said Simeon, camp and sulky. He gave a defiant flick of his head, hair swishing like a silky black cape. 'You know what he did the other night? He made them kneel in a circle around him then he fucked each one in the mouth. Called it his cocksucker clockface.'

'My God,' said Suzanne.

'It gets worse. Apparently, he has this regular thing where he gets them to bend over. You know, like over a rail or something? He pushes their clothes down to their ankles then selects who he's going to fuck based on how wet they are.'

'That's so degrading,' said Suzanne.

'Isn't it? I heard he walks up and down the line, wiggling his fingers inside them. Sometimes he writes a little number on their butt to denote their score.'

'Despicable man,' said Suzanne. 'He's just using those women. Using them for his own warped, greedy pleasure.'

'I know,' said Simeon. 'He doesn't give a toss about them as individuals. They're just orifices for his dick. He can't even be bothered to learn their names. Can you believe that? He calls all of them bitch. C'mere, bitch. Open your legs, bitch.'

'Jeez,' said Suzanne.

'Yeah.'

'That's so offensive, so demeaning.'

'Shameful,' said Simeon.

'Really crude.'

'Vile and humiliating.'

Suzanne cast him a glance. 'And totally fucking hot,' she said. 'I mean, *seriously*.'

'Oh, I know,' said Simeon. 'Wow, do I ever.'

Suzanne wrapped her fist into her hair, making skeins of honey-blonde silkiness, and pulled hard. With her head tipping sideways, she pushed her other fist between her thighs, rocking her hips back and forth.

'Hey, shall we role play?' she said in a low, throaty voice. 'You could be Christophe. I could be one of his bitches and –'

'Suze,' complained Simeon. 'You're always getting to be someone's bitch these days. I don't mind domming you *some* of the time. But, um, do you think every now and then you could switch? Let *me* be the bitch for once?'

Suzanne sighed and released her hair, shaking it out extravagantly like she was in a shampoo advert for the undead. 'Oh, I guess I ought. Trouble is, babes, I'm not so struck on switching right now. Maybe it's being back in Brooklyn. I dunno. I'm sorry. But I've been looking at what I do, examining my sexuality and the broader impact my expression of it has on society. And, um, while I feel kinda icky about using terms like "personal voyage" and "self-discovery", this has been a sort of interior journey for me. And I've come to understand that even though I totally love submission, I only like domming people when I can kill them.'

Simeon snorted. 'Well, yes!' he said, insulted. 'That's the ideal situation. But you could still dom me as a favour! Like, one friend helping out another. You don't have to dom me to death for us to –'

'I think it lacks integrity.'

'Ha!' cried Simeon. 'Integrity! In-fucking-tegrity!' He flung his gangly legs apart, sprang up from the tiny ghost car and began pacing along the track like a mechanised vampire from the school of Goth, albeit one who'd lost his cool. 'Since when did you care about integrity?' he demanded. 'You're a vampire. You're not meant to have scruples or . . . or integrity! Really, you should hear yourself, Suze. It's creepy. Sentimental. You're starting to sound like, ugh, like a human being!'

He stopped to glare at her, his ashen face stamped against the gloom like a moonlit rose petal.

'Human?' exclaimed Suzanne. 'Excuse me but weren't you talking about the ethics of feeding two moments ago? I ask you, *ethics*!'

'But that's different!'

'Why is it different?' scoffed Suzanne. 'Why?'

'Because . . . Because . . .' Simeon flailed helplessly as he stumbled for an answer.

'Because, see, my integrity is about me wanting to be true to my vampire sexuality,' said Suzanne. 'Whereas your ethics are just some pissy bit of squeamishness about feeding. Now who's sounding human?'

Simeon brightened. 'Actually, no,' he declared, jabbing a skinny finger at the air. 'That's where you're wrong. Totally wrong. Because my problem with the feeding, my real problem, is that ultimately, at the end of the day, when all's said and done, it's not actually very vampirey, is it? It lacks . . . What's that word again? Integrity! They've got some random mortal hooked up to a life-support machine and they're draining him for blood and —'

'So?' said Suzanne. 'What's the big deal?'

Simeon sighed heavily. 'That's what ants do to aphids, Suze. They milk them. Farm them and milk them. We're not ants. We're vampires! Monsters! We're evil. We should be out there killing people, not ... ew, milking them.'

Suzanne thought for a moment then laughed gleefully. 'You know what, Sim? You're right!' She raised her fist and they high-fived each other with a knuckle-knock.

Simeon grinned. 'And that poor bastard,' he continued. 'Kind of life is that for a dude? Strapped to a bed, full of tubes and shit? It's not like he's brain damaged or comatose or missing some limbs. If he was, cool. But he's young, fit and healthy. What a waste. If you ask me, he'd be better off dead.'

Suzanne narrowed her eyes. 'I knew you fancied him.'

Simeon shrugged. 'Hey, you've got to admit he is pretty cute.'

'True,' said Suzanne. 'So shall we dom him and kill him?'

Simeon laughed wildly. 'You're insane,' he replied, full of admiration. 'The guy belongs to Christophe. There's no way —'

'We could liberate him.'

Simeon considered it, his face darkening as the idea took hold. 'You mean,' he said with mock drama, 'we break into the funhouse and stage a daring rescue bid?'

'Yeah, why not? We could go during the day when they're all asleep.'

Nodding, Simeon said, 'I like it, babes. I really do.'

'Cool!'

'But supposing Christophe catches us,' said Simeon. 'Cos if he does, we're dead. Well, metaphorically speaking.'

'Then we'll just say we came looking for extra cock,' said Suzanne. 'It's not as if he'd find that suspicious.'

*   *   *

Coney Island's empty fairgrounds, poised between closure and redevelopment, lay sprawled along the shoreline like a dead Mardi Gras. In mellow sunlight, Simeon and Suzanne, wearing trench coats, fedoras and shades, drifted through the wreckage of graffiti and rust, of forlorn tattoo parlours, steel-shuttered clam bars and rides that once reached the sky. They looked like survivors of a nuclear apocalypse. Rats, cockroaches and vampires.

'I wish we'd come here in the 50s,' said Suzanne. 'Imagine the pickings.'

'Oh, man,' sighed Simeon, full of longing. 'Everyone so happy and off-guard. Although, to be honest, I struggled with the 50s. I never did find my inner Teddy boy.'

'Yeah, it's not really you,' said Suzanne.

Nerves had made the two vampires unusually subdued and they fell into silence as they walked through the desert of lost, broken decadence. Christophe, broad, beautiful and black (well, greyish actually; sort of an off-black), wasn't a vampire to be trifled with. He reigned over a harem of sycophants and sluts, women who adored him and men who admired him. His increasing megalomania had led him to cast off a slew of friends and move to Coney Island, taking over a defunct funhouse where he'd established a commune of dark, bloody perversion.

Simeon and Suzanne, much to their annoyance, hadn't been invited. Squatting the nearby ghost train seemed as close as they could get. Christophe rarely ventured out. He got his cronies to bring home victims for supper and, so the rumour went, when he'd mentioned his interest in having a life-support machine, the two vampires who'd provided this and fixed the electricity generator had promptly gained admittance to Christophe's inner circle. It wasn't fair.

'I don't recall that sign being there before, do you?' asked Suzanne.

On a boarded-up ticket booth, a printed sign said THE FUNHOUSE IS CLOSED MONDAYS.

Simeon shrugged. 'What's today?'

Suzanne laughed. 'Hey, I think the funhouse is closed *all* days. Has been for years.'

'Man, Coney Island freaks me out. I don't know what's real and what isn't.'

'Does anyone?' asked Suzanne. 'C'mon, round the back.'

Suzanne and Simeon had visited the funhouse often enough to know the various sneaky ways of gaining access. However, once inside and having shucked off their hats and coats, navigating the garish, lurching maze of corridors, obstacles and optical illusions proved mighty difficult. It felt as if the very structure of the building were shifting and spinning, the walls seeming to close in, slabs and spirals of clashing colours assaulting the vampires' minds.

'Makes me long for the Arctic,' said Suzanne. 'All that pure white space.'

'All that lack of food,' countered Simeon. 'If I never see another polar bear again it'll be too soon.'

Simeon strode through a hall of mirrors, eyeing the rippling silver glass as if his reflection were actually there. 'I'm afraid I'm missing the joke,' he said, standing opposite a mirror, his lanky debonair image failing to register.

Suzanne wandered off.

'We mustn't lose each other!' hissed Simeon. He stepped sideways to try another mirror, amused by the pointlessness of the exercise.

Moments later Suzanne called out, 'Hey, this way, Sim!'

'Where, babes? Which way?'

'Here!'

Simeon followed her fading voice, entering a dimly lit room whose walls, floor and ceiling were striped and zigzagged like geometric zebras. It appeared to be hexagonal or was that octagonal? No, it was worse. It was a dodecahedron. Or was it? There were dark doorways on each wall and as Simeon began to count, the room seemed to tip. Or was it his eyes? And was the ceiling on a slope? Actually, was that wall curved?

Somewhere in the distance, Suzanne yelped in pain.

'Shit! What is it?' Simeon spun around, regretting it at once. It was best not to spin in stripy rooms. 'Suze? Where are you?' He sidled along the edge, palming the wall to make him feel less woozy. 'Suze?'

'It's OK,' said Suzanne from a doorway to his left. 'I'm fine, babes.'

Simeon turned and was struck by how beautiful Suzanne looked. Framed by the darkness behind her, she had the allure of a Scandinavian ice maiden slurred by voluptuousness. The sapphire brilliance of her eyes gleamed in the half-light, and her hair streamed over her shoulders in waves of gold. She wore a girlish summer dress printed with cornflowers and even though Simeon had seen it all before, he still wanted to shove that dress high and fuck her to hell and back.

'What happened, hun?' he asked.

'We need to be careful. Follow me.'

'Shouldn't I go first?' said Simeon. 'You know, to protect you?'

Suzanne shot him a dark look.

Simeon shrugged. 'Just a suggestion.'

Suzanne leading, the two vampires crept down a black corridor lit with red. At the far end, a narrow door opened onto a room so orange it made them wince. Running along it and bordered by handrails either side was a walkway made of wood interspersed with bands of steel rollers which slipped and spun underfoot.

'Ouch!' yelped Simeon, stumbling on the rollers and grabbing the handrail. 'Fuck!'

'Oh yeah, don't touch the handrail,' said Suzanne. 'It's live. You'll get an electric shock. Sorry, I meant to warn you.'

Simeon waggled his hand. 'Man, this is a sadist's paradise,' he said approvingly. He looked at the rail, seeing now the strip of metal that ran along its length. He couldn't help but conjure up an image of Suzanne's face in pain. He loved to see her suffer, loved the way her composure crumpled as he dragged her down into humiliation and hurt. His cock twitched at the thought of threatening her, of forcing her either to suck him or to feel an electric current sparking in her fingertips. 'C'mere, Suze,' he said. 'I want to kiss you.'

Suzanne turned, lips tilting in a knowing smile, and sashayed towards him as best she could. The rollers clacked and whirred as she wobbled across them.

'So compliant,' murmured Simeon, drawing her body to his. 'Aren't you?'

Suzanne moved to kiss him, the two of them unsteady on their feet, but Simeon seized a fistful of hair and stilled her. He pulled her head back hard, making her neck arch with a beauty that was almost mortal. Suzanne grimaced, mewing in exaggerated protest.

'Little slut, aren't you?' breathed Simeon. 'Rushing in for a kiss like that.' On the rollers, they trembled in their embrace as, ever so slowly, Simeon licked Suzanne's cheek, leaving moisture shimmering on her pallid skin. 'So dirty, so shameless.'

'No,' whispered Suzanne. 'I'm a good girl, I swear.'

Simeon licked her neck, her ear, her lips, glorying in the tease, in her whimpers of frustration and the feel of her body quivering in his arms. She fought to stay motionless on the rollers but it was difficult and they wobbled again when

Simeon clasped Suzanne's wrist, holding her slender hand over the metal strip.

'No,' she wailed, trying to pull back. 'It hurts. Please don't! Please don't electrocute me!'

'Shut up,' growled Simeon, gripping her wrist tighter. 'I'll do whatever I want. You're mine. Hear that? All mine.'

'No,' said Suzanne. 'I beg you. Don't hurt me, please! I'll do anything.'

'I know you will,' replied Simeon. 'Because you have no choice. Now get on your knees. I want to see you with your mouth wide open and ready for my cock.'

'No!' cried Suzanne.

'You want to feel the electricity, sweet thing?' asked Simeon, pushing her hand towards the rail.

'No, please!' said Suzanne, wriggling in his arms. 'No cock! And no electrocution!'

In truth, Suzanne had a voracious appetite and would've merrily deep-throated him till her tonsils were sore. However, it was always fun to pretend otherwise, especially when there were no innocents around to genuinely debase.

'On your knees,' repeated Simeon and he edged her back until they were standing on a wooden section of the walkway. 'Now!'

Suzanne fell to her knees, doing her best to look distressed. With a smug smile, Simeon unzipped and his cock bounced out, thick and taut.

'Open wide,' he said in a persuasive sing-song tone.

Suzanne obeyed, gaping for him, and Simeon was about to sink into her pretty pink lips when a tannoy voice boomed out, deep and clear: 'The funhouse is closed Mondays!'

The two vampires sprang apart.

'Christophe!' hissed Simeon, tucking himself away.

'Bang on,' boomed the voice.

'Oh, fuck,' murmured Suzanne, scanning to see how they were being watched. 'Where is he? I kinda forgot we were on a mission.'

Simeon frowned. 'Remind me,' he breathed.

'Dude on life support,' replied Suzanne, as quietly as she could.

'Shit. Yes.'

'You want to see him?' said Christophe's voice. Above them, a trap door sprang open in the ceiling and a lime-green rope ladder tumbled down. 'Then come on up.'

'Balls,' muttered Suzanne. 'I guess we blew our cover.'

The green ladder dangled a few feet from the vampires. 'And that ain't an invitation,' boomed Christophe. 'It's an order.'

Suzanne looked at Simeon. 'You first,' she said crisply. 'You know, to protect me.'

'Touché,' said Simeon and swiftly set one pointy black shoe on a rung, gripping the ladder as it swayed. You don't scare me, Christophe, he thought, climbing higher. Then he changed his mind when he emerged on the next level: a huge room decked out like the laboratory of a mad scientist and lit like a murky disco, spots of blue, green and red glowing on mysterious pieces of apparatus. Vats, test tubes and pipes bubbled with coloured liquids; a small, half-dissected alien lay glumly in a clear cylinder; by Simeon's feet, a barrel on its side oozed acid-yellow liquid which appeared to have burned a hole in the floor; DANGER TOXIC WASTE said a sign.

'Hi there!' Simeon called out, seeing no one.

Silence.

'Hey, give me a hand,' said Suzanne as her head popped through the trap door.

Simeon noticed another room screened off by glass in a gloomy corner, and inside it was their mission: the cute mortal hooked up to a life-support system. Simeon had seen inside

65

that room before and guessed the glass must have been curtained off at the time. He certainly hadn't seen this crazy lab before.

'Cool,' said Suzanne after Simeon had helped her up. 'Experiments! Medical fantasies! I love – '

'It's not all fantasy, Suze,' warned Simeon, gesturing to the glass screen.

'It is if you want it to be,' came Christophe's voice, this time without the tannoy. 'Cos who's to say where reality stops and starts? Maybe my whole existence is a fantasy. Maybe yours is too.'

'Oh, for goodness sake,' said Simeon under his breath.

A thud on the floorboards made them turn and there was Christophe on the far side of the room, knees bent as if he'd just jumped from a height. Grinning, he swaggered towards them, looking oddly like a thuggish black Cossack, bare chested with fur-lined boots below calf-length combats. His hair was close-cropped, a shadow of wool over a menacingly strong head, and a neat goatee framed his plump lips. His skin was the colour of stale chocolate, muscular slabs of brown tinged with a bloodless beige-grey bloom, and tattooed inky flames licked up one big brawny arm. Whorls of dark hair clustered around his pecs and his stomach was a washboard. Around his neck he wore, like a symbol of defiance, a large silver cross.

Simeon's cock was rigid.

'Nice to see you, friends,' said Christophe and he clasped Simeon's hand, giving it a single shake. Around them, the light was low and purplish, and a stormy lilac glow shone on Christophe's body.

Before Simeon could reply, Christophe grabbed hold of his hair and plunged a fat, insistent tongue into his mouth. He kissed deeply, his thick lips pulsing, his beard scouring and, all the while, he kept Simeon's hair bunched, making his scalp prickle as if with a thousand tiny stab wounds.

When they broke away, Christophe smirking and Simeon stunned, Suzanne was gawping. 'Oh God,' she said weakly. 'I love watching men fuck. Keep going, please.'

Christophe gave an arrogant laugh. 'This ain't a floor show, lady,' he said, crossing to her. 'This ain't a pleasure palace. This ain't the fucking *movies*! This is about me. Me! Me and my dick. It ain't about you or what you want to watch. You don't count for jack shit. You getting that, missy?'

Christophe unzipped.

Suzanne smiled nervously and licked her lips.

'Now suck my cock, bitch. Show me you got the message.'

Simeon would've intervened to protect Suzanne's honour except he knew she didn't have any. Besides, if he squared up to Christophe, he'd end up the fool on the floor. This guy was twice his size, twice as solid, a statistic so hot it hurt.

Suzanne dropped to her knees. 'Message received loud and clear.'

Simeon throbbed with lust as he watched Christophe grasp Suzanne's hair, his forearms bulging as he held her steady in his grip. With slow showmanship, he eased his cock into her mouth, clearly revelling in his power and strength. Suzanne drew back and began slipping along his length, raising her eyes to him in search of approval. Christophe offered none.

'You enjoying that, huh?' he asked as if he were doing her a favour.

In response, Suzanne slurped faster and deeper until Christophe stilled her. He clamped her head in his hands and began driving harder and harder, neat hips thrusting against her face, his silver cross winking in the gloom. Suzanne spluttered once or twice, hands flapping in a weak gesture of surrender, but she was on her knees and she liked it nasty.

Simeon, standing there like a spare part with a boner in his pants, was wildly envious.

'You want cock?' asked Christophe, turning to him without breaking his thrust. 'Huh? You want a taste of my cock, boy?'

Simeon bridled at the 'boy' reference – he was nearly 300 years old! – but he was horny enough not to allow dignity to hamper his lust.

'The name's Simeon,' he said coolly, drawing himself taller. 'You know who I am, Christophe. And you know that I *always* want cock.' He flicked his sleek black locks and gave a stiff smile. 'And fortunately for you, I'm not too fussy whose.'

'Then get on your knees, slut,' snapped Christophe.

'Or else?' challenged Simeon.

Christophe moved vampirically fast, his arm a blur, and, before Simeon knew it, he'd been sent sprawling to the ground.

'Or else nothing,' said Christophe coolly.

'Bastard,' snarled Simeon. His mussed-up hair obscured half his face and, as he clambered onto his hands and knees, he looked ancient and savage, a creature emerging from the darkest of forests.

'What I say goes,' said Christophe. 'You got that?'

Simeon glared up at him. Man, but he was hot. His body was so big and muscular he might have been a machine built for efficiency, his grey-black skin concealing steel and circuitry rather than the vile needs of the undead. His cock, gleaming with Suzanne's saliva, poked from his combats, violet-tinged and brutal, and in the moody half-light, his eyes glittered like jet.

Simeon moved to kneel by Suzanne, aroused and fearful. 'I'm prepared to give it a try,' he said, attempting the breezy sarcasm of a man undaunted.

Christophe gave a light chuckle and slapped Simeon's cheek.

It was scarcely more than a chastising cuff but on Simeon's refined, high-boned face, the hand landed with a meaty thwack.

'Ouch! What *is* it with you?' said Simeon, gingerly touching his cheek.

'Slap me,' said Suzanne, tilting her face in offering. 'Slap me hard. Please!'

Ignoring her request, Christophe said, 'Open your mouths, bitches. I want to see what class of cocksucker we got here. Who's the best, huh? Which pretty little snow dog's gonna make me blow my load?'

'I taught him everything he knows,' said Suzanne, casting a sidelong glance at Simeon.

'Shut the fuck up and show me throat,' snapped Christophe. 'Both of you. And close your eyes. I got me a surprise for you.'

'No way,' said Simeon. 'No way am I closing my eyes. Suze, don't close your eyes. I trust this idiot about as far as I can throw –'

'Shut. Your. Fucking. Eyes,' said Christophe and the vampires obeyed at once. 'Better,' he said. 'Now stick your tongues out like good little doggies. Hands up. Higher. Beg nicely.'

Simeon and Suzanne begged.

'Real cute,' said Christophe, stroking Simeon's jaw.

Simeon tensed at the touch. He was desperate to peep, to withdraw his tongue, anything to make him feel less vulnerable, stupid and afraid. And yet at the same time, he wanted to remain like that because feeling vulnerable, stupid and afraid was so freaking hot. And it was always a delicate balance: the more real the fear, the hornier the scene. But take it too far and an excess of fear makes desire bolt.

Well, to be fair, it depended on which side of the equation you were on. Simeon knew only too well how delicious it was to have someone begging for their life. Hell, he could watch for hours as someone screamed for mercy. And no doubt Christophe could too. It was a shame they'd fallen out, although Simeon didn't know why they had. 'Was it something we said?' he'd asked Suzanne. But there was nothing they could recall. It seemed as if they'd simply fallen out of favour. Christophe could be so fickle.

'A little treat for you,' said Christophe.

Simeon heard a zipper open, sensed Christophe rummaging in his clothes, then he started as liquid spurted onto his tongue. After a split second's fear, he realised what it was. Blood! Beautiful blood! He'd barely tasted it when the source was withdrawn and, next to him, Suzanne gasped in pleasure. Then the liquid was back in his own mouth, streaming down his tongue, that familiar coppery tang catching in his throat. Christophe's cock nudged at his lips and Simeon sucked on its head, licking the blood which seemed to spill from its end. It was cooler than blood from a fresh kill but it was blood nonetheless. And it was sweeter, richer, smoother than any he'd ever tasted.

When Suzanne gasped again, Simeon peeked through his eyelashes to see Christophe aiming his cock at her gaping mouth. By his groin was a plastic pouch and from a small pipe, blood sluiced along his hard length, dripping from his fingers. When he entered Suzanne's mouth, rivulets of scarlet spilt onto her face and trickled into her hair.

Then Christophe swung back to Simeon as if he were pissing on them in blood. Simeon squeezed his eyes shut, gulping greedily.

'That's amazing stuff,' said Suzanne. 'So intense. I'm getting such a rush.'

And she was right. What the hell was it? Human blood? Manufactured? Had they improved that rotten synthetic Blud they'd had to drink in the Arctic? But right then Simeon hardly cared as long as it kept on coming, filling his veins with something so wonderful it had to be bad for you.

'You like it?' asked Christophe, swinging back to Suzanne.

'Oh, man,' breathed Simeon. 'I fucking love it. I feel high, so fucking high. Holy shit, I could conquer the world. I could . . . I could fuck everything that ever lived. I could stroll into an orgy with my cock so hard –'

'Last drop,' said Christophe.

Simeon swallowed. 'More,' he said.

'Yes,' begged Suzanne. 'More, please.'

'Taste each other,' said Christophe. 'There's more there.'

Simeon looked at Suzanne, at her mouth and chin smeared with blood, her golden hair lit with lilac and matted with crimson. She gazed back, hungrily scanning his face, her blue eyes unnaturally bright as if she were on the verge of killing. Yes, it was true. There was more there.

The two vampires flew at each other, kissing with feral aggression. They clutched each other's hair, tongues thrashing and probing as they sought the last traces of blood. When their mouths were cleaned out, they tussled and yelped, fighting to lick stains from each other's faces and suck the wetness from each other's hair.

'You missed a bit,' said Christophe, tapping the floor with his boot.

'Aiee! Mine!' Suzanne fell to the ground, tongue trawling over the splintered planks, scavenging for droplets.

'You bitch!' yelled Simeon, trying to drag her up by the hair. 'Give me some.'

'Good man,' said Christophe. 'Hold her like that. It's time she got worked over.'

'Get off me,' panted Suzanne, struggling against Simeon. 'I can see more. There's a splash by –'

'You greedy –'

'If you do what I say,' said Christophe to Simeon, 'I'll reward you with more.'

'I'm doing it!' cried Simeon. 'Just say the word and I'm doing it.'

'Help me spear her,' said Christophe. 'Shove your dick in her mouth while I fuck her pussy. We can –'

'And I get more blood?' asked Simeon.

'For certain,' replied Christophe.

'What do I get?' demanded Suzanne.

'Fucked,' said Christophe.

'But that's not fair. You get blood *and* my body, while I only –'

'Shut it,' snapped Christophe. 'Fill her mouth, bro. She talks too much.'

With a gleeful laugh, Simeon unfastened and angled his hard cock towards Suzanne's lips. Still clutching her hair, he slammed into her mouth, his stroke so sudden it made Suzanne's eyes pop in outrage.

'You like that?' he teased, shunting into her warm, wet throat.

'Good man,' said Christophe. 'Let's see how she squeals when she's got me poking her pussy.'

Simeon adjusted their position to accommodate Christophe, and Suzanne thrust her butt high, groaning in readiness. The rumble of her voice rippled along Simeon's cock.

'Oh, man,' he said. And again, 'Oh man,' when he saw Christophe kneel behind Suzanne, flip her cornflower skirt up, tug her underwear down and aim his big solid cock between her thighs.

For a small frozen moment, with the purplish half-light burnishing Christophe's torso, he looked like a statue cast in pewter, a fixed image of physical perfection, a monster made of metal.

Then Christophe drove into Suzanne, his body coming alive, the silver cross bouncing below his neck. His penetration jolted Suzanne forwards, pushing her mouth further onto Simeon's cock. She moaned long and loud, the tremors of her throat buzzing over Simeon's tip.

'There we go,' said Christophe.

The men quickly established a shared rhythm, Christophe's fuck urging on Suzanne's suck, everyone groaning, all their pleasures rising.

'She giving it to you good?' asked Christophe. He reached out to tug Suzanne's hair. 'You blowing my brother good, huh?'

Simeon and Suzanne moaned in unison. Yes, it was good. Everything was good, so fucking good.

'Feel this,' said Christophe, and he reached under Suzanne to work her clit.

Again, the snow vampires chorused their pleasure, Suzanne's excitement firing Simeon's. The strange sweet blood was still coursing through Simeon's body, and every sensation seemed wrapped in itself, shivering on the brink of becoming more than what it was. The timbre of Christophe's voice was wreathed in Suzanne's soft cries, a beautiful bass touched by the breath of angels, his own mind a cathedral echoing with the ragged hymn of a threesome. On his swollen cock, that mouth was a massage of wetness and heat threatening to drown him entirely, the spill of saliva cranking him tighter and tighter. Opposite, in the dim purple light, the sight of Christophe fucking was a vision of anatomical perfection, the black sweep of his musculature flexing with the strongest of drives, the drive to fuck.

Oh boy, was it good. Simeon felt he were chasing the fullness of sensation as much as the burst of orgasm, his perception on the cusp of mind-altering expansion. Minutes later, when he felt the rise of Suzanne's climax, his own groans rumbled through him like cascading stones, his pleasure landsliding. Around his cock, her breath grew short and urgent, and she lost her concentration, her oral skills slipping as nearness softened her body.

'Hot little slut,' gasped Simeon. 'Stuffed full of dick. So dirty, so greedy.'

Even as he spoke, Simeon knew that what he was really saying was 'Man, but I love you, Suze.' It was no big deal. He'd told her many a time before. He loved that she took it; that she gave it; that she wanted it; that you could not separate Suzanne from sex, perversion and appetite. When that was at the core of you and you met your soulmate, your fuckmate, you made damn sure you stuck together, especially in the face of eternity. So many mortals had it wrong. They thought sex was incidental, a thing apart like a hobby. They thought it was simply something you *did*. But Simeon and Suzanne knew better. Sex was something you *were*.

'Cheap little whore,' growled Simeon, plunging harder.

'Go on, go on,' said Christophe. 'Come for your boys. Come for us, bitch.'

Suzanne's eager moans thrummed on Simeon's cock then she wailed long and loud, bucking and twitching as she peaked. Simeon's climax tightened, and he might have come within seconds if Christophe hadn't snatched himself out of Suzanne.

'Take me, bro,' he said.

With his legs astride Suzanne, Christophe shuffled towards Simeon who opened his mouth to swallow Christophe's hard, handsome cock.

'Wicked,' said Christophe. He stood proud, clasping his hands behind his head and driving into Simeon's mouth. Simeon thought he'd died and gone to heaven, a cock in his mouth and a mouth on his cock. At that point in time, he didn't think he had any other requirements in life. When Christophe grew close, so did Simeon and, moments after Christophe roared and pumped his saltiness into his throat, Simeon gave Suzanne much the same. Release surged through him, squeezing him empty as he groaned around Christophe's cock, the taste of him still swilling in his mouth, a taste of peat, burned tyres and dark, forgotten shipwrecks.

When Christophe withdrew, he bared his palm for Simeon to slap. 'Gold star, dude.'

'Totally,' said Simeon, high-fiving him.

Suzanne pulled away from them and flopped onto her back, arms outstretched. 'Man,' she said. 'You guys are hot. Seriously.'

Simeon sat beside her, stroked sweat-sticky hair from her flushed face and printed a grateful kiss on her lips.

'And that blood . . .' said Suzanne.

'Yeah, what the hell *is* it?' asked Simeon. 'I gotta get us some.'

'Even crack addicts don't give me a buzz like that,' said Suzanne, toying affectionately with Simeon's fingers.

Christophe stroked his dwindling erection. 'It's from our friend over there,' he said, indicating the second room where the cute guy lay hooked up to equipment. 'Mr Tube.'

'Wow, is he on meds?' asked Suzanne.

Christophe shook his head. 'Ain't nothing in his system 'cept what we give him. Saline, food. Stuff that keeps him alive. He's just a scorching hot ethnic mix. It's a New York thing.'

'You mean the city's full of dudes this tasty?'

'Nah,' said Christophe. He zipped up his combats, sat against the overturned barrel and began rolling a joint. 'The blend's rare. No one knows the score. Two parts Armenian, one part Cuban, eleven parts Scottish, that kinda deal.'

'Yum. Does he have siblings?' asked Simeon.

Christophe shrugged. 'Believe me, we are looking! We are looking *hard*. Found a cousin but she was average so we ate her. I'm keeping him here. We got a nurse. He fixes the drips. Took a while to get the balance right. You know, input, output. But now we drain him regularly. Small amounts of blood but quality. He's getting weak though. And he's as mad as hell, totally pissed at us.' Christophe laughed. 'We give him a break Mondays, take him off the machine, tape up his tubes and holes, give him a little, ha, exercise. You know, check everything's still functioning. Torture him a while.'

'Cool,' said Suzanne. 'I guess some guys are too good to kill. Torture's neat.'

'Man, I'd like to see that,' sighed Simeon.

Christophe licked along the gummed edge of his joint and sealed it. 'Thought you guys got off on synthetic blood,' he said with a look of disdain. 'I heard that's what you were doing in the snow.'

'Bleurgh! Blud,' said Suzanne. 'That stuff is rank. I had to take mine with sugar.'

'Yeah, and it's only because we were starving,' protested Simeon. 'Give me mortals any day. Blud sucks.'

Christophe grinned, indigo smoke trickling up from his lips before he released a rich cloud. 'Then welcome back, friends! Hell, I thought you'd turned into a couple of pussies. I ain't got time for this new breed, those vamps banging on about morality and ethics. Dude, I think, get over yourself. You're a vampire. Ain't nothing gonna change that so get killing.'

'Totally!' chimed Simeon and Suzanne.

'So you wanna stay and play with my pet?' asked Christophe.

'Oh, let me at him,' said Simeon, taking the joint Christophe offered.

'Does he beg for mercy?' asked Suzanne. 'Does he plead for his life?'

'Oh, for sure,' said Christophe. 'He begs and he pleads and he wails. And you can tell he's hot for it. His cock's rock hard and he makes such a noise. But in the funhouse, no one can hear you scream. Especially when it's closed.'

Simeon and Suzanne also appear in Kristina Lloyd's Arctic vampire novella, *The Vampire's Heart*, published in the Black Lace collection *Lust Bites*. Kristina Lloyd is the author of the Black Lace novels *Darker Than Love*, *Asking for Trouble* and *Split*.

Vampires, Limited

Lisabet Sarai

'Next!' Lara stabbed the intercom button with a crimson-tipped finger. She tilted her chair back and closed her eyes, trying to summon some enthusiasm for the next sacrificial lamb. Who would have thought it would be so difficult? With the current craze for all things vampiric, finding a new model or two with the appropriate pallor and unearthly allure should have been a piece of cake. The city teemed with Dracula wannabes. Why were the ones who showed up at her office so lame?

She needed new faces, new excitement. The poster-sized cover images on her walls featured the dark-haired, chalk-faced, chisel-chinned hunks that her readers expected. Swathed in black, poised above the vulnerable flesh of their gorgeous prey with fangs bared, they reeked of danger and desire. An occasional female vamp joined them, jet curls tumbling into her pale cleavage, carmine lips shining as though already painted with blood.

The images were sexy, edgy and irresistibly hip. In its first year, *Vamp* magazine had broken the circulation record for a new publication. It had become the de facto authority for the burgeoning vampire subculture. It covered the fashions, the clubs, the bands, the latest pseudo-vampiric celebrities. In the back, advertisements for skin-bleaching cosmetics and fang implants mingled with the personal ads. 'Attractive SWF seeks dominant SWM for blood-sucking adventures.'

The cultural wave was far from cresting, but Lara knew that she had to keep innovating, or she'd be left in the dust by her copycat competitors.

A knock brought her back to the here and now. 'Come in,' she called, trying to erase the impatience from her voice. She flicked her black bangs out of her eyes and assumed what she hoped was a welcoming expression.

A man glided in through the door and Lara thought for an instant that there had been a mild earthquake. Reality somehow shifted. Her stomach dropped away, as though her roller-coaster car had just reached a peak and plunged down the other side. The office and its sombre furnishings suddenly looked more solid, hyper-real, every detail visible.

With some difficulty, Lara focused on the blond young man standing in front of her desk. 'Good afternoon.' Reflexively she took the portfolio that he handed her. 'I'm Lara Carter, publisher of *Vamp*.'

'Jim,' her visitor answered in a broad American accent. 'Jim Henderson. Thank you for taking the time to see me, Ms Carter.'

Jim Henderson was attractive, no question of that, but Lara could see immediately that he was all wrong. He was slender rather than muscular, though he moved well as he seated himself across from her. His straw-coloured curls and ruddy complexion fairly screamed health and youth. She'd never seen anyone who looked less undead. He had such an open, intelligent face that Lara couldn't imagine him looking crafty or menacing. He wasn't even wearing black. His tan slacks and robin's-egg sport shirt highlighted his trim physique and heightened the blue of his eyes, but no vampire (at least, no London vampire) would ever be caught wearing such a costume.

'You think that I'm the wrong type for your vampire mag.'

It was a statement, not a question and mirrored her thoughts so accurately that Lara was startled.

'Well, you certainly don't fit the stereotype. You're a bit too, um, wholesome for our readers.'

Jim's laugh held an odd, bitter edge. 'Take a look at my photos before you make a decision, Ms Carter.'

Lara flipped open the portfolio and leafed through the contents. There was no résumé. The first two pictures were head shots, clearly professional, and Lara had to admit that the man's smouldering gaze was dark and seductive enough to send a chill up her spine, despite the blue eyes and fair colouring.

'Do you have any experience?'

'Depends what you mean. But modelling experience, no. I've never been a model.'

'Why do you want to work for *Vamp*, then? What did you do before?'

'I was in college.' He didn't seem to want to say any more about his past. 'When I saw your ad, it seemed natural to apply.'

Lara appraised him with the hard-headedness that was her trademark. He was quite gorgeous. She wouldn't mind taking him home. However, she didn't need a dilettante, a college kid on a lark. At the moment, *Vamp* was her life's work. She'd quit a good job at *Vogue* to follow her hunch and it had paid off. She needed models who were as serious as she was.

'I'm not a dilettante. I am serious about this job.' Lara's eyes narrowed. His sensitivity was certainly unnerving. 'Take a look at the next few photographs. Please.'

She flipped to the next picture and sucked in her breath. The image was incredible. The scene was familiar but the intensity made it new. She scarcely recognised Jim. He wore a black velvet cape with a red satin lining and white gloves. His face was poised above an exquisite girl with long red hair that barely hid her obviously naked body. His full lips curled into a snarl, displaying the most realistic fangs that Lara had ever seen. Blood dripped from those fangs, pooling in shiny droplets on the woman's creamy skin. Blood welled from the puncture wounds clearly visible on her neck. The man's eyes were not on his prey, who wore a look of languid ecstasy. They were focused towards the viewer, burning with a palpable hunger that made Lara swallow hard.

'Wow,' she whispered. The photo had a dramatic, visceral effect. Her heart raced. Her palms became sweaty. Underneath her black jersey, she felt her nipples tighten into aching knots. 'That's amazing. How did you manage it?'

'Try the next picture.' The man's body was tense, as though he was working hard to hold something back. Slowly, tearing herself away from the soulful gaze in the photo, she turned it over.

The photograph that followed ripped her apart. Although vampiric in theme, it was nothing like the camp pictures that her publication featured. The same red-haired woman lay nude on a satin-draped bier, graceful and pale. Her wrists crossed on her abdomen, just below the modest swell of her perfect breasts. Her face was turned towards the camera, her eyes closed, her lips parted. A trail of crimson fluid trickled from her neck, across the white satin and onto the stone floor.

Behind the bier stood the vampire. His right hand held a white candle that fitfully illuminated the arches of the vault. His left cupped his victim's breast, thumb resting lightly on her prominent nipple.

His blond hair was pushed back from his brow, damp with sweat. His skin was flushed with the blood that he had swallowed, the blood that still smeared his lips. Looking into those eyes, eyes as dark as hell, Lara felt it all: his grief, his guilt and his awful, all-consuming lust.

Who was she, the ethereal, terribly convincing victim? And who, who was he?

She didn't see him move. Yet all at once he was behind her, his hands on her shoulders, murmuring in her ear. 'Barbara was her name. She was my girlfriend, back in college. A terrible mistake.'

He was so close, she should have felt the heat of his body, but it was as if a mannequin was pressed against her instead of a living person. She could smell him though, a sharp grassy scent that made her think of the country and wide-open spaces.

Casually he trailed a finger up the side of her neck and circled her ear lobe. A shiver raced through her, winding tight around her nipples, spiralling down to her sex. He nipped at her ear, playful, but hard enough to make her gasp. 'As for me, you know who I am, don't you? Or at least, what I am.'

Lara knew what he was saying. She just couldn't accept it.

'Here.' Still behind her, he grabbed her hand and placed her fingers on his throat. His skin was cooler than the air, as cool and smooth as marble. 'Do you feel any pulse?'

'No – but – it's just not possible. It's just a myth. A fashion, a fad. Everyone these days pretends...'

He brought her wrist to his lips, flicking his tongue over the spot where the veins were closest to the surface. His mouth was hot, unlike the rest of him. A violent shudder of desire rocked her body. 'Close your eyes,' he murmured.

I should call off this farce now, Lara thought, but she obeyed anyway. Something pricked at her flesh where he held it against his mouth, the tiniest sting, hardly deserving the name pain. Then there was heat, and a pulling, not at her wrist but somehow at her heart, which leaped up in response and began to pump at twice its normal rate.

Red flooded the space behind her eyelids, scarlet, crimson,

three-dimensional eddies of colour like billowing clouds. A brief icicle of fear stabbed at her, then melted as warm, sweet pleasure flowed through her limbs. Her nipples, her pussy, everywhere there was this hot wet current, aching and yet somehow not urgent.

'Relax,' he whispered. 'Let go.'

She heard his voice, coming from a long way off. She saw his eyes, burning through the red haze. They had darkened from blue to empty black. She felt herself tumbling into their depths. Some last fragment of self-consciousness cried out for her to resist, but she ignored it. He was too strong, his will irresistible, the gifts he offered too precious to refuse. She let herself drift. He cradled then released her. She felt herself beginning to drown in the scarlet river of his bloodlust.

The shock of separation drove black spikes of pain into her temples. She opened her eyes, gasping for breath. Motes of red swam in her vision. She twisted around to look at him, in wonder and terror.

'Sorry.' He shrugged. 'I didn't know how else to convince you.'

'You're ... You're the real thing, aren't you?' Lara thought her chest would burst. 'Nosferatu. Undead.' She rubbed at her throbbing head. 'I never believed ...'

'Believe,' he said, then all at once was back in his chair, leaving her heart slamming against her ribs. He smiled at her, that wide-open, American country-boy smile. Lara worked to catch her breath, to calm herself to some semblance of normality.

It wasn't possible. Vampires were a fiction, a legend. They were creatures of fantasy and nightmare. For some reason, the notion of vampires tapped into something fundamental in the human imagination. She knew dozens, maybe hundreds, of people who desperately wanted vampires to be real. These people were the engine of her success. However, even the most obsessed, the ones who caught and ate flies and slept in coffins in the cellar, knew the truth.

And now, here, that truth was being challenged.

He read her doubts, in her mind or on her face. He disappeared suddenly, then reappeared at her side with a glass of water. 'Looks like you could use this.' Another blink and he was back where he started, smiling at her across the desk. The water was there, at her elbow, proof that she hadn't been hallucinating. She took a sip and stopped fighting the evidence of her senses. It wasn't possible that he was a vampire. But it was true.

'Are you very ancient?' she asked finally. The question sounded absurd. What was she doing, continuing the interview? Jim laughed, wholeheartedly this time.

'I'm twenty-four. Or I was, that night five years ago at the frat party, when somebody's girlfriend's sister turned me. I admit that I was drunk. Barbara had just told me that she wanted a commitment, and I knew I wasn't ready. I told her I loved her, but that wasn't enough. So I went off, got plastered and the next thing I knew I was in bed with this slutty-looking brunette who had very sharp teeth.' Lara couldn't help giggling. His tale was such a contrast to the mythology that she marketed.

'And then? What happened next? What about Barbara?'

Jim's face grew shadowed. 'Look, I don't really want to talk about it. Not now, not here. Can we go somewhere quiet and dark for a drink?'

'You can drink? I mean, besides – well, you know.'

'Sure. I can't eat solid food, though. It's awful, because my senses are unnaturally acute. I can smell a juicy steak grilling half a block away. Pure torture.' He sighed. 'Anyway, what about the job? Do you still think that I'm unqualified, Ms Carter?'

Lara took note of the challenge in his voice. Her body still trembled at the proximity of an honest-to-goodness creature of the night, but her mind was working overtime. How could she best use him to further her goals? To expand her vampiric empire? His photos were far too raw for her audience. Could he project the same level of intensity in a less extreme scene? And what about his co-models? Could he elicit the same sort of rapturous response from them that she had seen in Barbara's face? Without actually taking them, of course?

She imagined herself in the woman's position, offering her throat to those vicious fangs. The notion was seductive. She had just been given a taste. To give in completely to that kind of power – to be overwhelmed, consumed by an unnatural hunger – the temptation was almost overwhelming. She'd always wanted the power, never considered letting go. Now the thought of offering herself to this creature made her damp with desire. A wave of dizziness swept over her, followed by a surge of fear.

'Don't worry,' Jim commented. 'Seriously, I know how to control myself. Every few weeks I raid a hospital or Red Cross blood bank, then fix up the computerised records so the inventory won't be missed. I'm only dangerous when I'm really hungry. And I don't mind if you want to use me to build your business. That's why I'm here.'

Lara blushed. It was difficult to remember that this apparently naive young man could read her thoughts. Did he know that her knickers were wet? His good-natured grin told her that he did.

She stood, working to regain her composure, and held out her hand. 'Well, Jim. I'm pleased to welcome you to Vampires, Limited. Shall we go for that drink?'

'Sure, Lara.' He helped settle her cape around her shoulders, then held the door for her. An old-fashioned gentleman, Lara thought. How charming. She pictured a shoot: Jim holding open the door of a crypt and politely ushering some juicy young thing into its depths. It might work. Then she noticed him watching her, a half-smile on his ripe lips. Damn. She couldn't get used to being so transparent.

Her assistant Felicia raised a carefully pencilled eyebrow when they emerged into the anteroom. Like everyone who worked for *Vamp*, Felicia wore black clothes and white make-up. 'Are you leaving, Ms Carter? There are still two candidates waiting to see you.'

'Tell them to come back tomorrow, please. I'm going out with Mr Henderson to discuss business.'

They walked in silence through the chilly overcast afternoon, heading for one of Lara's favourite pubs. The pavement was crowded. Businessmen and shoppers bustled by, not giving Jim and Lara a second glance. It would be dusk soon and rush hour would begin in earnest.

Lara stopped short, staring at Jim's figure, bundled up in his overcoat. 'It's daytime,' she accused, stabbing her finger into his chest.

'Yes, so?'

'Well, what about the sun? I thought that vampires couldn't be about during the day?'

'Not much sun,' Jim commented, peering up at the leaden sky. 'That's one reason I came to England, actually. I can't handle direct sunlight, but in weather like this I'm fine. Sunscreen or a hat helps, too.'

'But, then you're not really a creature of the night!'

Jim grabbed the hand poking him. Slowly and deliberately, he rubbed his thumb over the tiny puncture wound on her wrist. Lara trembled, remembering. 'Sort of depends on your definition, doesn't it?' His smile made her cringe with embarrassed desire. When he released her, she struggled not to sink to her knees. He took her arm and led her in the direction of the pub.

'Don't believe everything you hear. Garlic doesn't bother me. I could sleep in a church or take a bath in holy water with no ill effects. Electromagnetic radiation, on the other hand, could probably kill me. Even a cellphone makes me weak. A taser would likely do me in.'

Lara shifted the bag with her phone to her other arm.

'Loud noises are a problem, because my hearing is so sensitive. Explosions. Sirens. I went deaf for a week, early on, when my room-mate turned up the volume on Ozzy Osbourne. Now I always carry earplugs.'

'What about flying? Or becoming invisible?' Lara remembered the way he seemed to appear and disappear in her office.

'I can move extremely fast, when I want to. However, I have nothing whatsoever to do with bats!'

They arrived at Donnie's, the place she'd been aiming for. It was, as he had requested, dark and quiet, especially at four in the afternoon. Settling them in a booth at the back, Lara ordered a gin and tonic. Jim asked for a glass of Cabernet, grinning at her raised eyebrows.

They shucked off their outerwear. Jim sat next to her on the bench. His thigh was a mere inch from hers. It was just so strange that she couldn't feel his body heat through her tights. She wondered, suddenly, what his cock was like. Would it be cool like his neck or warm like his lips?

'I'd be happy to show you,' Jim laughed.

Lara felt the flush climbing to the roots of her hair. 'Damn it, can you hear every bloody thing that I'm thinking?'

'Not really. Sometimes it's all muddled together. But it seems as though the more emotion there is associated with a thought, the more clearly it comes through.'

Gently, he reached over and brushed her bangs away from her eyes. 'You seem to be quite an emotional person, Lara.'

Emotional? That certainly conflicted with her self-image. She saw herself as rational, businesslike, ambitious. She didn't let her feelings intrude on her life or influence important decisions. Her two ex-boyfriends had both called her 'cold', but never mind. She was simply disciplined. Self-controlled.

It was difficult to maintain control, though, sitting next to this beautiful and seductive . . . phenomenon.

'So, why did you answer my ad, really? What were you looking for? With your powers, surely you can get all the money you might want.'

'I was lonely. Even though I don't look much like Dracula, people sense something. They don't necessarily recognise what I am, but they know, instinctively, that I'm not one of them. Unless I use my abilities to charm them, they shun me.'

Lara nodded, recalling her odd sensations when he had entered her office.

'I thought that, working for a vampire magazine, I'd be surrounded by people who were used to the idea of the undead. Who found it glamorous and sexy. Maybe they'd react differently from ordinary people. But now I don't know.' A shadow crossed Jim's face. 'It might be too dangerous for me to be working for you.'

'Dangerous for you? Or for me?'

'Possibly both.' He sipped his wine. It stained his full lips purple. Lara briefly imagined kissing him, then struggled to suppress the thought before he could catch it. Lost in his own concerns, he didn't react. Lara fidgeted with the lime in her drink.

'Tell me about Barbara,' she asked finally. 'The woman in the photos.' As soon as she saw his ravaged face, she was sorry for the question.

'I was stupid, inexperienced. And we were so much in love. When I realised what I had become, I crawled to her on my hands and knees and begged her forgiveness. I was so terribly sorry to have ruined our plans for a life together. Barbara, though, had other ideas. She pointed out that, according to all information, we could now share eternity. All I had to do was turn her, make her into a vampire too.

'I was reluctant, but she convinced me. She was so beautiful, I couldn't bear the notion that she would eventually age and die while I'd live for ever.

'We planned the ritual carefully, almost as if it were our wedding ceremony –'

'The photos,' Lara interrupted.

'Right.' Jim laughed bitterly. 'I set up the camera to record it all. The initiation of my beloved into the realm of the undead. But it all went terribly wrong.' He choked back a sob.

Lara felt a sympathetic lump in her throat. 'What happened?'

'Everybody knows how you make a new vampire. First you drain the victim's blood, bringing her close to death. Then you allow her to drink your blood. That's what we planned. That's what we did. It was incredible, terrifying and ecstatic.'

'But?'

'But she died. I couldn't save her. I couldn't turn her. Since then I've learned the truth.'

Lara was silent, waiting.

'To create a new vampire, you must suck the victim's blood while you're physically connected. While you're having sex.'

'You're joking!' Lara struggled not to laugh.

'No, it's no joke. That's why I ended up this way. That girl at the party – all she really wanted was my blood. But one thing led to another, and eventually we were fucking. I don't think she really understood either.'

No wonder his little demonstration had produced such an intense effect. For him, bloodlust and sexual desire were inextricably entwined. The instinctive drive to reproduce, to bring more souls over the boundary of death into the shadowy world that he inhabited, this was something he could not deny and could only imperfectly control.

Lara knew she should be frightened. She should get out of his seductive presence before she made a final, incorrigible mistake. The risk, the pure reality of it, only made her want him more. He was watching her. She could feel his eyes on her lips, on her throat, on the rise and fall of her breasts as her breath quickened.

She glanced around the bar, filling up now that it was after five. Donnie's was not known as a 'blood' bar, but, still, she noticed half-a-dozen men wearing capes and pale make-up, plus two or three women in slinky black dresses and wigs. It was pathetic, the way they all craved a fleeting taste of inhuman power, a brush with immortality. And here she sat, thigh to thigh with the genuine article.

'I don't fully understand it,' Jim said, obviously catching her thoughts once again. 'Why would they want to be me? Power's nice, but overall I live a pretty lonely and miserable existence.'

'Maybe ... Maybe I can make you a little less lonely. For a little while.' Lara cradled his cheek for an instant, then pulled his mouth to hers. His lips were as soft as any flesh, warm and muscular as they met and moulded to her own lips. She tasted the wine he had been drinking, with background flavours of iron and salt. His tongue, too, felt human, jousting against hers, exploring, questioning.

Her rigid nipples pressed rudely through the stretchy fabric of her top, pleading for his attention. Of course he knew what she wanted. Without breaking the kiss, he cupped both breasts, tracing symmetrical circles around the tips. Her pussy clenched.

Her thighs opened involuntarily. She rocked back and forth on the bench, rubbing her clit against the hard wood.

'Please,' she moaned against his open mouth, and then was silent, realising that she did not have to say anything. He broke the kiss to throw a twenty-pound note on the table, then pulled her to his chest.

'Imagine your apartment,' he said, close to her ear. 'Think about your bedroom. And hold on tight.'

She took a breath and was swallowed by sudden, utter darkness. She could feel the bulk of Jim's body pressed against hers, but she could see nothing. A howling wind tore at her clothes. Her ears rang with the clang of a hundred untuned bells. Fear rose in her throat, but before she could scream, it was over.

Light returned. She stood on the shag carpet in her room clutching at Jim's shirt. Her knees buckled. He held her up, held her against him.

'I ... What ... How ... ?' she babbled.

'Hush, Lara. There's no need for talk now.' He bent to kiss her again and this time she felt the fire stirring deep within him. She sensed his unnatural strength as he lifted her onto the bed and knelt between her legs. He peeled off her tights and drew down her soaked knickers without comment. She felt the air stir as he bent his mouth close to her yearning pussy, but no breath. Her clit beat like a tiny heart, swollen with blood. She knew that he could smell the blood through her skin, that for him it overwhelmed the tidal scent of her sex.

Take me, she thought. Before the idea was fully formed, his tongue was gliding through her slit, slithering among her folds, lapping at her juices as if they were in fact the fluid that he most craved. She arched and twisted under him, opening herself to him body and mind. He stabbed his tongue into her depths, then pulled back to suck hard on the aching bead of flesh at the apex. Sensation rippled out from that centre to all her extremities.

She pinched her nipples through her top, shuddering as the pleasure looped back to her pussy where he stroked it to a higher pitch. He sucked vigorously, holding her lower lips apart so that he could penetrate more deeply, smoothing her soaked curls with his thumbs. Lara writhed against him, burying his face in her wet depths. He didn't need to breathe, she realised. He could go on like this forever.

It might have been that thought that pushed her over. It might have been the sudden pain of his teeth nipping her clit, or the invasion of a slippery finger into her rear hole. Whatever the ultimate stimulus, her climax seized and ripped through her. Ecstasy surged and then crested. She raced screaming and shuddering down the other side, spasms of pleasure shaking her until she was as limp as a rag doll.

'I want you naked,' Jim said, his voice soft but full of command. 'I want to be able to see your pulse. I want to feel the heat of the blood in your veins.' He lifted her to her feet, and she let him, still dazed and weak from her orgasm. He eased the jersey over her head, baring her small freckled breasts and taut wine-dark nipples. He reached around back to unzip her, giving her bottom a squeeze on the way, and guided her pencil skirt over her hips to the floor.

Lara let him undress her, passively enjoying his touch. She couldn't comprehend the lassitude that overwhelmed her. Normally she was the aggressor in the bedroom. Now all she wanted was to lie back and let him do whatever pleased him.

He arranged her on the champagne satin coverlet. The smooth cool fabric caressed her bottom and back. He crouched between her spread thighs, naked now himself. His cock was huge and pale with a livid purple head. Hot or cool? she wondered again. He half-smiled in response, and buried his undead flesh inside her.

Cold, deathly cold, and as hard as granite, he filled her, stretched her to the point of pain. Panic rose in her, fuelled by the weird sensations that his inhuman cock wakened. Surely he'd tear her apart. People always talked about cocks as if they were steel or stone, but this was no metaphor. Icy fingers crept through her depths, making her shiver violently.

Concern filled Jim's handsome face. 'Should I stop? Is it too much?' At the sound of his voice, something changed. The hard rod embedded in her flesh grew warm, melting her resistance and her fear. The pleasure began to flow again, as rich and sweet as honey. Full as she was, she wanted to be fuller. His cock owned her now and that was what she wanted. She wanted him to take her, to use her, to consume her.

He heard. He pulled his cock halfway out of her clinging flesh, then rammed it back in, wringing a whimper of pain from her. More, she thought. He pierced her once again, slowly, letting her feel the length and breadth of him taking control. Lara gasped. His smooth immutable flesh swept over her aching clit, waking shimmering echoes of her climax.

She gazed up at him and saw his eyes growing dark. His lips were parted. Peeking out she glimpsed the sharp tips of his fangs. A thrill raced through her. This was not fantasy. This was real.

More. He started to fuck her in earnest, thrusting hard and fast. She gripped the coverlet and arched up to him, still wanting more. The force of his strokes shook her whole body. Without effort, without expectation, she came, screaming and thrashing beneath him. Still he drove his cock into her again and again, until he had wrung a third climax from her ravaged body.

He hovered over her, supporting his weight with his arms

while his pelvis jerked, his cock drilling her pussy with metronomic regularity. His face was beautiful and terrible. His eyes were black pools of lust. His lips were drawn into a tense grimace, fully baring his fangs. His nostrils flared. Lara knew that he was scenting her blood.

It seemed now that she could read his thoughts. She sensed his desperate hunger and his fight to control it. He wanted her, wanted her body, in a way that no man ever would. The force of his need stunned her. She remembered the images he had brought to her office with new understanding. Being a vampire was not about power or immortality. It was about unending, insatiable lust.

Pity and desire welled up simultaneously. Nothing else mattered but this awful hunger, which only she could satisfy. She turned her head to the side, exposing the pulsing artery in her neck. 'Take me,' she moaned to him, inbetween thrusts. 'Taste me. Drink me. Make me yours.'

'No.' He forced out the words between gritted teeth. 'I can't. I won't.' His thrusts slowed, though his cock remained embedded in her pussy.

Lara tightened her inner muscles. His flesh jerked inside her. 'You need me.'

'It's not right.'

Lara reached down to where they were joined and dabbled her fingers for a moment, gathering her juices. Then she trailed her sticky fingers down from her ear to her collarbone, across her pulse, smearing the secretions across her blood-heated flesh. The smell of ripe pussy rose around her. 'Just a taste,' she cajoled. 'You know that you want to. You don't have to take me all the way.'

'I won't be able to stop.'

'I'll stop you.'

Jim laughed bitterly. 'Oh, no you won't. Don't you remember

my little demonstration? Would you have been able to stop me then?'

A tiny needle of fear pricked at Lara's heart. She ignored it. She wanted this and he would die without it. She knew that she could maintain control.

'Please?'

'No!'

Lara couldn't bear the anguish in his voice. She raised her wrist to her mouth, the one he had punctured earlier, and tore off the scab with her teeth. A crimson droplet welled from the spot. She forced it to his lips. 'Drink!'

With a strangled groan, the vampire seized her hand. He used his fangs to open the wound further. Pain flowed from her sliced wrist to her soaked pussy, where it inexplicably morphed into pleasure. She felt his suction pulling at her life-blood, felt her heart labouring to adjust. The sensation was familiar now, thrilling and yet soothing. With each of his swallows, her breathing slowed. Her limbs relaxed. Every nerve sang with delight. There was no striving for satisfaction. The truest and deepest pleasure was allowing herself to be consumed.

The sucking rhythm grew stronger. Dimly, through her trance, Lara understood that the vampire was fucking her as he drank. The sensations in her sex became more acute, the pleasure sharp-edged rather than mellow. She felt every detail of his movements, how his cock pulsed as he wallowed in her sex. She felt him tear at her wrist, felt the blood flowing lazily down her forearm. He lapped at the overflow. The warmth of his tongue made her pussy clamp down on his hardness. Her clit was huge and sensitive. Each of his strokes produced electric arcs of pleasure that sizzled through her flesh.

Crimson clouds swirled around her. She smelled cinnamon

and sulphur. Gradually, the more intense sensations faded. She did not miss them. The river was bearing her away, warm and wonderful. Her heart pumped sluggishly. She felt him, deep in her mind, sensed the way his terrible hunger receded as her life ebbed. She reached out to him, one last time, full of love and gratitude.

Agony suddenly replaced bliss, wrenching pain that filled the world. Seething blackness smothered her, roiling with horrible unseen forms. She couldn't breathe. Her throat was parched, her eyes stabbed by needles of anguish. Painful spasms racked her limbs.

'Lara! Lara!' Someone was slapping her face, stinging blows that rattled her teeth in her head. 'Come back, Lara!'

She gulped air and opened her eyes.

The room spun around her. Nausea rose in her throat, leaving an acid taste behind. Somehow she couldn't focus. Everything was blurry and the light seemed much too bright.

'Breathe, Lara. Focus. You're back. I'm sorry. I'm so sorry.'

Gradually the spinning stopped. The stabbing in her temples subsided to a dull ache and her vision cleared.

Jim looked younger and more vulnerable than ever. He knelt next to the bed, holding her wrist in an iron grip, trying to staunch the blood that still dribbled from her torn flesh. He looked incredibly relieved when she managed to prop herself up to half-sitting.

'How do you feel?'

Lara interrogated her body. 'Weak, and sore. But I guess I'm OK.'

'I told you. I told you we wouldn't be able to stop.'

'But we did. You did. I was ready to let it all go. But you're stronger than you realise.' She looked him over. His face was flushed and, though his fangs were no longer visible, there were traces of blood at the corners of his mouth. 'How do you feel? Better, I imagine, than before.'

Jim frowned. 'This isn't a joke, Lara! I almost killed you.'

'So? Then I would have lived for ever.'

'Is that what you really want?'

Lara remembered the terrible lust that she'd glimpsed in her vampire lover. She wasn't sure that she could endure that without going mad. 'I don't know. Maybe not. Maybe not yet.' He sat beside her on the bed. She reached out a finger and wiped the leftover blood from his lips. 'But with you – well, let me just say that perhaps you don't need to be so lonely any more.'

'Are you crazy? I'm dangerous. I warned you.'

'I'm willing to take risks.' Lara reached out and began to stroke his still-hard cock. 'At least when the payoff is worth it.'

Jim moaned. Lara wondered briefly whether vampires could actually come. She vowed that she'd find out. 'In any case, we're going to be seeing a lot of each other, now that you've joined the company.'

'I don't know, Lara.'

'Look, I won't take any argument. I'll appoint you vice-president, let you make artistic decisions, whatever you want. But I must have you.' She punctuated this with a squeeze that had Jim whimpering.

'Please.'

'Get over here. You haven't come yet, and just looking at you is turning me on.'

Jim straddled her and slid his cock into her sore but sensitive pussy. After all the previous fucking, after paranormal ecstasy and a brush with death, he still felt delicious.

'And based on what I've learned from you, I know exactly what will be the next big thing for Vampires, Limited.'

Jim moved inside her, slowly at first, then building up speed.

He smiled down at her. 'And just what would that be, Ms Carter?'

Lara clamped down on him, coming hard. She couldn't talk until after the spasms subsided.

'Vampire sex clubs, of course!'

Understudy
Angela Caperton

Blue lights bathed the vaulted ceiling of the tomb. The old Dutchman knelt, his silhouette cast up the arching wall. He wiped his brow and bowed his head above the long wooden box. Then his arm rose, its shadow enormous and black against the pallid azure stone, a hammer held high. He drove down, hard and sure as the fall of a tree, against the wooden stake.

The crack rang in the breathless theatre.

In the wings, Mauzy Lyman smelled wet wool and perfume, heard the shuffle and grunt out in the darkness, the indrawn gasp, and the little screams.

Behind the set, Count Dracula moaned like a beast in pain or a man in the throes of orgasm, his voice resonant and commanding in death, majestic even in pantomime absurdity.

The theatre rumbled with applause and the crew moved for the curtains and to clear the coffins away before the curtain call. Count Dracula walked stiffly into the wings, looking at no one, entirely in his role, as if he truly were one of the walking dead.

Mauzy loosened his tie and watched the curtains fall.

No work for Mauzy tonight. The star was never sick. In the two months Mauzy had been the understudy, he had only played two matinees when the Hungarian had assignations that he could not break, probably with Hollywood scouts.

This Hungarian, this Lugosi was the most famous man in New York City, *Dracula* the hardest ticket on Broadway and, in the spring, the show would be on the road for a national tour. Mauzy thought he could probably go along as the understudy, but, if the show continued on Broadway, he wanted the role itself, and who better than Lugosi's understudy? Who else knew every line, every gesture, as well as the Hungarian knew them, maybe better?

Mauzy lit a cigarette and wove his way backstage to the common dressing room he shared with the other male understudies. He changed out of the formal evening clothes and into his own heavy slacks and flannel shirt. A familiar tapping rattled the flimsy door.

'Come on in, Lia,' he said.

Lia danced into the room, her long red hair a lustrous velvet cloak that concealed her face. Her big brown eyes shone luminous for a moment. 'They asked me to go on the tour!'

'They did?' Mauzy's smile split his face even as a shot of jealousy pierced his heart. 'Lia, that's great. Of course they did!'

'I'm going to be Lucy!' She did another whirl in the small space. The last of Mauzy's second-tier compatriots mumbled congratulations before sliding out of the door, leaving them alone.

'Lia, zat's mah-velous. I cannot vait to bite you.' Mauzy hugged her and laughed.

She hugged him back, warm and close, and giggled. 'You sound just like him.'

Mauzy shook his head. 'Oh, no. I don't have his charm.'

'You might.' She kissed his cheek and hugged him again.

'May I buy you a drink tonight?' he asked. 'To celebrate?'

'I can't. Colin and Helen already asked. Tomorrow?'

'Of course.' He smiled an actor's smile.

Where was the fairness in it? Mauzy Lyman had studied acting with great men. He had been the star of *The Seagull* in Kansas City and *Desire Under the Elms* in New Haven, and now he was only an understudy to this Lugosi.

The crew made jokes about the lines of women outside the Hungarian's dressing-room door, the letters and packages, scarlet ink and purple paper, addressed to Count Dracula. There was magic in the role, Mauzy thought, though the play was nothing more than a romantic farce.

'Hey, Lia. Be smart. Don't fall under his spell, OK?'

She laughed and pressed her lips to his. 'Got to run, Mauzy. Be good!'

'I'll walk you out.' Mauzy pulled on his jacket and walked with her out of the Fulton and onto Broadway. Lia turned towards Times Square where a cab devoured her and sped away into the winter chill. He watched the river of lights flow slowly in her wake.

Maybe he would go with the tour after all. The show might not even reopen on Broadway. With Lugosi gone, maybe no one would come.

Mauzy pulled the collar of his coat up before reaching in his pocket for cigarettes. Low-hanging clouds turned the street lights misty and the cold December air smelled like rain.

He walked a few blocks west, bundled against the chill, then turned right into an alleyway. Out of the light, behind a fence, he followed wooden steps down to a panelled door, listened a moment and tried the knob.

Mauzy wasn't surprised when it opened. Selmo usually forgot to lock the door. Every cop on the beat knew the old Sicilian ran a speakeasy. In an hour or so, around midnight, the little joint would be full of dressers and chorus girls, some-times a writer or a choreographer.

Right now, Selmo's was almost empty, just the dark, heavy

bartender named Benny and a girl alone at a table. Mauzy dismissed her without a close look. Another out-of-towner, maybe a would-be actress. More grist for the mill. He took a seat at the bar.

Benny poured him a shot of the dwindling supply of genuine Woodford's and Mauzy put a dollar on the bar.

'Say it,' Benny urged.

Mauzy leaned towards Benny. 'I neffer trink ... Bourbon.'

Benny's chuckle rattled in his belly. 'That's really good. You sound just like him.'

Mauzy downed the shot and savoured the smoky burn. 'Wish I was him,' he said and tapped the glass for a refill.

'Nah, Mauzy. He's a oddball, right? I mean, the stories.'

Mauzy shrugged. 'Who ain't? Thing is, he believes in the role. It's like he turns into Dracula.' He shook his head. 'And the world turns around him.'

'An oddball.' Benny filled the glass and put a tumbler of water beside it.

Mauzy shrugged again. In the silence, a tickle of awareness shivered down his spine. He turned and saw the girl gazing at him. In the dim light, she didn't look like much, not very big, her hair pulled back under a black cap, her face dusky with shadows, but the intensity of her attention belted him in the stomach.

Benny winked at him as Mauzy scooted back from the bar, took the water glass and walked to the woman's table.

He started to ask if she minded him sitting and then realised the question's absurdity. Her gaze held his like a grape between sharp teeth.

The air in the room stilled.

'I was listening to you,' she said in an accented voice, perhaps French or Belgian. 'It is fascinating.'

He sat down facing her, suddenly self-conscious as her beauty was revealed. A miracle of symmetry, the woman's face glowed with a strange intensity. High cheekbones, the braziers for enormous black eyes, gathered the bar light into golden flames. A strong, slender nose and lips that parted in a glistening, nearly luminous smile left Mauzy's mouth dry. He imagined kissing her, the thought startlingly vivid. Skin as dark as a Polynesian's intrigued him and her hair, where it escaped her cap, was the pale silver of moonlight. She wore a coat cut like a shawl, loose around her shoulders, and a blouse of deep rich burgundy.

Her smile pulled him into her, but the depthless wonder of her eyes kept him, wound him in webs, turned the backs of his knees to water even as his cock hardened. He remembered the first act of the play, the women in Dracula's castle, the erotic pale trio preying on the traveller. A finger's grasp on the edge of reason, he stared into the fire-touched twin pools of her black gaze and believed in vampires.

Long lashes brushed the dusky skin of her cheek and an endless ache filled Mauzy's heart as she released him with a sultry laugh. The air in the room began to move again. 'It is fascinating what you do. Acting.' She traced one long finger over the edge of her wine glass, and Mauzy tasted her, the exotic spice of her sex as he imagined following just such a pattern with his tongue.

'It's what I want to do, but it is not easy.' An uneven tenor coloured the first few words.

'The man, the one who is Dracula? He is a good actor?' She didn't smile now, but lifted the glass to her lips and took a careful sip.

'Sure he is and in a real role, in a good play, I bet he'd show it.' Mauzy turned the tumbler of water, his mood dampened. Him. Always him.

'This Dracula is not a real role?' Her warm tone enquired, but held also a chiding humour.

Mauzy motioned Benny over and gestured towards the woman.

'I always drink wine,' she said to Benny, her foreign accent deliberately seductive, with just a hint of mockery. The bartender grinned like a schoolboy.

Mauzy ordered and, as Benny bustled off, asked her, 'What's your name?'

She gazed at him, her eyes depthless and filled with laughter and secrets. 'Anastasia,' she said with a little smile to show it was a lie and the end of the subject as far as she was concerned.

Benny brought the drinks, setting Mauzy's shot down and pouring Ana's wine with a flourish. He would've hung around the table if Mauzy hadn't waved him away.

'No,' he said, looking directly at her. 'This Dracula isn't a real role. It's a farce, a joke.'

'So you say.' She sipped her wine, the red liquid shining on her lips. 'Many people like it, yes?'

He shrugged. 'I suppose. There are so many better plays.'

'But this one, there is something of dreams in it, yes?' Her voice caressed him.

'Dreams? Nightmares is more like it,' Mauzy replied and lifted the shot.

'Do you know the difference?' She cocked her head and watched him, the tip of her tongue showing slightly as she sipped her wine.

Mauzy considered a moment. 'When I have a nightmare, I want to wake up,' he said before he threw back the whiskey and welcomed the heat as it coated his tongue and throat.

'Yes.' She smiled, her gaze suddenly intense, black fire flickering in her eyes. 'And when you are dreaming, truly dreaming, no matter how terrible or beautiful it is, you do not even know when you are dreaming, so you cannot wake up. Not until sunrise.'

A car roared wetly past. The promised rain had finally arrived.

'Plays though . . . they ought to be about something tangible, something real. Not some dream.' The edges of the conversation seemed to unravel around him.

'I do not agree.' She pouted a little and Mauzy heard the rain turn to sorrowful sheets. 'I have seen plays that are exactly like dreams and they are the very best. Why? Because they show us what can be true. Nothing is more honest than our dreams. They are our souls. You should listen to yours, Mauzy Lyman.'

Thunder rattled the door.

'Are you afraid of me?' she purred.

Mauzy's heartbeat quickened and for a moment air would not fill his lungs. 'Yes,' he admitted. 'Yes, I am.'

Her laughter joined the rain's snare drumbeat and her eyes danced, the dark flames deep within like melting stars in the night sky. 'Don't be. I will not harm you. Will you come with me?'

The invitation sent lines of tension into his groin, around his cock. The lines continued down his legs, feathery caresses until they circled over his feet and pulled them like a marionette's strings. He fell in behind her and together they went out into the night.

Mauzy wondered if Benny even saw them leave.

Rain blew in sheets like knives, winter's kiss in the quickening gale. Their cab, a gypsy sedan the colour of bone, floated towards them in the patchwork street-light glare. Beads of blown water glimmered like scattered diamonds, dazzling points of light that blinded and held all at once. The back seat smelled of oil and perfume.

She called out an address, her voice as warm as brandy. The cabby barked a short laugh, shook his head, and pulled fast from the curve, careened through slick streets, away from the comfort of the theatre district and into darker blocks Mauzy had never seen before. Soon, street lamps grew sparse and then absent as the cab raced down long avenues of tall shuttered houses, the shadowed giants of the island's fringe, alien in the whipping storm.

They pulled up before an ancient row house, its upper floor hidden in the blowing muck. A single light above the door beckoned to Mauzy.

Anastasia kissed the cab driver and he laughed, gleeful, almost crazed, and drove away.

She slid her arm through Mauzy's and led him in the driving rain up the sidewalk and steps and through the unlocked door.

The entry hall smelled of sandalwood and some sweet flower. When she closed the door, the rain's roar hushed to a grinding, rhythmic whisper like the noise from a thresher.

'My house,' she said, her gaze intent on him. 'Enter freely, of your own will.'

'You sound just like him,' Mauzy said, trying to smile.

She laughed lightly, chimes of pleasure that brushed Mauzy's groin with a flutter of seduction even as it shivered his skin. 'Only a joke, poor Mauzy. You really should relax.'

Her hand as hot as summer sunlight took his as she led him out of the entry hall and into her parlour. With surprising strength and a hint of force she pushed him onto a wine-dark velvet settee, then stood looking down at him, her dark gaze holding his. He thought of Theda Bara.

'Will you drink with me?' Her voice kissed him.

He nodded, his heart trilling. She glided away from him, her scent wrapping him in blankets of languid weight. With effort he looked away and up towards the ceiling invisible in the gloom, save in the corner where a single lamp burned. Golden fireplace light chased the dancing shadows.

Anastasia paused by the fire and shrugged off her jacket, then tossed it to the floor. The burgundy blouse shaped her breasts and the tight line of her stomach above a skirt as black as printer's ink. The fire glare behind her turned the skirt to grey mist and Mauzy's prick began to pulse. She wore nothing beneath the black silk and he saw with perfect clarity the dusky length of her thighs, the cut of her hip and the pale velvet of the patch that marked her sex.

She spun her cap onto the discarded jacket and shook out her hair in a fall of soft radiance, which framed her face and covered her burgundy shoulders like moonlight on a sea of blood. She stepped away from the fire to pour their drinks in shadow and Mauzy's spirits sank.

When she passed before the hearth again, his faith renewed, redoubled. The burgundy blouse, as thin and translucent as her black skirt, revealed for a moment her breasts, nipples erect and high, a perfect, naked shadow in an aura of fire. He barely breathed when she sat beside him, hip pressed lightly against his, hot and soft as though his woollen slacks had somehow melted away.

She handed him a glass half-filled with a thick golden liqueur and, as he took it, the glamour she had woven around him faded a bit and clear thought pushed forwards. He sniffed at the liqueur. The scent seemed familiar, earthy, sweet, with a flicker of heat, but he could not place it.

'Drink,' she commanded.

Mauzy raised the glass to his lips. The golden liquor burned his tongue, flowing into his chest and up behind his ears. Without hesitation he gave himself over to her. He knew he really had no choice.

No choice at all.

Ana unbuttoned her shirt and beneath was only Ana. Dark skin shone in the fire glow, her breasts, small and jaunty with stiffening nipples the colour of bruises. Mauzy ached to taste, to close his teeth around her breast, but he only stared, wanting. A smile, slight but smug tugged at her rich mouth and her hands went to the buttons of his shirt. As the heat of her caress set his chest afire, she leaned forwards, her lips wet and hot upon his neck, sank her teeth into the fragile flesh of his throat and drank him into darkness.

He opened his eyes beneath the cloak of night at the edge of the campfire's glow. He lived in the shadows beyond the wagons, and there he hungered. He heard a lively tune from the camp, flute and tambourine, and he remembered music as he remembered sunlight, precious and vanished things.

A south wind blew the Mediterranean's breath among the mountains, the smell of life and death. He himself stank of the earth where he lay each day, the brother of worms, dressed in linen finery, gone now to threads at cuff and hem. The watch he had worn every day of his life lay heavy in his pocket, no longer ticking.

He was the Romany night, the endless dark miles these people travelled. He was born of the cruelty they endured and the guilt and sorrow of unending departure. He was death waiting quietly in the shadows.

A girl left the fire and walked towards the wagon. The wind pushed him at her, his ragged linen rising like a cloak around him. He hungered like fire in dry leaves and drew her to him.

He was the dominance of mortality and the fever of desire. She could not resist him, did not even cry out or struggle as his teeth bit into the firm meat of her neck. Her whimper, between fear and pleasure, did not stir him, the sound of her surrender so common to his ears he hardly heard her. He knew only the rich life that ran from her and into him, the memory of lost pleasures, like music and sunlight.

'This is the seed of the dreams,' Ana whispered, her words as arousing as the press of her body against him.

Mauzy opened his eyes and saw her through a golden haze, naked, stretched out before the fire. She sat up, caught his bare thighs in her taloned hands, and leaned forwards, her hair a tickle of moonlight against his legs, her warm breath caressing his cock. She hovered over the plum-coloured head for a moment, licked her lips and slipped them, rose soft, around the pearled crown.

Mauzy inhaled the scent of candles and lamp oil, his vision fading behind closing lids. The room shifted like mist.

He heard the others out in the dim parlour telling tales of ghosts and monsters. He stretched in his bedroom, naked and sweating, his muscled thigh hot against the pale thin one of the young doctor.

'And thou art dead, as young and fair as aught of mortal birth,' he said in a husky whisper, languid and laughing at the doctor as he wiped his moist lips, the faint saltiness coating his tongue teasing his hunger and his sorrow.

'Oh no, your Lordship. Not dead at all. See?' Polidori purred like a cat, his beautiful body, lean and alive, young and perfect.

His gaze fell on the doctor's waist, the circumcised length of him already stirring, quite lively and ready for more.

''Tis why you keep me as your physician,' he smirked, cocky and confident, easy in his vitality.

He touched the doctor's staff, savouring the warm satin beneath his fingers. 'I will write a poem for you,' he promised, *and he knew in his heart it was one he would keep. 'An ode to the transcendence of flesh.' He bent to the feast, taking the flesh in his mouth again, devouring the inches of hot smooth youth as it pulsed along the cradle of his tongue.*

The doctor gasped as teeth found purchase, the sharp bite unexpected, but not unwelcome as pleasure's cry guttered the candle beside the bed.

Finished, sated, he wiped his mouth again, red this time, and rose from the feast.

He stood looking down at the beautiful body of the young man – his lover, his friend – and felt the weight of his own years even as the fragile shell of his renewal flowed from his throat through his body. A great sadness settled on him like a woollen cloak.

'I know not if I could have borne to see thy beauties fade,' he whispered in the darkness and kissed the doctor's prick. He left the bed and dressed, then returned to the parlour where the others still told their ghost stories.

Ana's mouth held him, her teeth sharp and hard against the tender skin, her tongue bathing the swollen head of his cock as her jaws worked, pulling at him in fierce rhythm. Pleasure pulsed through his veins, the aching edge of release a sheer cliff he raced towards. His fingers tangled in her hair, his hips thrust to meet her mouth. The sounds of her suckling and biting were music, and the perfume of sex and smoke and her relentless rhythm, wild tongue and – dear God – her teeth, threw him over the edge. He came in hot, shattering spurts, endless, floating. His back arched, his vision blind save the fire of his ecstasy.

'Blood and seed.' Her voice caressed his slicked cock as she released him and looked up with eyes as deep as the winter sky. 'Magic.'

The wind rose around him, blowing away the light, turning Ana to smoke, and he tumbled through a gulf, breathless, falling, lost to all hope of dawn, but her last word echoed and he knew she spoke the truth. The word opened doorways in his tumbling mind, her tight mouth on his cock a trigger and all of time and dream pulsed with the rhythm, the pounding of blood in a vein, the beat of wings against the night, the light of the golden moon, a stage light.

A dream, he thought. It had all been some dream in the moment before he went on stage.

There had been an incident, the Hungarian and some woman. Now Mauzy was the star.

He was the vampire.

Lucy waited for him in the silver moonlight, watching the mist for a sign. His will was hers. He had shown her the promise of eternal life and now he would take her across the border, into the transcendence of undeath. For ever young, vital in darkness.

He remembered the centuries in his home, in Transylvania, the war against the Turk, the land drunk on blood, death and rebirth, and then the stretched hide of the long decades when the fields had grown dry and his gypsy cattle thin.

Eastern darkness, ruin and rapine crept like dusk across the land, and he was the one who stood against it. He was its servant and its herald, prince of wolves, lord of bats, the Black Death and the bloody flux. In life and in death.

Faith was only the shadow of his power.

So out of darkness he had come, here to London, and they waited for him, the people in the theatre.

'New York,' he whispered, adrift in place and time.

A band of heat crossed his thighs where Ana sat astride him, tense, pressing down. His prick rose, hard and belligerent. She held him, long fingers caressing and cool around the swollen length. She pressed his cock against the glistening line of her sex. Ready and breathless, his hands gripped her hips, his thumbs playing at the edges of the moonlight triangle.

'Don't worry.' Her warm voice filled him with heat, as if he'd swallowed good brandy. 'This is only a dream.'

She settled on him with a squirm, her unsettling dark gaze hidden behind closed eyes. Her head fell back, the veil of white hair a canvas for the perfection of her body.

Lucy turned to him, her mouth a little 'o' of amazement.

He was the promise of wonders and terrors, of sensation beyond her skin, the survival of death. He was her hope and her salvation.

And she, his sustenance.

The beating of her heart welcomed him, like the blood in the doctor's prick, like his own body raised from death, water flowing in the ancient land, rhythms of creation and destruction, the very pulse of the world.

Then he tasted the ocean, salt and sweetness, and the essence of illumination beyond pale daylight. Lucy was his, divine in the moment, but destined for ruin, stalking the London night, preying on children, because on the other side of light lay nothing but darkness.

'Not in the play,' he protested, his voice thick, almost slurred. Ana gripped him with fierce, wet insistence, her sex tight around him, a velvet vice promising oblivion. She rode him hard, her head tossed back, moonlight hair a tempest around her dark shoulders. The heat of her body against his, enveloping him, shattered reality as she possessed him, absolute and overwhelming.

'No,' she panted, her voice sharp with arousal and control. 'In the dream.'

The churning beat of orgasm built within him, his cock held in slippery fire, her thighs gripping his. She leaned over him and pressed her hot small breasts against his chest. His fingers sank into her hip, gripping, desperate. He pulled her down as he thrust up. She gasped, clenching around him and slid up his shaft, angled her hips and settled on him again, spreading to take him deeper. He felt himself vanishing, becoming the moment and then her weight lifted from him, as she rose, gripping him. Ana cried out and shuddered hard, muscles throbbing along his cock. With a final thrust up into her, he came in gleaming sheets of sensation.

Silver pale, he crept from the ship's hold, walking among the slaughtered crew, the captain hanging from the wheel by his silver chain. Each of them had been a feast and a plaything in his turn. Each of the men was lucky to be dead, for they sailed with a cargo of plague.

Memory turned like a fat worm in his dead brain, soft and white, the flesh of a pretty sailor, briny with sweat beneath his thin lips, the coarse hair of the man's pale chest, the veins turned still and white.

His life had ended long ago but he saw the expanse of infinity, vast as time itself, beauty undreamed even by opium's dreamers, and he satisfied brief indescribable hungers with the pale forms that blew before him like dry leaves. After so many centuries, one leaf was much like another. Cattle. Sheep. Sometimes an intriguing pet.

Rats bloomed around him, an army of death, swarming over the docks and out into the town, hot and eager for the homes of men, where they entered unbidden to slay three in five with quick bloodletting.

Over his shoulder he carried the long box, the soil of his home-land within, dry and sterile. Nothing grew now beyond the mountains or in the wild places. No one ventured there any more and no beast could live. But here in the city, there were lives, beautiful women whose innocence burned like the sun he hardly remembered, sacrifices to the god he had become.

When he found a woman of sufficient innocence, he would take her and hold her close, share the fire with her, and then greet the dawn in her arms, wake and die in a sunrise kiss.

'The dream is a ritual,' Ana panted into his shoulder, her lips wet and cool. 'The dream is truth.'

They lay before the fireplace now. She milked him between her thighs and he rolled her over, pinning her, his cock still hard even as the light ran through him.

Quick wings in the noonday window, but he was quicker, first flies, then spiders, then fat sparrows lured to his ledge.

'Be sure you do not eat of the blood,' the quick things whispered in the voice of his father. 'For the blood is the life.'

Ana wrapped her legs around his waist and held him in her.

What was life to an abomination? Damned in the daylight, so only the master would have him, only the master loved him. Not the sparrows, not the cat. Certainly not the flies.

Now there was the nurse, the pretty one with hair the colour of bruised plums, lips like droplets of the Sacrament on skin as pale as cream. He crept towards her on hands and knees where she lay in the circle of her own skirts.

The nurse feared him and hated him. He smelled it on her, tasted it on the air when she came to give him tonics. When she made him hard.

The master came in the night and took Mina away to Carfax to make her his bride, and the nurse had fainted. All the others ran away, and now the nurse lay sprawled upon the stones, thighs round and white, his at last.

She lay on her back, the blood of her lips open and moving with the deep exhalation of her breath, breasts rising and falling.

The pulse in her thigh just above the garter, held him mesmerised, heating his scalp until sweat trickled down his cheek. With a shaking hand he wiped the drop away and bent to feed.

'Not blood,' Ana said. 'Dreams are the life.'

She lay beneath him, arching against him, her legs wrapping around him like satin chains. Still buried deep, Mauzy thrust again and her fingernails carved runes in his back. He came endlessly.

The painting moved and two figures faced each other.

The Dutchman's eyes flashed wild – the wooden stake clenched in his hand, the end of hope and redemption.

He opened his mouth in a hiss, the wolf in his heart raging against the foolish old man who faced him. The elder had run him to earth. Here in his own castle, they faced each other alone.

He allowed the wolf to take him, roared and growled, feral and snapping, as he leaped at the old man, knocking him over, trying to break bones. Spittle ran between his lips, dripping down onto Van Helsing's throat as he held him pinned. One snap, one perfect bite and the game was mate for ever.

But Van Helsing reached out with his withered hand and tugged at a cord and, with the tug, a window opened, dawn light scattered in diamond panes. His skin erupted in burning welts where the morning kissed him.

The Dutchman tackled him even as he writhed in pain. The old man sat astride him as so many lovers had before, and the stake that was awful nothingness nudged his chest.

Penetration, the unfelt centuries of agony in a moment.
Oblivion.

Mauzy lay atop her, her hands on his back gentle now, slowly stroking, tracing every line of muscle and nerve. She gripped him in the hot shackle of her legs and kissed his throat.

'Sleep now,' she entreated, tender and drowsy.

'Will I wake up?' He lifted his head and looked at her serene face. He thought of an infinite descent, transcendence and passage into another world.

'You will,' she breathed. 'In time.'

'Then you're not . . .'

'No, I am not what you think.' She lifted herself enough to kiss him, tenderness and amusement turning her lips to honey. 'I am something much older.'

He fell into a true sleep filled with visions. Desires and fears, guilt and hope for eternity, fantasies and doubts. Armies of the night, dark shadows of darker truth, lurid visions of flesh for feasts, dynasties of blood as old as Babylon.

He saw women more beautiful than eternity and men as dark and strong as death, a tribe as vast as the world, desirable, irresistible and sublime, rich beyond counting, near divine, but with the souls of preying beasts and immortal poets.

'The seed she took from you,' the creatures in the shadows whispered, 'breeds wonders.'

Then, if Mauzy dreamed at all, he dreamed of emptiness and silence.

Blue light painted the room when he woke, his head aching

and his hands shaking. He was – not surprisingly – alone. The room was nothing like he remembered it, the fireplace barren even of ashes, the furniture eaten with the slow hunger of moths.

No trace of Ana remained. He expected nothing else, but did not for a moment believe she had been a dream.

Warm wind blew from the west, bearing the scent of the night ocean. On the balcony of his seventh-floor room in the Arms, Mauzy watched the misty sky and listened to cars pass below.

The City of Angels.

The show had travelled across the continent on trains, to Chicago, Kansas City, Denver and half a dozen other cities. Each night he watched the Hungarian become the dream, but Mauzy understood now this was no pose, no pretence.

Anastasia had shown him the strength of the story, the dark hope at its core, the faith . . .

Maybe the Hungarian had met her too. Maybe one day Mauzy would ask him.

'Mauzy?' Lia stepped out onto the balcony, her gown blown against her, shaping the curve of her hip, the sharp tips of her breasts. 'You coming back to bed?'

'Yes,' he said, but he did not move.

She sat down beside him and he pulled her to him, enjoying the sweetness of her sleepy kiss and the perfume of her body. He smiled at her. 'It's like being drowned in a flower when I am with you.'

She looked at him, her gaze bright and alive. Lust rose in him, molten and blinding. He claimed her with his kiss and his hands, rough and merciless, peeled the gown from her shoulders, baring her to the waist. She struggled weakly and her breath came in quick gasps as he found her breasts and rolled her stiffened nipples under his palms.

'Lucy,' he whispered and bit her hard on the throat.

His will was hers. He had shown her the promise of eternal life and now he would take her across the border, into the transcendence of endless dream. The warm Pacific wind blew over them as he stripped Lia and fucked her against the balcony railing.

Shadows and ashes crept like dusk across the land, and he stood against them, prince of wolves, lord of bats, savouring the red passion and salty wine that kept death ever at bay, and sensation, desire and wonder fresh in the world.

Alive and dreading sunrise.

Paso Doble

Rhiannon Leith

His scent attracted her first, when Elena passed him on the street – a feral enticement to come and play. It lingered around her all the way home and disrupted her rest. The next night, she followed him, discovered his name and knew nothing would be the same again. His face haunted her. Even now, two nights later, the aroma enfolded her.

Elena opened her eyes as the sun set. A shiver crossed her skin, stroking down between her shoulder blades, following the ghost of his caress. She savoured the fading sense of his touch.

Near. So near.

Whether he would know her or not, she recognised the true identity of the man called Alex Vernon. Her body seldom erred on that subject.

My sire. My beloved.

Wrapping herself in a cream silken sheet, Elena rose from her bed. She swept the heavy curtains back and gazed across the city lights like the broken reflections in a windswept pool. High up in her eyrie, she lived with every modern convenience, every luxury, bought with much of the riches her sire had left her.

If he was back, would he claim it? Would he claim her as well?

She shuddered at the thought, picturing his hands, rough

against the smooth surface of her skin, olive against her porcelain complexion. She recalled the way she fell into his endless gaze and lost her way so long ago. His body, his kiss, the exhilarating agony of the turning bite and then ... the growing fire within her. An inferno drove out humanity and left a creature of pure passion and need.

The silk whispered to the carpet, pooling around her feet. Elena ran a hand over the swell of her breast, teasing the erect nipple. From the cold, she wondered, or thoughts of him?

Thoughts of Alejandro – Alex, as he now called himself – the vampire lord who was supposed to be dead, but walked as a human. A vampire who had made himself prey.

The point of a fang pressed into the ripeness of her lower lip, sliding into her flesh. Blood welled up, as sweet as nectar. She trailed her nails through her pubic hair and slipped a finger inside her own body. Like warm, wet velvet, she closed around herself and the muscles in her abdomen contracted as a single thought raced through her mind.

Alejandro.

She swirled the pad of her thumb against her clitoris and gasped. Sparks of electricity raced through her, like the first time he had taken her, forcing her against a wall in an unlit Seville alley. He had lifted both her legs, wrapped them around his hips and entered her in a single sublime stroke. His touch, his scent, the trail of his teeth down her throat – the combination of eroticism and danger sent her plunging over the edge in seconds. But he had not fed on her. Not the first time.

Alejandro's smile intoxicated her.

'Well-bred young ladies should not behave with such abandon,' he had said, his fingers pressing against her racing pulse. 'I will have to return, *amorcita*.'

Elena crumpled to the floor of her apartment, blood trailing from the corner of her mouth. She cried out his name, her body imploding beneath his phantom touch.

Alejandro Báez Ortega, Alex Vernon – whatever he called himself now. She would have him back. Then she would see him dead.

'So your papers are due next Friday and this time, when I say bibliography, I mean bibliography, not a list of the first ten hits off your favourite search engine,' Alex called over the bustle of thirty students leaving the lecture hall. His class laughed, scattering into the hall beyond, and he shut down his laptop in silence.

A discreet cough made him look up. A woman perched on the nearest study desk, long legs stretched out towards him, an elfin body with unexpected curves. Her cropped black hair framed a heart-shaped face and almond eyes which appeared to be all pupils and no irises – endless dark.

'Professor Vernon?' She smiled as she said his name and he knew it wasn't a question. Her eyes didn't ask questions. They demanded answers.

'And you are?' She couldn't be a student, not looking like that. A black leather coat fell from her shoulders to her calves parting below the cinched waist to reveal black jeans moulding her thighs. He couldn't recall ever seeing a woman who inspired such instant lust that he didn't dare move from behind the desk. Not that the desk could hide his interest.

The woman's gaze dipped to his crotch and her smile turned knowing. 'Call me Elena, Professor Vernon. I read your book, *Vampires Through the Ages*. It was . . . enlightening.'

Oh, one of those. Frankly, the last thing Alex needed was a wannabe vampire groupie hanging around, gorgeous though she was.

'I'm a professor of anthropology, Elena. Not a vampire expert.'

She sashayed towards him, the movement hypnotic. 'Definitely not an expert. Do you remember me, Alex?'

'No, I'm sorry.' Better get rid of her as soon as possible. He checked his watch. 'I have an appointment shortly, so if you'll forgive me . . .' He snapped the laptop over and found her right in front of him, the desk a flimsy barrier. She placed her hands on either side of the computer and leaned forwards. Her full lips parted and her tongue left a glistening trail behind it.

'Are you sure?'

Whatever he had intended to do evaporated from his mind as her eyes devoured him.

'Elena,' he breathed. He could sense her searching his expression, and deeper, searching through his conscious mind, as if somehow she had wormed her way inside him to flick through his thoughts and memories like a photo album. Elena tilted her head.

'Alejandro?' Her voice transformed, the command draining away. Sadness filled her features. Not just sadness, tragedy. Alex reached out before he was even aware of what he did. His hand touched her cheek, sliding along her jaw, her cold skin. She closed her eyes, a cat enjoying a caress. Her lips parted and he saw her teeth, just for a second.

Alex snatched back his hand. She moved in a blur, too fast for a human, too fast for anything natural, hurtling across the desk. Alex found himself slammed face first against the whiteboard, his arm pinned back between his shoulder blades. Her body pressed against the length of him, holding him immobile. She wrapped him in a scent like cinnamon and melted chocolate.

'I don't know how you pulled off a rebirth, Alejandro, but come near me and I will end you and you'll think Marika was gentle. Do you understand me?'

'Yes, but I'm not –'

Her mouth claimed his, silencing him. Her kiss ensnared him, demanding and at the same time enticing. Alex's heart thundered against ribs too frail to contain it. His breath fluttered in his throat like a bird in a trap. Teeth grazed against his lips, sharper than needles. Without releasing him, Elena allowed him to turn into her embrace. Her icy hands slipped beneath his shirt. His hard-on turned to iron, pulsing in counterpoint to his heart. Alex groaned against her kiss, wanting her and offering up everything to her. She pulled back his collar, her lips trailing down his neck.

'I'm not . . .' he tried to tell her, his erection straining against her firm thigh, his body beyond desperate with need. 'I'm not who you . . .'

Her mouth closed around the pulsing vein in his neck, two canines denting his skin. Her breath felt glacial, anaesthetising the area while at the same time heightening every sensation, lifting the hairs beneath, the nerve ends tingling with need. Need for her. For everything she was, whatever that meant. He waited, longing for her to bite, to take him.

She released him with painful suddenness.

'I should kill you,' she hissed. 'God knows why I don't.' She pressed her hand against his chest, covering his pounding heart. With her eyes closed, she lifted her chin, inhaling deeply. 'You're . . . You're not what I thought.'

'Elena.' She intoxicated him, left him delirious with lust. 'Please.'

Her face gentled and her voice came to him on a whisper, like the voice of another woman. 'I know. I remember. But believe me, it's better this way. I don't take thralls, nor feed from the living. I won't turn anyone. I'm not a monster.'

Alex stared at the gleaming points of her fangs, resting against her lips as red as the blood on which she thrived, and then into her eyes, like windows into the void beyond exist-ence. The desire didn't go away. It didn't even dim.

'Then what are you?'

'I think you know that, Alex.'

Elena did not flee. Vampires *flee* nothing. She strode from the lecture hall and out into the deepening twilight as quickly as possible while maintaining her dignity.

'Wait!'

Damn it, the man was stubborn! She slipped between moments, moving faster than his eye could follow, darting around the corner of the building. Alex ran on and, realising he had lost her, stopped. Elena drew the shadows about her body like a cloak and sank into their embrace. He turned in a circle, one hand raking through his thick black hair while his eyes – the colour of the richest coffee – studied the paths through the campus. His chest rose and fell as he struggled to catch his breath beneath the fine weave of his cotton shirt, muscled, toned. Alejandro had been nonchalant about his physique, but Alex, she guessed, took care to keep himself physically fit. Another drawback of mortality.

'Elena?' he called and her body reacted to the sound of her name on his lips. Within her, the ripples of desire started again. She wanted to go to him. It was impossible. Madness. This was not her Alejandro, no matter what ghosts lingered in the depths of her memories. Blood sang in his veins, the melody of temp-tation, the rhythm of his heartbeat enticing her, telling her to sink her teeth into his throat, to end his life. And to make him hers for ever.

He was not Alejandro. She knew that now. And knowing that, she could not kill him. No matter how dangerous she felt him to be.

And Alex Vernon was dangerous for her.

Far too dangerous.

'Shit!' Alex flung his arm down by his side and turned his back on her, wandering back towards the building. His shoulders slumped in dejection.

Elena let a sigh of relief slip from her. She never meant to kiss him, never meant to get so close. But holding him there, dominating him and feeling his instinctive submission, her natural impulse almost took over. His kiss burned on her swollen lips. She could still taste him in her mouth. The salt of sweat on his neck, the pulse beneath his skin . . . more than she could bear. Almost.

At times, Elena wished she was a werewolf instead. At least when they were in pain, they could howl.

She waited until he left. Not because she wanted to see him again. She just needed to know he had gone. He traipsed through the campus to the car park and she followed, holding to the shadows. Every so often, he checked over his shoulder. But he couldn't be sensing her. He was only human. Hadn't she proved that to herself? Yet the nagging feeling that he knew just got stronger. When he finally got into his car and drove away, she wondered why it felt like loss. More than that. Like bereavement. Again.

He was *not* Alejandro. She had no reason to feel like this. He was nothing to her.

Elena paced the elevator as she travelled up to the apartment. Once inside, she locked the door, slipping the security chain into place. Her clenched fists uncurled. Blood welled from the gouges in her palm where her nails had stabbed into the flesh. She licked it away, and the wounds sealed. Elena closed her eyes. She would have to leave the city, find somewhere else. Perhaps go back to the Old World and leave this new one far behind her. Because she could not stay, not knowing Alex was out there. Not if she wanted to keep her vows.

Marius knocked on the door three nights later, carrying the case from the blood bank. He eyed her up and down as he unpacked her order.

'You all right?' When Elena glared at him in response, Marius shrugged. 'Just never seen you hide from anything before, El.'

Every muscle tensed. 'I'm not hiding.'

'You haven't been out in three nights though. Someone's been asking questions about you downtown.'

Suspicion perked up her instincts. 'Who?'

'Just a guy. Not the usual type. Clean cut, you know? Saw him in a couple of places last night. And in Virtruvian's earlier, just after dusk.'

Elena's throat constricted. No. He couldn't have gone there. Alex wouldn't stand a chance. 'Virtruvian's is where Marika holds court, isn't it?'

She stared at Marius, but she didn't see his face. Alex stared back at her with wide, dark and endless eyes. Not Alejandro's eyes; his own innocent gaze filled with desire for her alone. He had gone looking for her. And her name on his lips would draw unwanted attention. Responsibility was a terrible burden, one Alejandro never understood, not really. But Elena did.

'Oh yeah.' Marius grinned, his fangs bright in the dim light. 'You and Marika don't get on no more.'

'Never did.' Refusing to be drawn further in, Elena strode from the kitchen. She grabbed the leather coat which swirled around her body like bats' wings. Her conquistador sword was mounted on the wall like a priceless decoration, its brass hilt entwined with a dragon. The carbonated steel blade still mirrored the world as it had when Alejandro gave it to her, and taught her to use it. He had been her teacher in so many ways.

She lifted it down, fitted the scabbard and belt across her body and sheathed it over her shoulder.

'El.' Marius's voice held a hint of concern, more than she

would have expected. 'El, Marika won't like you bursting in on her. It's been an uneasy truce. Since Alejandro . . .'

Elena glanced over her shoulder. Her smile would have been innocent, but for the glint of teeth. 'I'm just going for a friendly chat, Marius. Now get out. I don't trust you with my things.'

Alex woke to a pounding head and a taste in his mouth like something had crawled in, died and then dragged itself out again. He moved, only to find his wrists were tied in front of him with a thin leather band.

What the hell?

It all came rushing back: the nightclub, pulsing music and lights, trying to find Elena among the lowlife that thronged the place. A woman with a smile like poison had asked him to take a seat and offered him a drink. A woman called Marika with an entourage worthy of Hollywood.

'Elena?' Marika had caressed his shoulder like a butcher sizing up meat. 'Yes, Elena will come soon.'

So he drank Marika's rich red wine and slid into black oblivion.

Stupid fucking idiot!

The leather gnawed at his skin. He brought his hands up to his mouth and tried to worry it away with his teeth, but a soft laugh froze him. Looking around wildly, he could see nothing, no one. There was no light in this place.

'Human eyes too?' Marika said. 'Really, Alejandro. This reincarnation was something of a blunder, wasn't it?'

'Look, I'm not who you think I am,' he said. 'My name is Alex Vernon. I'm an anthropologist.'

Marika laughed again, the sound much too close. His skin contracted around his frame. It felt like being stalked.

A match flared to incandescence, blinding him. Marika lit a candle as thick as his arm.

'I met an anthropologist in Sarajevo,' said Marika, her slim face like a sculpture of the Madonna. 'He was sweet.' She lit another candle, illuminating more of the ornate room. Heavy drapes hung against the walls, a chandelier of wrought iron dominated the vaulted ceiling. Alex knelt on a crimson carpet in the centre, in front of a thronelike chair. All around him, twenty men and women, as pale and perfect as Marika, watched him with catlike curiosity.

He sucked in a breath. Vampires. Real vampires. His heart grew loud. He wondered if that was because it was the only heart in the room still beating.

Marika stopped in front of him, the match burning down to her fingers, the flame licking at her skin before she dropped it. It smouldered on the carpet. She crushed the embers out with one bare foot. Her toenails were painted the same shade of scarlet as her fingernails.

Alex sucked in a breath and forced himself to look up into her face, into inhuman eyes. 'I'm glad you liked him.'

'I wonder, Alex, will you taste as sweet when you die?'

All around him, the vampires laughed and Alex held himself as still as stone.

'I'd rather not find out,' he said.

She knelt opposite him, taking his hands in hers, stroking the sensitive skin beneath his thumb. More alien than Elena, her golden hair in its elaborate style and the long formal gown made him think of pre-Raphaelite illustrations of Titania, of Morgan le Fey, of La Belle Dame Sans Merci.

'Alejandro didn't taste sweet,' she said. 'I had to strap him down to drain him dry. He was old and bitter. He'd lived too long.' Her tongue flickered over his lips. 'Do you know where you are?'

'No,' he replied, unable to tear his gaze from hers. 'You drugged me.'

Her smile flickered across her lips. 'I didn't think you'd come willingly. Not knowing what we really are. You do *know*, don't you?'

Marika drew him to his feet and turned him around.

'Sit down,' she whispered, and pressed Alex back into the chair. She stood behind him, her hands trailing down through his hair. Her scarlet nails scratched lightly against his throat and then her hands came to rest on his shoulders, kneading the bunched muscles there.

From a doorway beyond the watching crowd, a high-pitched giggle broke the oppressive silence. The other vampires faded into the background, not quite invisible, but not noticeable. The eye just slid over them. A young woman ran into the centre of the room, a bottle of champagne clutched in her hand.

'Wow! Would you look at this place?' she exclaimed. Two men followed her. One was blond, his skin gilded, a perfect quarterback, while the other would have fitted into any Goth band rather too neatly. Quarterback smiled, pulling his party girl to him, lifting the champagne bottle to her mouth and encouraging her to drink. Goth looked directly at Alex, then raised his questioning gaze to Marika.

'It's all right,' Marika whispered, her voice trembling on the air. 'Carry on. Think of it as a demonstration.' The slight nod of his head looked like a bow. 'They chose well.' Marika's breath played against Alex's ear. 'Don't worry, you can answer me. No one will hear you. We hide in between the shadows. It is one of our gifts.'

'They're going to kill her?'

'Perhaps. It's up to you, Alex. You get to choose.'

'What the . . .' He started to rise, but Marika pulled him back into the chair, her grip on his shoulders impossibly strong.

Quarterback and Partygirl kissed between mouthfuls of champagne. Goth just watched for the moment, his hand busy at his own crotch. The woman gave a throaty sex laugh and tipped the remaining champagne down her cleavage. Grinning, Quarterback began to lick the swell of her breasts, pulling the chiffon blouse out so he could run his hands over her wet skin. Goth pulled her to lean back on him, then nuzzled her neck. He took her hips in his hands and moved them in a sultry dance, pushing against his compatriot's hard-on. Partygirl gasped and her head fell back against Goth's shoulder, lolling like a rag doll. Quarterback took the material of her blouse and ripped it open. He pulled off her bra and took her aroused nipple into his mouth, working the other with his hand and fingers.

'Jesus,' Alex hissed. 'This isn't . . .' He felt Marika's head dip, her lips trailing along his neck and his cock strained stupidly against the restricting fabric. His breath hitched in his throat. He couldn't be aroused by this. That wasn't in his nature.

'Yes it is,' said Marika and she reached around him to undo the buttons of his shirt.

Alex wriggled his hands, hoping to loosen the leather binding, but it just chafed at his wrists, another heightened sensation joining the mix that made his blood race faster. Marika pulled open his pants and sat on the arm of the chair, the curve of her ass pressed against his side with uncomfortable intimacy.

Goth slid Partygirl's skirt and panties down and lifted her so he could kick them away. Naked now between two lovers, she writhed and called for them to take her, to fuck her, to make her come.

Marika's hand closed around Alex's pulsing cock, her fingertips running over the head, setting little flashes off in his head. She caressed the length of him but her gaze was consumed with the scene before them. All around them, the vampires turned on each other, caressing, kissing. Mouths, tongues and fingers engaged in pure pleasure. Someone groaned out loud. Partygirl.

Alex looked back to find Goth naked, burying his tongue in her anus. Quarterback switched breasts. His fingers dug into her vagina.

She started to come, her abdomen trembling, and the two vampires rose together. Quarterback lifted her from the ground, wrapping her legs around his hips, his hands buried in her ass cheeks, parting them. He slid into her and she cried out. Not words, just inarticulate sounds. Goth pressed his erect cock to her other hole and slowly, deliberately, forced his way inside. Partygirl screamed in abandon. She shook her head, her hair tumbling over her face, her tits jigging up and down as they fucked her in unison. Her jaw hung slack, her mouth open with moans of pleasure. Her eyes fluttered wildly.

Goth's eyes met Marika's again. Alex saw the hunger there, recognised it for what it was. Raw, immortal, dangerous. Goth's fangs rested against the throbbing vein in the woman's neck, dimpling the tender skin.

'No,' Alex whispered. Marika's hand tightened on his cock and it throbbed beneath her touch, straining for release.

Partygirl came again, her howl breaking against the vaulted ceiling. Goth plunged his fangs into her jugular. Partygirl cried out, a shout of something trapped midway between pain and pleasure.

'Does she die, Alex?' asked Marika, working her hand up and down so fast that his brain could not keep up with her words. 'You choose. Does she die or does she live?'

'Let her go,' he gasped. 'Let her live.'

'And what will you give in return?'

'What?' He couldn't think. A fog had settled over his mind. All he knew was the surging of his blood, the dammed sperm straining in his balls and the girl, the girl thrashing, shrieking as she came, as she died. 'Stop. Stop them.'

'You owe me, Alex,' said Marika, and let him go.

Quarterback bit down on the woman's breast, closing his mouth around the wound. They took her together, drinking in the glistening blood that spilled out of her, pumping their bodies into hers until, finally, she fell still. She hung between them, limp as an old rag doll. They released her, lay her on the floor and licked clean the blood from her neck and her breast, the semen from her labia.

Marika stepped in front of him, blocking his view of what they did next.

'Stand up,' she commanded and Alex found his body moving in spite of himself. Inside he trembled and wept, but outside a shell formed, a crystalline surface that felt nothing. Marika ran her gaze over him so intimately that it was worse than her touch. Alex felt his skin tightening, shivering. He couldn't move.

He'd come for Elena. Like a fool he had stumbled blind into something far worse. Elena had terrified him but also filled him with such desire that he thought he could never experience the like. This was not the same. Mortality had never loomed so vividly before him. He had never thought he would welcome it. Marika took his bound hands, lifted them to her mouth. Her fangs sank deep into his wrist. Alex jerked back, but her grip was like a vice. There was no pain, just a sense of drawing that left his legs weak and his head dizzy.

Marika broke off her feeding and smiled. His blood stained her lips, but her teeth were as white as ever.

'Sweet,' she said, with a satisfied purr. 'I knew you would be sweet.' She pushed him back into the chair. 'One of my court had your book about vampires,' she said, circling him. 'We found it most amusing. You said ... What was it? Oh yes, that the vampire myth is based in a deep-rooted desire to return to primal instincts, where there is no responsibility for anything other than self, when all that matters is food and sex. Is that right?'

Alex didn't answer. The bite on his wrist burned. Blood welled up in the puncture wounds, dripping down the length of his fingers.

'Well, let me tell you something, Alex. When a vampire is turned, when they first reawaken, they must feed. They are at their most vulnerable and their most dangerous in those first moments. A newborn vampire needs to hunt, even another vampire. That's why we always make sure there is a ready victim to hand. Food and sex, Alex, food and sex.'

A soft groan filled the room. Marika stepped behind him and lifted his head. Partygirl rose to her feet, naked, beautiful, her eyes empty. She sniffed the air and, catching the scent of his blood, her head snapped in his direction. Her mouth opened, revealing fangs, and she surged towards him. Alex scrambled back but Marika held him firmly, her nails digging into his shoulders, piercing cloth and skin.

'Alex!' Elena shouted. She leaped from the crowd of leering vampires surrounding the doorway, a sword flashing like an arc of silver before her. Hitting the ground, she rolled, her nimble body intersecting the path of the oncoming vampire. Partygirl went for her instead. Elena sidestepped, her sword blurring, moving faster than the eye, and Partygirl's head toppled from her shoulders and thudded against the polished floor. Enraged, Goth charged Elena, and she pivoted, her sword leaving a gleaming trail of light. He dropped to his knees, clawing at his spilling entrails. Quarterback retreated, his hands held out before him in placation.

Elena froze. Marika's hand closed on Alex's throat, lifting him from the chair. Her fangs slid into his jugular like a hot knife through butter. Alex tried to gasp for air, but nothing would come. His body spasmed and a wave of darkness rose beneath him, endless dark, like Elena's eyes, creeping up to smother him. Elena called his name, her lyrical voice echoing through the hollow expanse of his mind, and Alex wished he could have had one more moment, one more second with her alone.

Marika dropped him and Alex wilted to the ground. Elena shuddered in disbelief, the bowstring of her anger tightening in the face of such horror. To lose him once was bad enough. To lose him twice, to the same bitch ...

'Too slow, Elena,' said Marika, wiping her face with her sleeve. Alex's blood smeared across her cheek. 'Yet again. The human body can withstand the loss of up to forty per cent of their blood, but I'm not sure how controlled I was.'

Alex's chest rose feebly. Elena heard his heart flutter, struggling to beat, to keep him alive. So weak.

'What do you want, Marika?' asked Elena, in her most controlled voice. Her grip on the sword tightened. Her muscles burned.

'I can't kill you, Elena. We both know that. Not without losing more than half my court. My strain is not as powerful as yours. I accept that.'

'I had no quarrel with you.'

'I killed Alejandro. And now I have killed him again.' She smiled – that sickening smile which meant she held all the aces, and probably had a few extra tucked up one of her voluminous sleeves. 'But this time, Elena, you can save him.'

'He's dying.'

'So? What is that to us? Take him. He's yours.'

'And what do you want in return?'

'Leave, Elena. Go away, as far and as fast as you can. Never come back to this city. It will be mine.'

Elena tipped her head to one side. Marika feared her and grew more desperate by the second.

And Alex was dying.

Choice? What choice?

'Very well. Step back from him and clear a path to the door. If anyone hinders me...' She lowered the sword and glared down the length of the blade at Marika's sculpted features. '*Anyone*, they die.'

Marika's court drew back. Sliding between moments, Elena darted to Alex's side and flung him over her shoulder, the scent of his remaining blood maddening. Her nostrils flared. His dwindling heartbeat echoed within her body.

Elena sprinted from the chamber and up the subterranean tunnels leading to the world above. Behind her, she left silence.

Elena carried Alex up, right up to the roof of the building that towered over Marika's domain. The moon grinned skull-like at her, yet lit the way, as bright as day to vampire eyes. She laid him out on the rooftop surface, shed her sword and her coat and knelt beside him.

'Alex?' She searched his face for any reaction. 'Alex, can you hear me?' His eyelids fluttered. His chest stirred, then fell still again. 'Alex, I can save you but...' She broke up, startled to find tears stinging her eyes. 'Do you want to live, Alex? Do you want to live for ever?'

He didn't answer. Elena closed her eyes so hard that black and white dots burst behind her eyelids. She'd vowed never to do this. She swore she would never make the same mistakes as Alejandro did.

And yet, here lay all that was left to her of Alejandro, no matter how small a trace, slipping through her fingers.

Elena closed her hand around the blade of her sword and squeezed, letting the razor-sharp edge slice into her palm. She closed her hand to a fist and held it over his mouth; blood dripped onto his lips.

'Please, Alex. Please, don't leave me. Not now. I can't lose you again.'

Tears leaked from the corners of her eyes, rolled down her face, joined her blood. Alex parted his lips, drinking in her blood and tears. His breathing eased, the heartbeat fluttered one last time and then fell still. The moment passed.

He opened his eyes, the rich brown bleeding away to the endless black of vampire eyes.

'Run,' he whispered, his voice hoarse, hungry.

'No.' She placed her uninjured hand against his cheek, ice cold to the touch, flawless.

'A newborn vampire needs to hunt, Elena. I understand that now. So run. For me. Now.'

Fire ignited under her skin. If Elena's heart still beat, she knew it would thunder. If her body still needed breath, it would be caught in her throat, dammed by her pulse. She edged backwards as he drew himself to his knees, his fingers splayed apart like claws. He looked so familiar, so like her sire, and yet . . . nothing like him.

'Alejandro?'

Alex bared his fangs, his eyes blazing with need.

Elena ran. She threw herself over the gap between the buildings onto the next roof. Alex leaped after her. A newborn was the vampire in its purest form, and a vampire sired of her strain, Los Vampiros of Andalusia, direct descendants of the mantequeros, the offspring of Lilith herself, purest of all. Alejandro Báez Ortega had been the most powerful vampire in countless ages. He sired only Elena and all his powers passed to her. And Elena had sired no one else. Until now.

The thrill of the chase consumed her, exhilarating whether hunter or prey. Up ahead, she saw the roof-access door. Elena threw herself at it. She grabbed the handle, her hand slippery with blood, but as she turned it, he grabbed her. Alex tore her shirt away, shredding it in his eagerness and Elena fought back, even though the last thing she wanted to do was to repel him. It was part of the game, part of the ritual, and something lesser vampires like Marika and her countless watered-down scions would never understand. The rhythm of their paso doble seized her. Alex ripped her jeans down her long legs and she kicked back. He was too quick, sidestepping her, pouncing on her before she had a chance to use her newfound freedom. She tried to turn on him, ready to scratch and bite, but he slammed her body against the door, twisting her arm up between her shoulder blades. He pulled all but the last scrap of clothing away, his tongue sliding down the length of her spine, teeth grazing over the point of each vertebra. At the base of her back, where her hips flared out to the globes of her ass, he paused, his fingers skirting the lacy film of her underwear.

Elena pressed her bare breasts against the smooth coldness of the metal door. He held her there, his hands travelling over the slender columns of her thighs and up to toy with her labia through the near-transparent material separating them.

'Say my name,' he growled. She stayed silent, defying him with the only means she had left. Her body longed to betray her. Hunger boiled in the pit of her stomach and her hips undulated towards his mouth. Need, desire, lust . . .

Alex slid up her length. He pressed against her, from foot to neck. His mouth grazed her shoulder. He reached around to cup her breasts. They fitted into his hands as if they had been made to nestle there. She felt his shaft against her ass, like steel wrapped in velvet, pressing into her skin.

'Say my name, Elena.'

'Alex.'

'Not *Alejandro*?' he taunted.

Her nails scraped gouges in the door. She pushed her hips harder against him. 'Alex!'

His right hand slid down the curve of her waist, fingers probing beneath the flimsy material. Down further, going where only her own hand had ventured in a hundred years. He slipped one finger inside her, then two.

Elena's fangs distended with unsatisfied need. He thrust against her from behind, trapping her between his body and his hand, and his hand between her body and the door.

'Say it again.'

'Alex.'

Withdrawing his fingers, he ripped the lace away and lifted her from the ground, pushing her harder against the door.

'Tell me what you want, Elena. Tell me now.'

'You, Alex. I want you. Inside me. For ever.'

Alex entered her in one sweeping motion. His cock filled her, pressing the whole way into her welcoming warmth, stretching her. Elena cried out, his name ragged on her lips. He thrust, withdrew, almost pulling out completely before he drove himself into her again. Rising within her, the orgasm built beyond control, beyond sanity. Alex roared, his voice breaking with need as he pounded into her body, tipping her over the edge the same moment as his teeth sank into her neck. Elena threw back her head in ecstasy and howled. Not in pain. This could never be pain. This was fulfilment.

She came to herself in a tangle of limbs, with his weight on her body, his tears on her face.

'Did I hurt you?' he asked.

A smile flickered over her face, teasing the warm glow that spread through her. 'Hurt is relative, Alex.'

'I went too fast. Next time we'll make our hunt last longer.'

She felt her smile broaden. She couldn't help herself. 'Alex, my love, you and I can hunt each other across eternity.'

Sometimes They Come Back

Portia da Costa

What's with the shutters? When the hell did she have those fitted?

It'd been three weeks since Richard Lacey had visited the house that he'd formerly shared with his wife Melinda, but even in that short time he could see there'd been changes. For some reason best known to herself his wife had installed heavy metal shutters on every window. Horrible black things they were, grim and bleak and ugly, making the place look like a fortified bunker in the heart of suburbia.

We'll soon see about this!

Richard frowned as he pulled into the drive. What on earth was going on? Mel had ruined the house's aspect completely – when he still owned half of it. She'd no business making drastic alterations and knocking down the value his property like that.

Staring at the dour, uninviting façade, he took a deep breath.

He wasn't here to argue. In fact quite the reverse. Trying to think positive, loving thoughts, he turned off the engine. He planned his little speech and how the scenario that accompanied it might play out. But still he felt uneasy, and it wasn't just the fucking shutters that were to blame.

Stepping out of the car, he stared around him. More shocks.

The garden, always Mel's pride and joy, was looking terrible.

Her roses were in a pathetic state, with dead blooms hanging forlornly on their stems, and ranks of sly, greasy-looking little weeds had popped up in between them. It was a pleasant evening and the twilight was golden, but a dark, unsettling miasma hung over the entire garden. Clutching his peace offering of an expensive bottle of wine and some Belgian chocolate truffles, he strode to the front door and tried to shake off the sudden heebie-jeebies.

Out of courtesy, he rang the bell. Mel was mostly in. She didn't go out much. In fact her lack of interest in social activities was one of the main reasons they'd split. Well, correction, *he'd* walked out. A grinding pang of guilt tightened his gut as he remembered her pleas for him to stay and her floods of tears. But the prospect of life with a party girl like Susan had seemed so much more exciting. As had the copious and uncomplicated sex, a relief after Mel's intense emotion and her frequent, unexplained melancholy.

No answer. Was she even in? With those hideous blinds it was impossible to tell.

Tucking his bottle and his box under his arm, he fished out his key, already feeling the bright edge wearing off his reconciliation plans. Trust Mel to be out, just when he wanted to spring the great news that he was coming back home for good.

The hall was pitch dark. Which made him realise that there were metal shutters even on the sidelights and the fanlight above the door. What the fuck was that all about? He'd get them removed as soon as he was settled back in again. They were an eyesore, not to mention depressing and unnecessary.

Pausing to switch on a lamp, Richard wrinkled his nose.

Christ, what's that smell?

A heavy, pungent fragrance hit him in the face. It was so powerful he half imagined he could see motes of it drifting in the flat air. It reminded him of the crumbling roses outside, but laced with unfamiliar spices and herbs and with something earthy and disturbing at the back of it.

He'd never smelled it before, and it was nothing like Mel's light floral cologne, or even the many polishes and cleaning products she used.

He quite liked it though. In fact he more than liked it. It had a dark and sexy kick that gave him the horn.

Which was a good thing, really. He was planning to fuck Mel anyway, to seal his return with a reunion shag. She'd be so grateful and, since Susan had turned sour on him, he was missing regular action.

He set down his gifts and walked into the lounge. It was in darkness, just like the hall. Switching on another lamp, he went to the window, but he couldn't find the controls for the blinds anywhere. How the hell did one open the bloody things?

Weaving carefully amongst the furniture, he made his way back to the hall.

What the hell is going on? And why am I so incredibly randy?

It was getting pretty serious now. He was rock hard in his jeans. God, he hoped that Mel came home soon from wherever it was she'd gone.

Upstairs, it got worse. The fragrance was stronger and he was so stiff now it was uncomfortable to walk.

At the end of the landing, the door to the master bedroom was slightly open, and when he reached in and tried to switch on the light inside, nothing happened. Bulb out?

He padded into the room, negotiating by the glow from the hall. The unsettling floral scent was so thick here that it felt like he was struggling to walk through it, like he was wading through treacle. Flopping onto the bed, he was forced to clutch his aching, throbbing groin.

Oh Mel, oh Mel, he thought, stricken by a sudden gouge of desire for his wife. He'd treated her so badly. He hadn't valued her when he should have done. He'd do better now. He'd do everything she wanted him to.

A heavy lassitude drifted over him, and he leaned back on the bed, kicking off his shoes. Wherever she was, he'd wait for her, and be good to her when she got back. Better than he'd ever been.

Stretching out, his hand connected with something soft and flimsy and, drawing it to him, he discovered it was an item of lingerie. A camisole-type thing, he realised, holding it up in the light from the doorway. It was black, and made of silk, and encrusted with lace. Nothing like the sensible white cotton bras and knickers that Mel usually wore. The soft fabric slid through his fingers like fluid, and his cock leaped as he imagined the silk between Mel's legs. Not the delicate cloth, but the satin feel of her arousal.

Desire gripped him by the balls, sluicing through his body, choking him.

Why had he left her? He struggled to remember. He must have been insane. How could he have forgotten how sexy she was? Her perfume filled his brain. Or was it her perfume? What was happening to him? His head seemed to whirl while his cock pulsed and raged, dragging at his belly with an agonising need to fuck.

A raw pitiful sound echoed in the room and he realised it was him, groaning aloud, like a beast in pain.

He was lying on the bed, still in his coat, but, with fingers that shook as if he had a palsy, he ripped at his belt, his trousers, his zip. Opening his fly, he reached in and rummaged in his shorts. Finding his burning cock, he wrapped the cool silk around it, wishing it were Mel's fingers, or her lips, or the soft, liquid paradise between her legs.

He pumped and pumped himself, almost in tears, crying out her name, 'Mel! Mel!'

How could he have left her? She was a goddess ... He was unworthy of her, he'd been lucky to have been allowed anywhere near her.

His hand was inept and clumsy, not like her gentle hand, the way she'd always held him. Caressed him. Pleasured him. The exotic perfume that reminded him so perfectly of her seemed to be drenching his brain and creating pictures, memories, longing, longing, longing ...

Confused and frustrated, he felt orgasm barrelling towards him, but as he reached for it, almost clawed for it, a subtle displacement of air stopped him dead in his tracks. The shock of it held him, kept him still, denied his release.

A figure rose with utter grace from the chair in the corner of the room, strangely visible in the darkness as if he were suddenly granted special senses to see it.

'Mel?'

She was here. Walking towards him. His Mel, of whom he wasn't worthy, so familiar yet strangely, utterly different.

'Ah-ha, sometimes they come back it seems, these errant husbands.' In the strange light he saw the ghost of a wry smile on her familiar face. 'Regardless of whether you want them to or not.'

Richard tried to rise, but he'd lost all his strength. It'd been leached out of him by his lust, his remorse.

'Mel ... oh, Mel ...' he managed to gasp, staring at her as he still held his cock in his fist.

How the hell could he have forgotten she was so beautiful? He frowned, his vision blurring and shifting. For a moment, the notion that she never *had* been quite this beautiful flitted through his brain and nibbled at the edge of his consciousness. But then his perception seemed to phase again, and he acknowledged his beloved wife's supreme loveliness.

Her pale face shone in the gloom, her skin white and pearly. Her lips were like bloody rose petals, her eyes like dark stars. Black, thick and shiny, her hair cascaded lusciously to her shoulders. Had she done something with it? No, it had always been like that, hadn't it? So lustrous and so sensuous, so seductive.

And her body . . . Oh, her body.

She was wearing a dark silk and lace robe that seemed to be part of the same set as the camisole with which he was rubbing his aching dick. The sleek fabric was mutable, like black liquid metal, forming to the lush contours of her breasts, her thighs, her delicately curved belly and the little mound of her pussy.

She was close, so close now, and the way she'd moved made him feel giddy as if he'd been on a merry-go-round too long. Had she walked, or had she glided somehow?

No, that was ridiculous. People didn't glide, especially his wife. And yet somehow she was here, sinking gracefully down onto the bed beside him, having traversed the room without any discernible effort.

'Mel, I'm so sorry,' he whispered. He couldn't manage more because his cock was pounding with blood, and he felt as if there were a great weight pushing down on his chest.

'Indeed you are.'

Her voice was as quiet as his. She'd always been soft spoken. Yet the words seemed to resound against his eardrums as if she'd roared.

Reaching out, she dashed away his fingers from his cock and folded her own around it. They felt cool through the silk of the camisole.

Stark fear washed through him. A terror he didn't understand. Dear God, might she wrench his dick off as a horrific retribution?

The way her red mouth curved, promising yet cruel, seemed to suggest that she'd read his very thought.

She began to pump him, slowly and teasingly, her sultry body rocking and weaving as she did so, as if she were pleasuring herself at the same time, rubbing her sex against the mattress as she moved.

Maybe she was? Her crimson tongue flickered out like a serpent's kiss, moistening her lips as her eyes closed and she undulated her hips.

Then she let out a little gasp, as if, astonishingly, she'd come.

A thought whipped across his mind like a bullet train, yet he managed to grasp an impression of it.

Hadn't Mel always been hard to rouse, slow to climax?

Not now though. Oh, not now. She threw back her head, keening her triumph to heaven. Her perfect white throat rippled as she cried out in pleasure.

How? How?

Confused, he found himself noting, as if through a haze, that her throat wasn't quite as perfect as it had first appeared to be. There was a delicate yet pronounced red scar close to her chin, a few inches beneath her ear. It was faint, like two minute red spiderwebs, but it had the look of a fierce wound long healed.

He'd never seen it before, although they'd been married for seven years.

A moment later, she worked her shoulders, opened her eyes and focused on him.

Richard flinched. Was he imagining things or were there glittering specks of red in her pupils?

She looked down. So did he.

Good God, he'd almost forgotten that she'd got his dick in her hand.

With a little 'humph' of displeasure, she whipped the camisole from around his shaft and flung it away. But when her fingers closed on him again, they were still as cool as the silk had been. They felt delightful, sweet and soothing against his feverish, rigid heat.

He looked into her eyes again, but the red flecks were scary. He closed his own eyes, not able to face her, reluctant to think.

For a few moments, she played with him, manipulated him, flickering her cold fingertips up and down his length as if he were a flute and she was picking out a tune.

He still didn't dare open his eyes, but behind his eyelids her image danced and terrified him, all crimson pupils and wild Medusa hair.

When cold moisture hit his glans, he shouted out loud.

His eyes shot open again, and the sensation of being consumed by something cool and wet and mobile compelled him to look downwards at his dick.

Mel was sucking him, her ruby lips moving up and down along his shaft, as her tongue plagued and tantalised him. He shouted aloud again as her teeth grazed his hardness.

And she was naked too, her robe flung away across the carpet, and her lush body curved over him, utterly graceful. Her magnificent breasts brushed his thigh, her nipples as hard as two studs of icy metal.

Oh God, she's going to bite it off!

Black fear gnawed his gut, but insanely it made his dick even harder. Her soft laughter around his flesh nearly finished him, but she did something infernal with her fingers that kept him hanging, unable to climax.

Releasing his precious member from immediate danger, she straightened up, smiling.

'It would have served you right if I had done it, darling husband,' she purred, her voice low and terribly thrilling. 'But why bite off your dick to spite my face?'

With a toss of her head, she slithered forwards and crouched over him like some beautiful but deadly spider, moving strangely.

Terror surged in his belly as she climbed on top of him and sank down.

The shock of her around him seemed to fracture his perceptions. For a few precarious moments, he grabbed at consciousness, and clarity, and realised he'd been stupefied.

His wife's slick body was cold, so cold around him. He started to soften, but then she gripped him and massaged him, and he stiffened again.

The room rocked and revolved, circling like a carousel, but he clung to the fragments of his sanity.

'Why the . . . the shutters?' he gasped, his voice rising to a squeal as she rotated her hips and jerked his erection this way and that, clasping him and milking him at the same time. 'What's going on?'

He felt like a worm, a peon, gazing up at her. She was goddess, an icon of sex, deigning to look at him, deigning to fuck him, deigning to touch him.

For a while he thought she wasn't going to answer. For a while he thought he was going to pass out or that the top of his head was going to fly off.

How in hell could he have left a woman who could do this to him? Fucking Susan had been like fucking a log of wood by comparison.

'I had an intruder, my dear. Someone broke in,' she cooed, leaning down over him, her sex never faltering in its grip and squeeze, grip and squeeze. 'And you weren't here, so I decided to take precautions.'

'I'm sorry . . . I'm so sorry,' he gasped, not sure what he felt. It was difficult to think straight with his dick plunged into a cold silky paradise.

'I believe you are, Richard.' Her voice was like honey in his ear, and her cool lips were satin against his neck, as she kissed him there. He felt her tongue pop out like a little dart and work delicately against a patch of skin as if preparing it for something. 'Do you still love me?'

The words should have been a shock, but somehow he'd been half prepared for them. And half prepared to give a fully truthful answer.

'Oh yes, Mel . . . Yes, I do!' Her lips pressed against the moistened patch of skin, right over his pulse vein, as her satiny channel rippled around him, a perfect counterpoint. 'I was stupid and cruel and thoughtless, but I won't be again. I won't be again. Believe me.'

She was licking, licking, licking, but somehow at the same time smiling. He could feel it.

'No, you won't, that's very true,' she confirmed, in a zephyr of breath against him. 'And in spite of everything, *I* still love you, Richard. Which is luckier for you than you could ever possibly know.'

Her hips rose and fell, her body, inclined over him, as supple as a contortionist's. Her mouth was open now, against his neck, her sharp teeth grazing.

Sensing his climax near, Richard tried to grab her, but somehow without even touching him she dashed his hands away. He lay stretched out on the bed like a frozen starfish, unable to move, unable to do anything but feel.

She was nipping him now, nibbling and worrying his neck, moaning at the same time, a deep and feral sound. Her vulva fluttered as she was orgasming almost continually.

Richard screamed as she bit hard into his neck, not from the pain of it but from the intensity of coming. Cold light flooded his head and his pounding loins began to empty.

The next day at work, he felt nervy, out of sorts, lacking in energy. He couldn't concentrate on his job and he could barely remember his own name.

His neck hurt and his dick felt as if it'd been through a mangle. Every time he touched it – and he touched it a lot – it tingled with pleasure as if it could remember details he'd forgotten.

He couldn't do anything without thinking of Mel, and yet he couldn't really remember what had happened with her. His brain was fuzzed apart from the remembrance of pleasure. Acute, intense, painful pleasure, the like of which he'd never realised was possible. He couldn't even recall how he'd got out of the house or whether she'd said he could return to it again.

The hours dragged. His neck throbbed and burned. The day was too hot and muggy and the sun was far too bright. All he could think of was the cool darkness of the bedroom back at home and the cool darkness of plunging his cock into his wife.

When evening fell, he left his hotel room, jumped into his car and drove home at faster than the speed limit. For some reason he wasn't sure of, it'd seemed important to wait for nightfall . . . but now, he was in a hurry. He hungered.

Tearing through the streets like a madman, he felt his spirits rise, and his cock too. Soon he would be with her. Soon they would be alone. And fucking.

But outside the house, in *his* drive, there stood another car. A sleek black beast of a car, a beautiful Aston Martin the like of which he would never be able to afford even if he lived for ever. Confusion whirled in his gut, a nausea of panic. Who was here? *Why* were they here? Why couldn't they leave him alone so he could convince the woman he loved to let him come back home for ever?

He rang the bell. He rattled the door. He rang the bell again. It seemed important to observe the courtesies now, and yet the dark churning bile of fear and jealousy overcame him. He pulled out his key and, scrabbling and scratching furiously, he finally let himself into the house.

Again the darkness. Again the overpowering scents. Rotting roses. Ancient spices. Something not quite right that nevertheless wound itself around his aching cock and seemed to caress it.

Richard dashed through the dark house, barking his shins on furniture and cursing. He had to get to her. Where was she? Who was she with?

The savageness of his jealousy gnawed on him like a rat on a bone, and yet, dimly, he was aware that it served him right that he was feeling it. How much of this dark acidic emotion had he inflicted on Mel? She must have felt it, knowing he'd been with Susan, living with her and fucking her.

Sounds from upstairs nearly made him faint in an agony of mental pain.

It was voices. Mel's and that of a man. Low with pleasure and ragged, as if deliciously close to orgasm.

He almost flew up the stairs, more sure footed now, his anguish lending him wings.

In the bedroom, as he burst in, exactly the tableau that he'd feared assaulted his eyes.

His Mel, astride another man, her body magnificent in torn black lingerie, her eyes wild with lust and hot dark glee as she gazed down at the pale muscular form of her lover. A lean man, ripped and powerful, with long flaxen hair.

Richard froze, unable to speak or move. He could do

nothing but watch in a saturation of horror and grinding despair.

Slowly, slowly, Mel undulated and rocked on the body of her paramour, her slender form hypnotic in its grace and almost glowing, fluorescent with sensuality. Slowly, slowly, she turned her head to the side and looked straight at Richard, her beautiful face a disdainful mask of passion. Her eyes still on him, she reached down, to the apex of her thighs, where she sat on the slim hips of her lover, and languidly, almost insultingly, strummed her clit.

Her lips were red, decadently stained, and her neck was bleeding, just as Richard's had been, and just as the neck of the man beneath her was doing.

Only her blood, and her companion's, was almost black.

Confusion surged like bile in Richard's throat. What did it mean, the biting? The blood? Absurd concepts tried to present themselves to him, but his mind was so blank with shock he could not get a grip on them. Even though she was fucking another man before his very eyes, Richard wanted to go to her, but when he took a step forwards, she growled out a warning, low and ferocious.

As if turned to stone, Richard could only watch.

Mel lifted herself, and slammed down, lifted herself, and slammed down. The blond man made sounds just as unearthly as she had, his long narrow hands coming up and roving all over her body, sliding beneath the remnants of lace and silk and squeezing and fondling possessively. Richard cringed and ached as he saw those alien fingertips slide into his wife's bottom cleft and toy with her there, inducing fierce groans and shimmies of lewd ecstasy from Mel. Tears filled his eyes and streamed down his face when the lean and hungry lover reared up from the bed and latched his stained mouth onto Mel's nipple and began to suck and bite.

The unholy communion went on and on. How long could they last? How long could they torment him with their writhing and mutual pawing?

Sick with humiliation, Richard unzipped himself and took his cock in his hand. He wanted to die, but he wanted to come too. As Mel and her lover fucked and writhed and humped, he wanked himself furiously, barely even feeling any pleasure in it, just driven by a gnawing, raw compulsion.

As they roared in triumph, he sobbed and spurted on the carpet. Staggering and falling, he curled up into a ball, unable to face the loss, the shame, the sadness.

Richard lay there for an indeterminate period, frozen, paralysed by the weight of his own shortcomings, the faults that had brought him to this misery. Who could blame Mel for taking a lover? He'd done it, and he had much less reason to than her. His anguish was so intense, he wanted to drown in it. He wanted to die.

Then, before he really realised what was happening, he was lifted up. Bodily. Like a feather's weight, like a child.

Stark terror and a strange sense of being nurtured made him keep his eyes closed. It had to be the strong-looking blond man who carried him to the bed, surely? Only a man had the muscle to lift another man.

So why did he imagine, in his fever, that it was Mel? Why did he feel scraps of lace and her sumptuous breasts pressed against him.

'Richard, open your eyes.'

It was a command, all wrapped around in the perfume of dead roses. Fearfully, he obeyed, looking upwards at two faces looking down at him. Unable to help himself, he scowled and twisted away from the blond man.

'Now, now, now, darling, don't be like that.' Mel pressed a long crimson-tipped fingernail to his brow, then his mouth, smoothing out the displeasure. 'This is Sylvester, and he's our friend ... You'll grow to love him.'

What?

Richard shook his head, trying to clear it. Him, love a man? That was bullshit.

And yet a moment later, he succumbed, when the handsome blond touched him and began to kiss his heated skin.

Sylvester smelled of roses, and also of blood, sharp and metallic. His long tongue was pointed like a lizard's, as it flicked his throat and his jaw, and slid momentarily into his ear. In Richard's mind it seemed to coil around his cock. Helplessly lost, he closed his eyes and slumped back against the pillows, all the while aware that Mel was working on his clothing.

Her hand slid beneath the panels of his shirt, peeling them back like wings and baring his chest. As Sylvester tongued his neck and shoulder, she pressed a fingertip to his left nipple and delicately swivelled it around, then went in hard, with an excruciating little pinch. The pain was sharp and sweet and he groaned and wriggled, breathing in the man's fragrance, which smelled identical to Mel's.

Then it was his trousers that were torn off him, and his boxers with them. His sticky cock came bounding up, aroused anew. Struggling to find his thoughts, his will, he tried to fight them, but it was hopeless. He was overwhelmed, he was their toy, just eager flesh to play with.

Eyes tightly closed, he tried to ignore the second presence on the bed, but it was impossible. He sobbed, acknowledging that they'd now changed places and it was Sylvester attending to his cock, while Mel kissed his naked chest and bit at his nipples.

Tears streamed down his face as a cold mouth took him in, and he screamed like a child as he smelled blood, dark and coppery. His consciousness wavered, then he realised it was from his chest, not down below.

Pleasure flooded through him, dark and tainted. Hands and mouths roved over his body, touching fondly, kissing, licking and biting. Tongues and teeth grazed and tasted his naked skin.

Finally, he was enveloped again. Cool, lush liquidity around his cock, which made him whine and squirm.

Mel? Sylvester? He could no longer tell, they seemed one being, one lover, all devouring.

When sharp teeth plunged into his neck, his cock jerked and jerked again, disgorging semen. His world went white, the pleasure unbearable, his soul extinguished.

He felt odd, strange, not himself.

As Richard struggled to wake, it seemed as if his body wasn't his, but someone else's. It felt weak, empty and feverish, yet still aroused.

He couldn't seem to move, but the smell of roses made his dick leap.

'Open your eyes, Richard. Open your eyes.'

He raised his heavy lids and saw his wife, naked and entwined with her lover. Sylvester's hand was between her thighs, slowly moving. Her smile was silky, her body gleamed.

Her eyes were red.

A curtain of misdirection fell away.

'Wh – What are you?' Richard gasped, trembling in fear and sweating with horror, yet still cruelly turned on.

'Oh, I think you know, Richard, don't you? Surely it's obvious?'

'But they're not real . . . V –'

'Hush!' Her soft hand stopped his mouth, even as she writhed in obvious pleasure.

'But how?'

For several moments, she rocked and swayed, then groaned with pleasure.

A second later, she looked straight at him, cool and level.

'I had an intruder, remember?' Leaning over, watching him from the corner of her eye, she slowly licked her lover's neck, scooping up his unnatural blood with her questing tongue. 'But he came back too, and made an offer that I simply couldn't resist.'

Richard felt like weeping again. He loved Mel. He wanted her. And now this . . .

'But I love you,' he said in a small voice, his body aching.

'And I love you too, Richard. Really, I do. And so does Sylvester.'

As if to prove it, the handsome blond reached across and casually and with fingers of ice, stroked Richard's cock.

Intense pleasure speared through him and, at the same time, familiar visions from a dozen movies filled his mind.

He saw the legendary sinister European aristocrat, a familiar archetype with pointed teeth, crimson eyes and a billowing black cloak.

And beside him, his voluptuous bride, voracious, cold and beautiful.

Mel smiled, as if delighted that he finally comprehended. Her sharp white teeth appeared to sparkle and the wound in Richard's neck began to throb.

'Am I like you?'

A great peal of laughter rang out, like a tumbling bell, filling the room.

'Oh no, my sweet. You left me, remember? You don't deserve the big prize.'

Shivers, both cold and febrile, racked his body. He knew he was different, but if not like them, how had they changed him?

'You're our servant, Richard. Our toy, our food, our plaything . . .' She paused, not looking at Richard's face, but watching Sylvester's slender fingers ply his pulsing, aching flesh. Despite everything, Richard was rigid, stiff, responsive. Despite everything, he was enthralled by the touch of another man.

'Don't you know the Dracula story, husband? Don't you realise? ' Mel purred in Richard's ear while her lover pumped his cock. 'You're our Renfield, my love. Our creature. For all eternity.'

As Richard sobbed and jerked and climaxed, he felt quite happy.

Portia Da Costa is the author of the Black Lace novels *Continuum*, *Entertaining Mr Stone*, *Gemini Heat*, *Gothic Blue*, *Hotbed*, *Shadowplay*, *Suite Seventeen*, *The Devil Inside*, *The Stranger*, *The Tutor* and *In Too Deep*. Her paranormal novellas are included in the Black Lace collections *Lust Bites* and *Magic and Desire*.

The Man-eaters

Carrie Williams

Sara never told him what happened that day down by the Ganges, as he lay sweating and shivering in their room, fearing malaria. All he knew was that she was never the same again. By the time he actually asked her, she was so far away from him that he knew he had lost her for good. He knew, too, that he loved her in spite of how she'd been, the disdainful way she'd treated him of late, of how she'd changed. Perhaps even more – the sex ... Well, the sex was just *extraordinary*. Exhilarating to the point of frightening him.

I know now, he said to himself as he preceded the girls down to the water, that I would do anything for Sara.

She didn't mind at all when Neil cried off; in fact, she was pleased that she was going to have Banhi to herself for the evening. Half-Indian, half-British, Banhi was like no one she had ever met before. She was so interesting, so full of fascinating anecdotes and tales, so full of life. She was also ravishingly beautiful. Beside her, Neil, God bless him, paled into insignificance.

As she eyed the menu, waiting for her new friend to arrive, she thought about her boyfriend. All had been well, or perhaps seemed well, until this last week. After meeting in their last term at university and going through the stress of finals together, they'd rewarded themselves with this six-week trip around India. She'd enjoyed it, enjoyed his company. But these past few days she'd begun to wonder: Was he enough?

And the sex? That, too, had started well. Excellently, in fact. But then didn't it always, or almost always? Just about every relationship she'd had had begun with that honeymoon period in which the new lovers just can't keep their hands off each other. It was whether it could carry on like that that counted. And in her experience, it didn't.

Perhaps that was it: perhaps the honeymoon with Neil was ending and she was crash-landing back in reality. Perhaps she was getting bored. Closing her eyes for a minute, she relived the previous evening. The half-hearted blow job she'd given him, hoping he would come quickly and exonerate her from her duties. She'd told herself she was tired, but deep down she knew that she could, even when tired, if she really wanted too. That in fact some of the best fucks had happened when she was tired, woozy, yielding; that that was when she opened up best, as if submitting herself to a universal force greater than herself.

'Sara.' Banhi was sitting opposite her, as if she'd materialised from nowhere. She smiled, revealing perfect white teeth. Sara didn't know what to say: Banhi always made her breathless, left her struggling for words.

She smiled back. 'Hi,' she managed at last.

Banhi picked up a menu and, as she perused it, her eyes kept darting back to meet Sara's over the top of it.

'Decided what you fancy?' she said at last, and this time she held Sara's gaze.

Sara squirmed a little in her seat. She wondered, sometimes, if Banhi was flirting with her, or whether she was just like this with everyone – intense, making one feel as if one were at the centre of the universe, or caught in a spotlight. As if one were somehow special. No one had made her feel this way before, and it both excited and terrified her. If Banhi wanted something from her, could she, Sara, live up to the other girl's expectations?

They shared a large vegetarian *thali* and, as they ate it, talked of this and that: of what Sara and Neil had seen on their sight-seeing excursion that day, and of what Banhi had done at the university, where she was studying Hindu mythology.

'I've been learning about *you*,' she said with a mischievous grin.

'How do you mean?' said Sara.

'The goddess Kali,' said Banhi. 'She of the four arms. You know – there are statues of her everywhere.'

'The one with skulls around her neck?'

'The very one.'

'So where do I come into it?'

'Well, it turns out another name for her is Sara, or the Black Goddess. That's what the gypsies called her. I never knew.'

'Sara? That's an odd name for an Indian goddess.'

'Well, it's all crazy and mixed up, as always with these myths and legends. There's a place in southern France called Saintes-Maries-de-la-Mer, where the Roma people go to worship their patron saint, Sara, who is also known as Sara-la-Kali, which means "Sara the Black" in Romany.'

Banhi drummed the tabletop with her long slim fingers. 'In short, some scholars claim that the Romany Sara and the Indian Kali are one and the same.'

'On what basis?'

'On the basis of the word *kali* and also the similarities between the gypsy pilgrimages and the worship of Kali – both involve immersion in water. They claim that Sara is not a real saint but a transference of Kali to a Christian figure.'

'And why is she – are they – black?'

'Kali, who might or might not be the same as the goddess

Durga, depending on who you listen to, is usually depicted with a black face. Have you seen that on statues? She's black because she's the goddess of creation, but also of sickness and death.'

Banhi paused for a moment and Sara felt transfixed by her dark gaze. The other girl's pupils seemed unnaturally large, all-devouring, as if they were trying to suck all the light into themselves.

'She's a most interesting creature,' Banhi went on at last. 'Both a giver and a taker of life. A redeemer and a mother-goddess, and yet unspeakably vile. Vengeful and monstrously violent. In one famous myth, she fights Ruktabija, the king of demons, who duplicates himself with each drop of his blood that is spilt. Kali wins out by sucking the blood from his body, then putting all of his duplicates into her vast mouth. She finishes up by dancing on the battlefield, on the corpses of those she has killed.'

Banhi sat back, as if exhausted by her tale. 'Am I boring you, Sara, my black goddess?' she said, brow creased.

'Of course not,' said Sara, a sudden vehemence to her, a new energy. Being with Banhi, she realised, made her feel so . . . so *alive*, in a way that being with Neil didn't. Neil was fine, she said to herself, but beside Banhi with her vast knowledge of things so alien to Sara, he seemed rather grey and humdrum. She could listen to Banhi all night and beyond.

'How about dessert?' she said, conscious of Banhi's eyes on her. She wondered what interest she could possibly hold for her new friend with her fascinating tales, her glamorous jet-setting life from one university to another. Banhi was ever-questing, voracious, and next to her Sara felt she knew nothing, had nothing to say.

Banhi shook her head, and was already standing up and gesturing to the waiter for their bill. 'Let's walk,' she said to

Sara, and Sara felt boneless, malleable. It was as if she was being drawn along in the wake of some incontrovertible force, a force of life impossible to resist.

'Let's walk by the river,' Banhi said, and her eyes shone like pools of dark liquid in which Sara feared she might drown.

There wasn't a soul by the river – the curfews imposed by the religious hostels, where most of the Western travellers lodged because they were so cheap, saw to that. Sara expressed concern that they would be locked out for the night, but Banhi just waved a hand dismissively and said they would find a way back in if that happened.

That same hand found its way to the small of Sara's back somewhere along the riverbank, and Sarah felt as if some kind of electric pulse was travelling through her, stimulating all her nerve endings. She was wearing only a vest top, and through the flimsy fabric Banhi's hand felt hot, almost as if it were branding her. Sara was certain that there'd be a hand-shaped mark there, the imprint of Banhi, when she got back to her room. How would she explain that to Neil? She hoped he'd be asleep when she returned.

They talked as they walked, but thinking about it afterwards, Sara had no memory of the contents of their conversation. She put that down to the disorienting effect of Banhi's hand on her, of her own confused thoughts. She had felt, she realised with hindsight, almost as if she had been hypnotised – by Banhi's slow, measured voice and, behind it, echoing its lulling rhythm, the gentle lapping of the water against its banks.

But she would never forget what happened as they approached the guesthouse and Banhi stopped and turned to face her, her hands now moving to Sara's shoulders, pulling her in towards her. The night was almost moonless and there were no lights in the buildings around her, she supposed due to the nightly power failures that afflicted the town. Yet there was an odd red sheen to Banhi's eyes, an otherworldly patina that made Sara's head reel.

Banhi's hands moved down to Sara's hips, making sweeping, caressing motions. As she smiled, her teeth glittered like shards of glass despite the lack of light. Sara shivered, though the night was still balmy. Her life, she felt, hinged on this moment, on what she did now. What did she want? More of the same with Neil, or with someone like Neil – an endless procession of Neils down through the years? Or whatever Banhi was offering her?

The other girl's hands had moved to her breasts. Sara knew what she wanted and, in a spasm, she threw back her head and let out a long moan into the silence of the night, the pale flesh of her neck exposed.

He didn't know exactly how she'd changed, only that she had. At first he'd put it down to his malarial feverishness, the way the sex had taken on an almost hallucinatory intensity. It had surprised him all the more in that he'd been worried of late that Sara was going off him. She was always crying off, making excuses and, when she did submit to his advances, making him feel like she was doing him a favour. She claimed to be too tired, most of the time, but there was no reason for it – it's not as if they had kids, for heaven's sake.

But that night she'd been out with Banhi – that's when it all started. This time it was he who was not really up to it and she who had insisted, stalking into the room in silence, not even asking him if he was feeling any better, just crawling over to him on the bed and taking him into her mouth before he was fully erect. As she'd coaxed his cock into life, she'd palpated his balls, softly at first, then with greater fervour. He'd arched his back then, pressing himself into her eager fists, enraptured that she'd come back to him at last after the waning of her desire.

Swapping over, she'd taken his prick in one fist and one and then two balls in her mouth. As her hand had moved up and down his shaft, she'd reached under him, clutching at one buttock. His excitement mounting, he'd felt her growing more frenzied too – her nails dug into him and she'd begun to let out strange guttural moans that sounded almost like some kind of religious chant. Rearing up and away from him, she'd stared down and he'd been frightened then by her eyes – there was some kind of emptiness to them, despite the ardour of what he had taken to be her love-making but would now hesitate to describe as such. He smiled at her, for reassurance as much as anything else, but she failed to return it, instead yanking down her shorts, pulling the gusset of her knickers aside and impaling herself on his straining prick. He'd come with a yell, in a mixture of awe and terror at this new creature that seemed to be manifesting itself in someone he had thought he knew so well. He barely even noticed, as he did, how she had shot one finger up into his arse.

Dismounting, she'd remained astride him, her sopping pussy on his belly, and, reaching down, frenetically massaged her clit with the heel of one hand until, leaning away from him, head thrown back, she'd come with an unholy shriek that sent a chill through him. It was as if he'd made out with an animal and, although he couldn't miss the increasingly passive Sara of yore, he wasn't sure what to make of the new incarnation. She felt, if anything, more distant than before.

She remembered going into the room, seeing Neil on the bed, naked, a book by his side. Then things became both hazy and, almost paradoxically, hyper-real. It was as if all her senses had been cranked up several gears, as if her whole body had been retuned. The smoothness of his prick, the clean salty taste of the pre-cum on her tongue. The silkiness of his balls as she had rolled them, first one then the other and finally both, in her mouth. The feel of her juices flowing over her fingers as she'd bought herself to a climax, like a wash of pure satin.

But yes, there was a haze there too, the feeling that she'd been in some kind of fugue state, the remnants of her experience down by the river. That, too, seemed both heightened in intensity and woozily unreal. She'd felt Banhi's mouth on her neck at the same time as her friend had pushed one hand down her shorts and knickers, then the flutter of soft fingertips at her clitoris. She knew she'd come then, too, head still thrown back to the stars as they wheeled above. But after that ... How had they got back? It was only a matter of steps to the guest-house, but she remembered none of them. Had they been locked out, as she had feared they would be? She had no idea of the time, of how long she and Banhi had tarried by the river. It was curious: she'd have suspected drink, only it was one of the state's all-too-frequent dry days. They had drunk salt *lassis* with their *thali*.

Now, sleepless still, watching as dawn stripped the sky beyond their window of light, she reached for him across the bed, her hunger for him renewed.

It was almost like the old days, when she had never been sated of him, when she had cycled to college in the dead of night to hand in an overdue essay and then raced to his room, woken him up and demanded that he take her. When she'd gone to find him in the library, given him glorious head in the philosophy section, ignoring his protests that he was supposed to be revising. Not that he'd really minded: he loved it, he told her on numerous occasions, that she was a woman of appetite. He loved that she made him feel so wanted, so necessary.

He opened one eye as she swung one leg over him, took his prick in her fist again. With her free hand she took one of his and guided it to her pussy; instinctively he bunched his fingers together and she fed him into her, without the need for lube. He had known her horny, but this was something else.

She moved against him, pushing herself onto him harder and harder, until he was afraid he must be hurting her. Her face, though, bore an image of an almost religious transcendence, like the statue of a saint. He spoke her name, quietly, and she didn't react. He said it louder, and then still louder. Her eyes remained closed; she was far away from him, somewhere else.

He half sat up, eager now to penetrate her, to find some kind of connection, but she pushed him down, her movements shockingly forceful, and brought her mouth back down around him. He tried to hold off, but in spite of himself he began to buck his hips beneath her, losing control. As a jet of come issued forth, he felt her mouth tighten around him, form a sheath so close and avid that he feared he would be sucked dry, drained of all his vital juices.

She left him in the room, shellshocked. Banhi was out on the terrace, watching the slow, almost imperceptible flow of the river.

'Time,' she said as Sara took a seat beside her, without taking her eyes from the water, 'seems not to exist here.'

'Perhaps that's why you like it so much,' countered Sara. 'Perhaps that's why we all like India. Everything slows down, or appears to.'

Banhi turned her gaze on Sara, and Sara had to look away, so powerful was the surge of emotions inside her. This girl, this almost obscenely beautiful creature, had made her come only the night before. Did she really expect them to just be able to sit here and chat about things as if nothing had happened? And what did it all mean? Would they do it again? Were they lovers now? Did she, Sara, want them to be? And how had what Banhi had done to her down by the river made her want to go and fuck Neil with an ardour she hadn't felt in months? It was all painfully confusing. Part of her just wanted to run away from it all, but she knew that she couldn't. That Banhi had some kind of hold of her.

'. . . heard of kundalini yoga?' she heard her friend saying.

She shook her head. 'I don't think so.'

'Kundalini means coiling, like a snake. The snake is a symbol of energies that haven't been tapped into, of new possibilities.'

'Do you practise it?'

Banhi nodded. 'Every day. Without fail.' She smiled, but she was already looking back at the slow-flowing Ganges. 'I have transformed myself,' she said. Her eyes flicked back to Sara. 'Let me show you how.' She rose.

Banhi's room, Sara noticed as her friend ushered her inside, was the same as theirs, give or take a few square feet, only it smelled of incense – sandalwood, thought Sara, and something else that she didn't recognise. Something more earthy, almost feral. There was only one small paneless window at the front of the room, equipped with bars – presumably to keep out the monkeys that patrolled the walkway outside. Banhi lit a candle by the bed.

'Lie down,' she commanded and, at Sara's raised eyebrows, added, 'Just watch, for now.'

Sara did as she was bidden and observed as Banhi slipped off her clothes and knelt in front of her, her feet hip-width apart. Between her legs, Sara could see the fuzz of her sex. Her own pussy stirred and dampened. She struggled not to touch herself, or to reach out for Banhi.

'This,' said Banhi, 'is the Hero Pose, also called the Celibate Pose. It's a meditative pose designed to channel sexual energy up the spine. Now –' She brought her hands up in front of her – the same hands, Sara thought, that had brought her to a climax the night before – and interlaced the fingers of each.

'This,' she continued, 'is called the Venus Lock. It works by applying pressure to the Venus mounds at the base of the thumb, which channels your sensuality and ensures a glandular balance, which in turn helps you to concentrate and focus.'

She relaxed the pose. 'It's all,' she said, her eyes boring into Sara's, 'about what you want and how much you want it.'

Sara swallowed almost painfully.

Her friend continued and again Sara thought she saw a strange red glow to Banhi's eyes, a brilliant flash of teeth as she spoke. 'What is it that you want, Sara?' she said.

Sara sat up, reached out. She knew without any doubt, in a sudden burst of clarity, that she wanted Banhi. That no one else would do.

Neil was waiting for her, but this time he was afraid. This time he wanted to talk first, before submitting to her new-found appetite. There was something odd about it all and he suspected that it had something to do with Sara's new friend Banhi.

He'd been suspicious of Banhi since the moment they'd met, down by the Ganges. It was Sara who'd insisted on going down to see the bodies being burned; he'd thought it was ghoulish, this desire of hers, and had accompanied her only because he was uneasy with her going alone. Banhi had approached them, had latched onto them, or rather Sara, like a leech. Within minutes they'd seemed like best friends reunited after years apart, which was unusual for Sara – she was usually quite wary and reserved when it came to new people. She generally withheld her trust for a long time. Neil had felt elbowed out from the start; even when Banhi had deigned to address him, he'd felt there was something a little mocking in her eyes. He knew he held little interest for her.

He didn't care much, at first, but Sara hadn't stopped talking about her – how interesting she was, how exotic, how gorgeous-looking. It was as if Banhi had cast some kind of spell on her. He'd wanted to throw his hefty guidebook at Sara, insist that they leave Varanasi right away, if only to get away from the damn woman who seemed to have taken over her mind, brain-washed her with all her hippy talk of chakras and goddesses and all sorts. Sara, on the other hand, had insisted on extending their stay here, had all sorts of new places to add to their itinerary, all of them suggested by Banhi. He'd found himself being dragged from temple to temple, to gaze at erotic carvings and shiva lingams and yoni stones, when he'd been expecting by now to be in a national park, riding elephants.

He sat up in bed, expectant and nervous, sexually charged and yet reticent. What was she going to do to him now? His fever abated, his concerns about malaria receded, he felt eager to be gone from this place, leave all this strangeness behind. He wanted to find the old Sara, the Sara he knew, even if it meant that their sex life died down again. This girl, he saw in a flash of clear-headedness, was an impostor.

The door opened. Sara crossed the threshold and stepped up to him. There was a curious fire in her eyes.

'Sara,' he said.

She made no response. She seemed to him like a sleepwalker, devoid of all intent, manoeuvring on auto-pilot.

'Sara, what's happened to you?'

She came closer, and he became aware that he was holding his breath. He wanted to tell her to go away, but some deeper, darker part of him forbade him to speak.

She climbed onto the bed, pushed him backwards, suddenly all too full of intent, although a certain robotic aspect to her remained.

'Sara,' he beseeched her. 'Sara, please.'

She was the master now, he understood that. He'd fallen in love with her for her appetite; it had been the spark that had lit the conflagration between them. But he had met her passion with an equal one. This time Sara seemed to be fired by a flame he couldn't match.

She pressed her lips to his torso, moved up, clamped her mouth on each of his nipples in turn. He let his head fall back, utterly submissive. He was hers, whatever she wanted of him.

Driving her nails into the flesh of his shoulders, she took him inside her, up to the hilt. For a moment he felt he was going to pass out, felt he was being pulled into a vortex or a black hole from which there would be no return. Bringing his hands down from where they had been behind his head, clamped around the bedposts, he seized her hips as she rode him wildly, baying like a she-wolf, seemingly lost to everything but the sensations that were ripping through her. He didn't know where she had gone, but he knew that she was far from him.

Sensing his climax near, she rapidly dismounted, brought her hand and mouth to his prick and squeezed it hard as the pearlescent white stream gushed into her mouth. Raising his head, he watched her drink as if struck by a thirst that could never be slaked. He came and came, as he never had before, unsure whether it was her need that was somehow calling forth such unprecedented reserves in him, or his own excitement at watching her drink him in.

Afterwards, too exhausted to attend to her, he lay and regarded her as she pleasured herself, although as soon as the word 'pleasure' flitted across his mind, he wondered if it could ever do justice to the waves of rapture that rippled across her face.

She left him, asleep or unconscious she knew not which, and directed herself like a noctambulist towards Banhi's room. Her friend was waiting for her.

'Well?' she said, one expertly plucked eyebrow arched. 'Is he ready?'

Sara nodded. She'd thought she loved Neil, once, but everything that had gone before had been swept away by the tidal wave that was Banhi. She took her friend's lovely oval face in her hands, kissed her with savagery. Banhi responded by biting Sara's bottom lip, and as their tongues slipped and slid around each other like writhing snakes, blood mixed with saliva to form a pinkish foam.

Banhi stepped back at last. 'Cigarette?' she said, wiping her mouth and chin with the back of her hand. Sara acquiesced.

'Who *are* you?' she said as her friend lit two cigarettes and handed one over.

'Who are *we*,' said Banhi. 'For we are the same. Sisters and lovers, with souls as black as night.'

'I need to understand,' said Sara, 'if I am to stay with you. To – ' She stopped, unable to say Neil's name.

Banhi studied her coolly. 'You meet all kinds of people,' she said at length, 'in my field. Sceptics and believers, rationalist and mystics, angels and daemons.'

'Are we angels or daemons?'

'Perhaps a little of each. We cannot know ourselves, not fully.'

'Is there a name for ... for people like us?'

'I really don't know, Sara. But when I think of us, I think of the *rakshasa*.'

'What are the *rakshasa*?'

'A species that was first created by the Brahma to protect the sea from those who wanted to steal the elixir of immortality from it – a least that's one version of the myth. They are shapeshifters, sometimes appearing as tigers, or if in human form as seductive women who lure men to their deaths, drinking their blood, sometimes eating their flesh.'

'And you really believe all this. Believe in them?'

Banhi looked back at Sara dispassionately. 'I don't know what I believe,' she said. 'I know only,' she went on, 'that you, Sara, are the black goddess for whom I have been waiting for so long. I sought you out because I recognised that you, like me, are a woman of appetite.'

Sara thought, a little guiltily for a moment, of Neil, back in their room. Neil, whom once she had loved, who had once used the same words to describe her. Then she looked back at Banhi and her remorse dissolved like smoke in the sunlight.

A knock at the door interrupted her reflections.

'Neil,' said Sara flatly. It was as if he had materialised from her thoughts.

'It's time,' said Banhi, her voice equally level. She held out her hand to her friend.

Neil stood and watched, for the second time, as bodies burned slowly on small pyres by the river before the ashes were scattered in the water, or, in some cases, were thrown in as they were, wrapped in traditional cloths and garlands of marigolds, weighted down by rocks. Death, he saw clearly, could be a beautiful thing. A desirable thing even. And to die here in Varanasi was supposed to be the best death of all, releasing one from the cycle of birth and rebirth.

Like the Hindus who came here in their thousands, he accepted his fate, welcomed it, in fact. He was so very tired.

Sara had been feeding off him, he realised now, draining his very lifeblood. Her reawakening, he understood, had nothing to do with sex. It had been a slow dance with death.

She had sucked him dry, leaving a husk of a man, a bloodless being. He turned to her. She stood behind him, hand in Banhi's. Their eyes blazed back at him, incandescent in the blue light of dawn. In them he thought he could see something like eternity.

From his pocket he extracted the box of matches that Banhi had handed him on the way from the hostel. Striking one, he brought it towards the pale paper of his flesh.

Banhi was already turning away, eyes brighter still, as if she were lit from within by the rising sun. She squeezed Sara's hand as they climbed the steps back up to the town, oblivious to Neil's cries. Her lips curled into a smile.

'Who next?' she said.

Carrie Williams is the author of the Black Lace novels *The Blue Guide* and *Chilli Heat*. Her third novel, *The Apprentice*, is published in early 2009.

El Alquimista
Madelynne Ellis

Cheap hotel. Flock wallpaper curls from the walls and the stench of urine suffuses the dingy corridors. What little light there is bleeds through the broken slats of the blinds. It's the right sort of place to be hunting lowlifes, because it's teeming with them. *They're stretched out across the carpet, or poised, shaved and sultry in open doorways.* Unclear. But I'm not here for any common or garden bag-snatcher or drug-pusher. I'm aiming for the top of the food chain, the kingpin, and I'm under no illusions that he's here out of anything other than choice.

I assumed money and security meant a mansion, patrols, guards and barbed-wire fences. My mistake. Big one. It's cost me a year of my life. Clever of him, though. Why waste resources unnecessarily? Why isolate yourself from your food supply, when it's more convenient to live among it. Especially if, like this guy, you get a kick out of poisons. Most of the occupants of this hellhole deserve their own biohazard warning labels. I don't even want to touch them. But I guess he likes them rough and dirty. Maybe barbiturates and amyl give O neg an interesting piquancy.

El Alquimista – the Alchemist, they call him. His fingertips are stained golden brown, the nails blackened at the tips. He smells of camphor and linseed, and keeps thick juicy leeches as pets. At first I thought they were a form of filter, but I know now they are just a cruel and pointless torture. And maybe a convenient midday snack. I can picture him sinking his fangs into the soft swollen bodies and letting the rivulets of harvested blood trickle over his jaw. He has a very distinctive jaw. But everything about him is distinctive, from his soulless eyes to his magician's robes. His head is shaved. Tattoos cover his scalp. Each dark line of ink is burned into my brain. I see them in my sleep. I won't ever forget them. I won't ever forgive him.

He stole something from me so precious that even after a year grieving, I can't think of it without a lump forming in my throat and the pain of loss prickling over the surface of my skin. I shake off the memories. Today, I need to remain focused, only then will I succeed in taking something equally precious from him.

Jade-coloured flowers with vulgar pink tongues at their centres mount the walls of the stairwell. I get two flights up to a place where the carpet is worn thin before the trouble starts. It begins with a gong. The brassy sound peals through the nicotine haze of the building, and numerous figures spill onto every landing. I don't take the time to count them. Three lie dead beside me, and another lies, skull smashed, by the basement door, before the first of them even cries, 'Stop!'

When they raise knives and firearms, a solemn rictus smile spreads across my face. I can kick arse, but I know my limits, and I can't take out thirty of them at the same time without blowing the building apart, and that wouldn't serve my purpose. Instead, I allow them to surround me and take me captive. I've an inkling in this instance co-operation will get me where I want to be a darn sight faster than if I put up a fight. None of these men have the capacity for independent thought. Sure enough, their strategy of dealing with intruders consists of taking me to their leader.

They swarm around me, a multitude of black beetles with carapaces of leather, and for a moment I feel like royalty, protected by a guard of honour. Except, there is nothing honourable about them. They are like worker drones: sapped of individuality and programmed to enact a simple function – protect their master or die.

'El Alquimista welcomes you, senorita,' one man cackles when we reach the fifth floor. His work-roughened hand locks around my wrist and bites into the flesh. 'He hungers for the sort of blackness that resides in your soul.'

I still at his touch and meet his gaze. 'There's no deceit in my heart.'

God, how I pity him, this creature before me, not truly a man any more, just the empty shell of one. Once he must have been lovely, a glowing golden angel. The Alchemist's foul chemistry cannot erase all of that beauty from his form. His eyes are the pure turquoise of an idyllic paradise lagoon, but they are dead. That emptiness chills me. There is no soul left in their depths. The Alchemist has siphoned it off, little by little, alongside every drop of blood he's fed upon.

I wonder just for a moment if this man had a lover before his current master? Was she as young and bonny as he must once have been? Did they hang out together in parks and coffee bars? Did they plan a future involving one another: mortgage, children, retirement? Trips of a lifetime, snow, skiing, sand and surf ...

'Murder for revenge is still murder,' says my captor and, for a split second, I see a sliver of pain contort his hollow features. I wonder did he come here like me, seeking vengeance? Is his slavery the price he paid for his foolishness?

'You can't murder that which is already dead,' I reply.

The Alchemist was first committed unto the earth five centuries ago. He is not a living man. I've seen the church records that detail his human life. I pride myself that I am perhaps the only living being that knows his true name. And from those humble beginnings on Mersea Island, I've followed his footsteps through the ages and across the continents to find his current abode. He's been a Venetian nobleman, a conquistador and a silent movie star, but always he returns to his magnum opus, the divinisation of man into god.

'My comrades weren't dead.'

'They were dead. They just hadn't realised it yet. You're all dead.'

His grip slackens, but another of my escorts takes offence at my words and smashes me head first into the steel door that marks the only exit off this landing besides the stairs. Pain slices across my brow and explodes inside my ears, but he fares worse. I aim for his jaw, and leave him spitting teeth onto the floor as the space-station-style door slides open and I'm swiftly ushered through.

What lies beyond that wall of brushed steel is an oak-panelled wonderland. The scent of beeswax polish lingers by the entrance, but just a few paces further in a multitude of sharper chemical tones dull the warm fragrance. Before me, endless worktables are littered with alembics and beakers. Brightly coloured liquids bubble inside intricate glass assemblages. There are no sinks, I note, and no running water.

'Leave her here and depart.'

It's the first experience I've had of his voice and I drink it down. I let each syllable entwine itself around my subconscious. He has an accent. English burred by the centuries and flavoured with a Latin rumble. Anticipation has me easing onto the balls of my feet. There's something captivating about his voice.

My escort backs away, and the door slides back into place, locking me inside.

'Come closer.'

I obey, simply because on this point my will and his are in alignment.

His laboratory is a place of eerie shadows. I make my way cautiously among its mazelike furnishings. Each piece is lavishly old. An ossuary occupies the whole of one corner. Bones stacked with precision to fashion a morbid bed. The thought of him lying there entertaining his victims, brings a wash of acid up from my stomach that almost makes me gag. This ivory cradle is not so very different to a once beloved white sofa I curled upon to chill out after work. The same sofa Billy died upon.

'Your victims,' I blurt.

'My lovers. Alas, time isn't so kind to them as it is to me.'

I turn to find him just a yard away from me. Our gazes meet and I stare into his black eyes until I can feel their pull as if they were a gravitational force. They glitter with the malice of the coldest, foulest magic. And something else, something that almost entrances me.

'Should I bid you welcome, my unexpected guest?' His voice is a disrespectful purr. It tweaks my senses, mocks me and, at the same time, begs me to be party to his mirth. 'Unexpected,' he muses, 'though perhaps not entirely unanticipated. You can't let go, can you? It's always the ones who are stuck in the past that seek me out. They believe I offer closure.

'Take a seat, my dear.' He gestures to the bone garden with a sharp flick of his wrist.

'I'm not sitting there. But then I didn't come here to talk.'

'No.' He smiles, a thin toothy grin. 'I imagine you came here to kill.' He extends his neck and for a moment scents the air. 'Four . . . no, three. The other is merely injured.' He shakes his head, then with a tut turns his back on me. 'Do you know how long it takes to make an able servant? The procedure is fraught. The specimen has to be perfect and then not all of them survive.'

'Spare me your hardship, Gulielmus de Vere.'

'Spare me your heartbreak, little girl. Our tragedies are what form us.'

I grasp tight the crucifix that lies concealed within my pocket. 'The devil formed you.' I spring forwards, catching him unawares, and press the warm silver into the skin of his cheek. We stagger backwards, locked together and crash into vast arrays of equipment. But to my horror, there's no scent of burning flesh and, as we topple to the floor, the Alchemist is laughing.

Glassware shatters beneath us releasing clouds of vapours and lakes of fizzing solutions. As we roll, acid burns new scuffs into the leather covering my back and the acrid scent of vinegar floods my nostrils. His touch is tart too. It sends a slow shiver rolling through my insides. I cling to him, even as I fight with him for the dominant position. There is something horribly familiar and undeniably erotic about the weight of him above me. He is the same height and build as Billy.

We roll, and the scent of vinegar is replaced by the sweeter scent of pear drops. His hand curls tightly over one of my breasts. His black talons dig into the warm flesh and my nipples steeple. One such point presses hard against the centre of his palm.

'Vampire!' I accuse. 'You stole him from me. He was mine. My beloved, not yours to prey upon.'

Our eyes meet. I find that his are not black. They are mahogany, like the dregs in the bottom of a wine glass.

We're just millimetres apart, but only my breath mists the space between us.

'He was mine to do with as I pleased. But what makes you think I'd destroy that which I need?'

'He bled out. You gouged too deep.' I can still see the blood upon my hands where I pressed fruitlessly against the wounds. Blood everywhere, soaked into my skin, splattered across the carpets, and bright scarlet against the white leather of the month-old sofa.

'Your Billy tasted of soap and soda, too sickly sweet to be permitted to survive, not at all what I was after.'

How, I think, does he know Billy's name, when I haven't told him it? But my lips won't move to present the thought. Instead, my mind conjures a memory. I remember Billy tasted of freshly baked apple pie and of thick Turkish coffee.

The Alchemist tastes of cracked leather, musty and worn thin with age. I don't seek his kiss, but he forces it upon me, and when he does I respond with surprising passion. His tongue thrusts deep and curls deep around my own, whilst the hand on my breast squeezes harder until it's on the edge of painful. And even as I fight his manipulation, I realise I'm becoming aroused.

This man that I hate, that I've studied and plotted against, whom I've made into an obsession, has a power over me I never anticipated. Just his nearness, his exotic creepiness and ruthless dominance make me want him. I wonder, is that how Billy felt too, in the moment's before his demise?

Only when the Alchemist has wrestled both my hands above my head and holds them pinned in one of his, does he draw back to look at me again. 'Of what do you taste, little flower?' he asks. 'Are you spicy and bitter like your scent suggests, or is that merely a mask for your sweetness?'

'How should I know? I'm not in the habit of tasting myself.' I bring my knees up, trying to find a way to throw him off me, but all I succeed in doing is providing him with a simple means of getting between my thighs.

'Sweet,' he declares, and he drags his talons down my stomach. When he reaches my fly, he makes a big display of popping each button. 'One ... two ... three ... four.' The anticipation is killing me. 'Have you never dipped your fingers into your cunny and brought them to your lips before?'

He slides his fingers under the elastic of my panties and his hand covers my mons. I clench every muscle tight, but his fingers are gentle as he dips into my heat. I don't want to react, but he knows what he is doing, and all too soon I'm soaking, and I can't unlock my gaze from his. His fingers glide between the lips of my sex, until they are thoroughly coated in my juices. He teases my clit with an idle flick before bringing those fragrant digits to his nose. He scents them, but he doesn't taste them. Instead he offers them to me to suck.

When I resist, he forces his fingers between my lips.

I don't like this game. I didn't come here to play.

A deep groan escapes me as the taste of my body floods my mouth. I taste of old memories, strawberries and champagne as Billy and I rolled upon the grass on our very last day together. The fizz bubbles on my tongue. I lie in his arms, content and gaze at the sky, the same shade of crystal blue as Billy's eyes. Fleecy clouds are stretched high across the heavens in lines, like the bubbling surf upon the tide we paddled in that morning.

The Alchemist crushes the recollection into a crystal tear, which he plucks from between my lips and holds between this thumb and forefinger.

'Shall we barter now, sweet Jessamine? My life for yours? I can take away every dream you ever had, every precious event, every friend, every good lover and leave you with only the bad. Or I could leave you contented, with not a care in the world, and a single ruby tear for you to treasure.'

His slaves are bound with such jewels. My escort up the stairs wore his dangling from his ear. I think it is formed from the first drop of blood the Alchemist takes.

'You make these offers as though I had a real choice. I've no wish to die lonely, and that is all you're offering. No, I came to bring your menace to an end.'

'You know nothing of my menace.' He chuckles and scores a line down the centre of my vest top with his talons. He peels the cotton aside and scoops my breasts from my bra. 'What you need is a lover. Someone who can stoke that fire in you until it burns with something other than rage. Billy was never yours, my dear. I'd known him, nurtured him since birth.'

'Don't be ridiculous. He told me all about himself. He mentioned nothing of you.'

He continues to stare at my tits as he talks, as if fascinated by their soft rounded form. And his attention makes the nipples crinkle. I start imagining the feel of his mouth around them.

'Deny it all you will, but it is the truth. Do you want me to fuck you?' he asks. 'Shall I prove how closely Billy and I are related. I think you'll know the truth once I'm inside you.'

'You're close enough already.' I look up at his mouth and, for the first time, real fear shakes me as I catch a glimpse of his elongated canines. 'You're a walking corpse,' I hiss. 'I'm not a freak, I don't fuck with the dead.'

'I'm not dead, Jessamine.' With his free hand he grasps a handful of my hair and tugs really hard. 'I'm very much alive. Once we're connected, you might even hear my heartbeat.' He forces his lips upon me again and this time, as we snarl and kiss aggressively, I feel the silk of his old-fashioned robes brushing against my skin, and I feel his erection nuzzling against my sex.

My body wants him. It screams for the pleasure he can offer. There's been nobody since Billy. And the Alchemist is right, he is the perfect weight, the perfect double of my lover. If I close my eyes and blank out the world it could be him. He liked to play rough sometimes, though he was soft and kind-hearted. Somehow, I let my eyelids and my defences droop.

The Alchemist's kiss moves to my ear. His tongue troubles the tender surface making it tingle, while his fingers coax my nipples into even higher steeples. 'Shhh, it's all right,' he whispers when my breathing becomes ragged. 'I'll only take what you don't need. Just enough to give you the pleasure you so desperately crave.'

Slowly his hand moves lower, his thumb brushes over my clitoris and draws erotic circles around it. Billy used the same technique. He'd torture me with it, until I was plumped and overeager and then he'd put his mouth down there and continue the tease with his tongue. Billy never entered me without bestowing an orgasm first. He used to say he liked how slippery it made me feel and how hot around his cock.

I'm like a furnace now, burning up. But the Alchemist never stops coaxing. 'You shouldn't have gone so long without a lover,' he says. 'Your hunger is consuming you. I can ease that. I can make it all go away. Just give me the word and we'll make a bond.'

I want him; crave him with every ounce of my being, but the price he's asking is far too high.

When he nicks my ear lobe, panic floods my veins and I rise up beneath him. I don't escape. Our bodies just press closer, but he does release my wrists. 'You must know how this works,' he says. 'I need to take a little the better to give.'

'No. I saw what you did to Billy, you won't take that from me.'

'Are you implying your boyfriend was bisexual? Do you imagine I fucked his arse as I took his blood?'

'No!' I don't know what I'm protesting at: the implication that I'd imagined it or the image he is planting. Billy was true to me. This beast preyed upon him. They were never lovers.

But I can see them entwined now. Billy's knees on the floor, his upper body supported by the white sofa and his hand on his cock, wanking himself while the Alchemist thrust roughly into his arse.

'Stop it,' I gasp. 'Stop planting these images.'

'Why?' he laughs. 'They're turning you on.'

'They're a lie.'

'A fantasy,' he counters. 'Indulge it. Indulge me.'

He lifts himself from me and comes up onto his knees astride my hips. 'Taste me.'

I struggle into a sitting position, drag the robe from over his head and fling it as far as I can. Beneath it, he wears only soft woollen leggings tied with a drawstring. I wrench open the bow and pull them down to reveal his cock. His skin is smooth and completely bare. There is no trace of hair; Billy was just the same.

His cock rears towards me, pumped with blood, thick and hard. High on bittersweet memories, I run my tongue around the head and swallow him down as deep as I can go. I try not to rationalise my eagerness as I do this. It's all consuming and once he's actually inside my mouth I can't get enough of the taste and size of him. I suck him and I groan. I curl my fingers into the firm muscles of his arse and work his hips faster.

'It's not enough.' He undoes the knot that binds my long hair upon my head and lets it fall in a chestnut cascade over his hands. 'Though I can see why Billy loved you.'

He did love me. We loved each other.

Anger rips through my innards again. I jerk away from this monster and make a bid for freedom by scrambling away from him on all fours. Between the tables' legs he chases me. Glass splinters bite into my palms and knees. This meeting was never supposed to be like this. It was supposed to be efficient and quick. I still carry upon me all the tools of my new trade, but none of them can ward me against his pursuit.

His hand closes around my ankle and I reach out to the nearest solid object for support. His ossuary. I scream. Bones tumble around us and form a cradle. I cling to the ivory shin bone that was so recently the leg of his bed as he climbs on top of me again. His weight presses my breasts hard against the varnished hardwood floor.

Drunk on terror and arousal, I squirm beneath his weight, begging, sobbing, but I'm not sure what for.

The Alchemist scoops my hair away from my neck and sinks his fangs deep, at the same time his cock slides with joyous ease into my sex.

And we fuck, and he drinks, and I writhe, while memory upon memory drips through my brain. Like tears falling into a coffee cup, they make little waves and spread out. I know that he sees these snapshots too, just as I see glimpses of his past.

I see Billy, here in this lab, sucking the Alchemist's cock with relish as I have just done. My heart is breaking even as I rise steadily towards climax. I thought it was already smashed in two. Now I realise it was merely cracked.

His pace becomes more urgent, the wound in my neck deeper. Dizzy and breathless, I listen to the drumming of his heartbeat in my veins. Orgasm rushes up fast. A single touch to my clit is what tips me over, but I curse him as I come. Nothing will ever make right his theft, but that doesn't mean that my revenge can't be sweet.

We roll once he has emptied his seed into me, so that I finally lie on top. My blood stains his lips. I wipe it off with my fingertips, but stop myself from licking them clean.

'You need to accept that Billy was mine.' His expression is serious. 'You've seen it. You know it's true now. He was never going to be more than a momentary blip in your life. He was a fling. Whatever else you imagined wasn't real.'

I don't know that I believe his visions. Considering the strength of his science, I think he could make anything seem real.

'It's a defence. I understand that.' He gently strokes my face. 'But you have to understand that he was not a real human being. He was a construct. My homunculus.'

'No!' I will not believe it.

I see Billy on his knees again drinking down the Alchemist's sperm as if it's the sustenance upon which he feeds in order to survive.

Theirs is not just a homosexual bond. They are part of one another.

'No-oooooo!' From my pocket I bring the first of my weapons.

The brown paper bag splits and I tip the millet into his open mouth. He chokes on it, splutters the tiny seeds into the air. But it matters not, because I've a gun in my other hand. I pull the trigger at point-blank range. One shot, straight through the heart. For a second I hear his laughter. He thinks I've made a mistake. 'Wooden bullets.' There's no mistake. I stripped the branches from the oldest hawthorn tree I could find and whittled them into shape myself.

His eyes are no different in paralysis than they were a moment before at the height of ecstasy. If indeed that's what he felt. I slip the blade from the holster on my thigh and trail the ruthlessly sharpened edge across his bare throat. Blood beads in the cut and trickles down over his chest. But I don't take his head. I'm not ready for a journey to the crossroads yet. I just need time to think and plan a bargain.

If he made one Billy, why can't he make me another?

I sit propped against the ruins of the ossuary and drag his suspended corpse over my lap so that I can stroke his cold brow. 'Shall we bargain?' I ask. 'Your life, for another chance to live my own.'

Madelyne Ellis is the author of the Black Lace novels *A Gentleman's Wager*, *Phantasmagoria*, *Dark Designs* and *The Passion of Isis*. Her paranormal novella *Broken Angel* appears in the Black Lace collection *Possession*.

There's a Sucker Born Every Minute
Sommer Marsden

Tyson thought he was a vampire. Sheila told me he'd had these little tattoos put on his neck to resemble bite marks.

'I swear to fuck, they look like a beaver got at his skin and the gangrene set in. He really, really thinks he is one of the undead. He keeps the schedule and everything.'

I shrugged. 'So, what's the harm?' I asked. 'I mean, it's clearly insane but he's not hurting anyone else.'

'His kids.' Sheila lit a cigarette and I had a moment of brief hot jealousy. I had quite five months before.

'His kids hate him anyhow. He's divorced. His kids know he's a nut. He's back to the ups and downs of singlehood and he's doing nothing but partying.' I snapped my fingers to stave off the craving for a smoke.

'Did you hear me, Jules? The man thinks he is a vampire. A bloodsucker! He vants to suck your blood.' She did her best horrible accent.

'Blood. What about the blood? Does he drink that?' I thought I had her. I wanted to rub in my victory. But she shuddered and I swear to God, for just a moment, she gagged.

'From what I've heard it can be summed up with one word,' Sheila hissed.

'Well?'

'Butcher,' she hissed and my stomach rolled.

'Eew.'

'Exactly.'

'Well, it's not our problem. It's really sad but not our problem.'

Sheila puffed and looked up to the heavens. Her dark-red dreadlocks tangled in her multiple chunky necklaces. Silver and crystals and beads. Baubles and the biggest fucking crucifix you have ever seen. 'Sheil?' I asked.

'Wanna go to a party?' She took a final puff and crushed the smoke out under her big-ass stripper boots.

'Oh, Jesus. You are kidding me.' I was curious though. I could feel a tiny burn of excitement in the pit of my stomach. I fidgeted with my blue silk jacket. I twisted my hair up and then let it go before I could secure it. 'I knew you wanted to go out but you want to go visit the nut who thinks he's the Vampire Lestat?'

'Come on, Jules.'

'Fine. Fine. But you drive and I swear to fuck if he bites me, I'm gonna beat you to a pulp.'

'Deal.'

Goddamn, I did my best not to stare at those hideous tattoos on his pale freckled neck. I diverted my gaze to his too-long red hair. It was bound loosely in a messy ponytail with a piece of leather thong. My eyes returned to the greenish-grey puncture wounds. I wanted to stick my fingers in the faux holes and yank. Strip the flesh from his throat and toss it over my shoulder like a used tissue. It was morbid and disgusting and fascinating, too. I couldn't stop looking no matter how hard I tried.

'I have relics,' he said.

I glanced at Sheila's wide green eyes and felt a tickle of fear work across my skin. Not because of his so-called relics but because he was a full-on fucking lunatic now. That much was clear. 'That is . . . lovely.' I was struggling for words. I downed my beer and wished for another. Alcohol would help. It would give me lots to say. What I ended up saying might not make sense but I doubted Tyson would notice. And if he did, I doubted he would care.

Sheila handed me a bottle. It was warm but it would work. 'Relics?' I asked. Damn. I wished I hadn't.

He nodded. His eyes lighting with a fantastic excitement that made me feel almost cruel. 'Let me show you. Come on.' His grin was fierce and scary. My stomach seemed to shrink in on itself but I followed, pushing Sheila ahead of me. If she thought she was getting away she was as insane as Tyson.

We followed him up two flights of steps to the attic. It was as big as the house but seemed somehow larger. Double the size of the floors below. 'I keep them over here,' he hissed and the hair on the back of my neck stood up.

'Fucker is creepy,' Sheila hissed against my ear as we followed.

'This is entirely your fault,' I reminded her.

'I know, I know,' she snorted. Her Chivas sours had caught up with her and she stumbled forwards in her pole-dancer boots with a dirty kind of grace.

'Let's go see his relics,' I said, effecting my best vampire accent.

'Right you are, dearie,' she said and hooked her arm through mine. We skipped forwards like Dorothy and the Cowardly Lion, fuelled with courage by spirits that lived in bottles.

'Here is the latest,' he said. His eyes were full of a sort of green and lavender light. It was surreal and I felt fear prickle the skin along my spine. He whipped around clutching a plexi-glas box as if it were the Holy Grail. Inside was a perfect set of white teeth. White white teeth. White like bone. White like new fallen snow. Not just any teeth. Vampire teeth. The canines were long and curved like a battle sabre. Sharp like a weapon.

'Wow,' I breathed. It was an involuntary response. I certainly didn't want to add fuel to his fire. But they were impressive. Whoever had created this fake 'relic' was an artist. They truly did appear real.

I touched the small clear box and Tyson flinched. 'Careful, please, they were expensive.'

Because a sucker's born every minute. I smiled. 'Sorry.'

He nodded, regaining his manners. Sheila touched a small hand mirror that rested on the table and he nearly had a coronary. 'Careful!'

'Sorr-eee,' she snapped, 'just wanted to check my make-up.'

'That is a mirror that was said to be the first to fail in showing Vlad the Impaler his reflection.'

'As if drinking blood can steal your reflection,' she snorted, but she set it down.

'What are those?' I pointed to what appeared to be little yellowish rocks. About the size of large potatoes, they sat at the bottom of a woven basket.

He selected one and turned it to me. 'Baby vampire skulls.' He smiled as if this were the best news in the world and I noticed his teeth. Wickedly sharp and white. He was either wearing a special bridge or he'd gone and had implants. It was all the rage with some of the Goths: find a crazy dentist and have dangerously sharp canines added.

'Jesus Christ, Tyson!' I barked and he hissed at me. Hissed. The man had gone off his rocker.

'Please, Jules. Watch your language.'

I inspected the small skull he held and consoled myself in the knowledge that they absolutely, positively had to be small animal skulls. Since there weren't vampires, there could not be vampire babies. Plus, did vampires even have babies? No. I shook my head and snorted. That was stupid. Vampires turned others into vampires. Then I realised that was stupid, too, because there was no such thing. Tyson's lunacy was contagious or I was drunk. Or both. My money was on both.

Sheila had dropped onto a shabby brown sofa and was snoring lightly. Tyson frowned at her. 'She can't stay there. She'll wake up and touch all my stuff.' He sounded like a petulant child.

'I'll stay until she wakes up. I'll make sure she doesn't touch anything.'

He looked unsure and then the sound of breaking glass floated up from the floor below and his face went from unsure to panicked. 'OK, but please, Jules, don't let her break anything. You have no idea how much this stuff cost me.'

I nodded as he ran off. No, I had no idea. But I could guess it was a lot. Idiot.

I sat down next to my very best friend. She was drooling just a little over her faded-out black lipstick. 'What have you gotten me into, Sheil?' I sighed. I let my head fall back and yelped. Over my head was a bigger than life Dracula. I should say, a life-size cut-out of Gary Oldman *as* Dracula. 'Nut,' I said. Because Tyson really had become a nut. I closed my eyes and waited for Sheila to wake up.

I knew I was dreaming when the teeth started to chatter inside their plastic prison. They chomped at the lucite wall with a vicious ferocity. I laughed a little because the dream was completely ridiculous. Too odd to be even slightly scary. 'If you think I'm letting you out, forget it,' I said to the teeth.

The scraped against the box so hard a horrendous noise assaulted my ears. Much like nails on a chalkboard, it made my teeth itch to hear it. I stood and walked to the table and squinted at the teeth. They chomped at me as if they could see me staring down. I touched the box and the most amazing sensation overtook me. My skin felt warm and lucid, like someone had just drizzled some hot glowing liquid over my body. A slow line of pleasure slid down my spine. I yanked my hand back and the feeling disappeared.

The teeth, stilled during my touch, now chattered and shook in their confines. My heart was banging under my breastbone but the pulse had travelled further south. Contractions and flickers of pleasure worked through my pussy and I sighed. This dream had taken a severe left turn. The teeth did a creepy disembodied jitterbug and I reached out and pressed my fingertips to the box.

They stilled and a hot ribbon of excitement curled low in my belly and wet the soft skin between my thighs. 'Oh my,' I breathed like some prudish schoolmarm. I glanced around the room and found myself still alone. Sheila still snored and no one had joined me. The pulse between my legs started a more erratic tempo. The force of the pleasure nearly stole my breath. I pressed my free hand to my mound and pressed one finger to the seam of my sex. I heard my own moan before I even realised I had made the sound. I pushed my finger harder and the tip found the swollen button of my clit even through my skirt and panties. The teeth made a soft *shhhh* sound. It was impossible, really, but they did.

I licked my lips and tried not to think about it, but it just got worse. The constant *thump, thump, thump* in my sex that made me just want to come. Right then. Right there. I pushed my hand down into my skirt and past the cotton triangle of my panties. My fingers found wetness and then slid back up to rub eager circles over my clit. I sucked in a great breath of air when spots appeared before my eyes.

Faster. Clear as a bell in my head but not my thought. It didn't scare me though. I was clearly dreaming. A wet dream, sure, but nothing to be scared of. So I went faster. Stroking myself with one hand while stroking the little warm box with the other. The teeth were still as if they were watching me. I slid a finger into my hot sex and flexed against my G-spot. I growled in the quiet room as orgasm came towards me more swiftly now. I prayed Sheila wouldn't wake up and catch me. I stared at the teeth, stroking faster. I wondered what they would feel like rasping over my skin. Sinking into my flesh.

We can find out. I smiled as the warm sweet release rolled through me. Wave after wave, as slow and golden as raw honey. 'We could, couldn't we?' I snickered when my body was through.

I took my hand away from the box, wondering if I would wake up now that I had peaked. But no. I didn't and the teeth went berserk, bouncing and clacking, until I was fully annoyed. 'Oh, now just stop it. You can't do anything for me. You are nothing but a set of teeth. I will not open the box.'

Track lights ran the length of the ceiling. Several were aimed at the teeth and their container. I assumed this was because Tyson considered them a prized possession. It occurred to me that the teeth must be terribly hot. Which was insane. But I picked them up to move them to a darker spot on the table. When I sat the box down, I realised that my free hand had moved up to pluck and pinch at my hard nipples through my blouse. I didn't normally wear a bra and the force of my pinches ground my tender flesh against the over-washed cotton. The sensation was decadent and my pussy fluttered back to life.

I can make you feel good, Jules. I can make you come and come and . . .

I pinched harder and flexed my sex muscles as the teeth tried to woo me. The sensation was so intense that if I kept it up I wouldn't need the teeth. But I wanted them. I was intrigued. And after all, it was my dream. I could fuck teeth if I wanted to.

I fingered the thick slit where the box lid met the box. The box was a completely clear cube so the teeth could be seen from all angles. I finally found the hidden hinges and I pushed lightly until the lid popped up just a bit. 'There it is,' I said, mostly to myself but the teeth seemed to vibrate with anticipation.

Hurry.

I pushed back the lid and put my hand into the box. I rested my hand, palm up, and waited. I guess I figured the teeth would hop into my hand like those little walking teeth that you wind up and they take off chattering. They did not. The teeth were motionless. 'Well, be that way,' I grumped. When I went to shut the box they went berserk again. 'You have to make up your mind.' I tried again. Waited. They sat completely still. I sighed.

You have to pick me up. I swore I detected a hint of exasperation. But I wanted to feel good as the teeth had promised. So, I ignored the tone and picked them up. Before I could even pull my hand free, a canine had scraped the pad of my thumb and drawn a perfect red bead of blood.

No pain, just warm silvery pleasure sliding under my skin. Making my skin flush and my body contract on an intense orgasm that seemed to travel everywhere. My pussy, my thighs, the tips of my finger, even my scalp. I moaned lowly, the force of it all stealing my voice almost completely. The needle-point canine stayed put, still puncturing my skin as I made my way to a huge overstuffed armchair in the corner. My knees felt weak with the fear and the aftermath of coming.

I curled up in the chair. It smelled like old damask and dust. My eyes drifted closed and the teeth moved softly over my skin and up my wrist. Gently scraping and lapping like a bony tide at the beach. I kept my eyes tightly closed, instinct dictated. I lost track of the teeth, as crazy as that sounds. But it was a dream, so no reason for concern.

Naked is better...

I totally agreed. I tugged my blouse over my head, pushed down my simple black skirt. I nearly left my panties but pulled them down. In for a penny, in for a pound. I let my fingers graze my swollen and abused clitoris. I hummed deep in my throat as the teeth scraped the hollow between my breasts. My nipples pebbled quickly, the fragile delicate skin drawn so tight it almost hurt. I rubbed my clit again and the teeth latched onto one rosy nub and bit me. Gently enough that I did not scream, hard enough that I felt the urge to shove my fingers deep into my willing pussy. And I swore I felt a tongue. A tongue with those teeth.

But I kept my eyes clamped shut. I didn't want to know. I just wanted to feel.

The canines slid through my skin easily. Heat blazed in their path, causing me to contract against the chair and suck in a great breath of air. Something rubbed my breast. It felt like a jaw. A stubbly jaw. But they were just teeth. I ribbed my clit harder, spread my pussy lips wide with my other hand. Scissoring my fingers on either side of the hood, I pinched my swollen button fiercely until bright dots of red and blue bloomed in the blackness behind my closed lids. 'Oh, again,' I said.

Bite me again. And they did. Dragged dryly and slowly over my chest to the other nipple and then slid into my pink ready skin with great ease. I clamped my fingers, pinched again and another bright orgasm hit me. How many could I have? I wondered. I was game to find out.

Many, many if you stay with me.

I nodded. I could do that. The teeth slid along my skin and

the sensation of that stubbled jaw followed. Up and over the hollow of my collarbone. I jumped a bit, it tickled the way they skimmed over me. My skin broke out in goosebumps and I could hear the music from downstairs. Something from the original Goth genre. I think Gene Loves Jezebel singing 'Jealous'. I could smell smoke, cigarette and otherwise, and hear the easy drunken laughter of the party. And Sheila snoring. Then there was the sound of the teeth. Like a letter opener being dragged over an envelope and I was the envelope.

For the first time it occurred to me that this might not be a dream, but instead of fear when those teeth reached my throat, I felt a wave of excitement crash down over me. Liberating. They brushed the sensitive dip where my throat met my shoulder. My nipples puckered in response and I arched up as if in a strong lover's embrace. The teeth pierced my skin with a bittersweet pain that made me sigh softly. What felt like silken hair brushed over my shoulder, tickled under my chin. He was coming back to me. For me. The thought popped into my head uncalled for but as clear as a bell.

Yes. For you, lover. And then what felt like dark velvety laughter echoed through my head. I arched up further, baring my throat, making myself more vulnerable to the bite. To being devoured. The tongue lapped at me even as the stubble chafed. I could see him in my mind as clearly as a Polaroid picture. Chin-length hair the same shade as dark chocolate. Green feral eyes with strands of gold and flecks of brown. Stubble along a well-chiselled jaw and lips as red as ripe berries in the summer. As for his teeth, well, I'd seen those.

Almost, love. I am almost the man you feel in your head.

The more deeply he drank from me, the more my body hummed with a steady erotic rhythm. A beautiful beat that ricocheted from breast to sex from sex to the very soles of my feet. I was one big nerve ending finely attuned to his touch and the wet velvet tongue he now dragged down the length of my throat.

Hands lifted my breast. Yes, hands. Big cool hands that hefted my breast as if weighing it and then sampled more of my blood by sinking his teeth into my areola. His teeth so sharp they caused no more pain that a fine hypodermic needle sliding past the thin barrier of my flesh. But once the sharp pinch rippled through me, a pleasure so white hot followed that my throat constricted from the strong emotion.

I wanted to ask his name. If I was his dinner, I should know his name. I couldn't. My strength had been drained along with my life force. I felt at one with the chair, boneless and stuffed.

Dorian. My name is Dorian. And don't worry. You're not dinner. You may be dessert for the rest of your life, but you're not dinner.

I could only nod as the bites were replaced with soft kisses. Kisses with potential pain. The curved, wickedly sharp canines dragged over my lips as he took my mouth with his. Cool and hard, he slipped between my thighs and parted them as wide as they would go. I dragged my eyes open just a bit as he draped first one leg then the other over the chair arms. He was beautiful.

As are you. So beautiful you woke me from the soundest sleep yet.

He was still talking with his mind but that was OK. It was all OK because he had now parted my sex with his long cool fingers. He rocked back to examine me as if I were a work of fine art. Gorgeous. He positioned the large white head of his cock at my entrance and made eye contact with me. Despite my lethargy I felt an excitement stir in my belly. He grinned at me and slid home. He fucked me smoothly, his eyes never leaving mine. I knew he could read my thoughts and somehow that was more intimate than having his cool smooth dick deep inside of me. He stayed cool, like marble as he thrust high and hard. When his movements were more animal than man, his eyes flashed silver and magical like a cat's.

Forgive me, it's been about 200 years.

I didn't acknowledge him because a pure sweet orgasm was wringing what energy I had left free from my body. I wanted to cry out and embrace him but I hadn't the energy. Dorian gave a great roar as he emptied into me but only I could hear it. I could hear it in my mind and feel it bouncing around in my chest like a ball of bright yellow light.

My love.

Yes. My love.

When he nodded, satisfied, I knew he had heard me answer. When he used one ragged nail and then offered me his wrist, I didn't think. I drank.

It all flashed through my head so fast. A freight train of fear and worry. Now I had to change. It would be painful. I would die and be racked with great shivering spasms as I ceased to be human and became one of the undead. All the things I had read came back to me. Every bad movie I had ever seen. Anxiety filled up my solar plexus and seized my throat. What had I done!

His quiet laughter brought me back and I caught his humorous gaze. I frowned.

'None of that will happen,' he said. His voice was as warm and smooth as really fine coffee. 'You will feed and feed until you can control your hunger. You will have a slight discomfort as your feeding teeth come in. No more than a human infant getting its first set of teeth. Whiskey will do wonders as they push the old teeth out and take their place.'

He pulled me in and kissed me and it soothed my terrors. His tongue tasted like blood and I could suddenly smell us in the room. Sex and blood and awakening.

Sheila continued to snore and I could feel Dorian's hunger. When his eyes lit on her, I shook my head. 'No. Never her,' I said.

Footsteps echoed on the attic stairs and when Tyson turned the corner we all froze. His blue eyes bounced from me, naked and unkempt, to Dorian, naked and reformed, to the empty box. 'What?' That was all he said.

'Ah, my keeper,' Dorian said softly. The softer his voice the more menace it contained. 'Just in time. I'm hungry.'

I felt it swell up in me then. A cavernous hunger that all but shut my mind down. It was all I could think about. All I could feel. I felt a little bad for Tyson.

'And look, he marked our entry for us,' Dorian said, grabbing the other man and hauling him forwards. He pointed to the shabby tattoos and I couldn't help but smile. He really was clever.

'You?' Tyson said to me. His eyes grew even wider as if I had betrayed him. 'Why? How?'

I leaned in and sniffed him. My stomach rumbled and my mind went blood red. I shrugged. 'I can't help it,' I said. That's as far as I got. The hunger took over and I sank my normal teeth into his throat. Messy.

I felt Dorian rooting around in my head and then more of his soft laughter. He finished my sentence with a stolen thought, 'There's a sucker born every minute.'

The Oasis at Night

Madeline Moore

He remembered that he'd dreamed.

Or did he dream that he'd remembered?

She was tiny and exquisite. Her eyes were bright and proud but her soft-lipped mouth was as voracious as a lamprey's. She was grieving the deaths of two heroic lovers. He was weary from too much – everything. They consoled each other with lust and love bites and promises of sweet surcease.

When her body grew cold he brought a snake to her bed to tell its serpentine lies for her. Her personal maid and two trusted servants spirited her body away that it not be violated. He took the blame and was cruelly punished, even unto death.

Thus, they both found rest and, in their own ways, they slowly healed.

When Charles Lomax was seven his history teacher closed the unit on the Stone Age and opened the one on Ancient Egypt. Young Charles learned about the annual flooding of the Nile and about the use of the *shaduf* for irrigation. He found it all very interesting, but then he turned a page in his history book and was gloriously stunned.

Hieroglyphics! They made so much sense. At first, he thought that he didn't even have to know the language to read the pictographs. Later, he found that it was a bit more complex than that, but still fascinating.

He was already advanced in his English studies and doing well in French and German but from then on he was obsessed – by languages and archaeology. A tutor remarked that it seemed that Charles wasn't so much learning Attic Greek as *remembering* it. By the time Charles was sixteen he was also fluent in Aramaic, Latin, Hebrew and Egyptian Arabic and had mastered French, German, Italian and Spanish. His teachers considered him a prodigy, which freed him to study anything he liked, at his own pace. He took his Bachelor's at eighteen, his Master's at nineteen and his PhD at twenty-two. The British Museum consulted him and gave him free access to the resources of the Egyptology department, including those relics that weren't available to the general public.

A senior professor who yearned to touch Charles in tender but inappropriate ways invited him to a dig in Normandy. Charles wasn't interested in Viking mounds, but it was all experience. The professor never summoned the courage to act on his desires, but his wife did. Charles was introduced to the pleasures of the flesh by a voracious fifty-year-old who taught him everything she'd ever learned about sex, both practically and from her multilingual studies of pornography.

Inspired by his new interest, Charles took a second look at some ancient scrolls that he, and many scholars before him, had dismissed as nothing but hieroglyphic erotica. He read about what Bast did to the Sphinx and about Horus' contortions with the seventeen virgins and was getting bored when he came to a scroll that claimed to describe the perversions of Cleopatra VII, the last Pharaoh. A month later, he was convinced that the scroll was authentic and contained clues as to Cleopatra's last resting place.

His university was glad to grant him funds. If his search was successful, it'd be a more important find than that of the tomb of King Tut by Lord Carnavon. All that remained was for

Charles to chose a graduate student to accompany him on the trek. Many applied, included Sarah, the pouty blonde he'd had his eye on all year. One didn't mess with the students, not on campus, but on field trips, as he'd learned, the rules changed.

(It was funny, watching the Professor's lips start to make the sibilant 's' sound of 'Sarah' and then close into an 'em' and spout *her* name, *Miriam*. She'd known he'd choose her, but she didn't know how she'd known. The feeling wasn't new. It seemed all her life, *and even before*, she'd known things without learning or seeing them. No, she wasn't the brightest of his pupils, nor the prettiest, though her sloe eyes and olive skin attracted those who liked the type, but she was the one for this field trip. Whether Charles'd known it or not he knew it now. Sarah looked surprised, almost as surprised as Charles. Miriam dipped her head in modest thanks and set about making the travel arrangements.)

They got to Heathrow at 3 p.m. for the 4.35 flight, which was delayed. As they were travelling first class, they were led to a luxurious lounge for lobster puffs and dry Martinis.

Miriam asked Charles, 'Was she really as bad as they say?'

'Cleopatra? How do you mean "bad"?'

'She married her little brother, didn't she?'

'That was common for royalty in Ancient Egypt. It was to preserved the bloodline and to prevent civil war.'

'How?'

'Better to share your throne than fight over it.'

'So the marriages were in name only?'

'No, they were consummated and produced offspring.'

'And the other things they say about her? Didn't they call her "the gobbler"?'

Charles didn't smile, though he liked the way this was going.

If Miriam wanted to talk about Cleopatra's sex life even before their expedition started, chances were she'd want to emulate it before they were finished. He might be naive but he wasn't so innocent as to think a woman's conversation didn't send signals.

He said, 'She was reputed to be an incredibly skilled fellatrice. It's said that she could bring a man to climax in seconds, or keep him on the brink all night. Some say that the tale of her bathing in asses' milk was a euphemism.'

Miriam's eyes widened. 'You mean . . . ?'

'She kept a personal guard of large and lusty men, just as Catherine the Great of Russia did, and for similar reasons, I imagine.'

Miriam said, 'She was a fascinating woman, wasn't she?'

'Consummate linguist, diplomat, politician and seductress? I'd say so.'

'You admire her, don't you?' Miriam asked.

'I've devoted years to studying Cleopatra and her times.'

'I've got so much to learn.' She glanced up from beneath half-lowered lids.

God, how he wanted to see them darkened by tears. Or lust. Tears of lust. He shook his head. 'About Ancient Egypt?'

'About all sorts of things.'

It was 10.15 by the time they boarded. A flight attendant brought them champagne and menus, but they were past eating.

Miriam asked for a blanket and pillow. When they were brought, she tilted her seat back.

Charles followed suit. Miriam spread the blanket across both of their laps. That was nice, and it got nicer when the girl closed her eyes and snuggled down. Her head lolled. Her cheek rested against his upper arm. She had heavy eyelids. Her lower lip was so full it was almost everted. There was an enticing pulse in a pale-blue vein at the base of her slender throat. It made Charles feel protective. It made Charles feel predatory. No logic in that, so he dismissed both thoughts. Thirsty. When the flight attendant passed by again he asked for red wine.

A while later, Miriam murmured and moved again. Under the blanket, her hand came to rest high on Charles's thigh, warm through the denim of his jeans. Had it been any other girl, for example, Sarah, he'd have taken it for an obvious ploy. But this one seemed so innocent that he, who could still count his conquests on one hand, felt guilty for letting her fingertips rest on his growing erection. He was afraid to so much as touch her hand, for fear he'd plunge it down the front of his jeans and mash it, splayed, across his crotch. Christ! He shifted suddenly, turning his body away from hers, and stared out the window. This passion, surely it was for the game afoot, the treasure, not the girl. He was closer to Cleopatra than he'd ever been but all he wanted to do was grab Miriam by the hair and shove her face into his lap and scream while she sucked him dry and then do it to her, suck her dry, as dry as a fig. Charles groaned and closed his eyes.

(In fact she had been sleeping. Dreaming. She was the student in the story; she dare not make a mistake. She dreamed she bowed to another's passion, so all-consuming it seemed like rage. All-consuming. That was the part that made it sad, sort of, the part that gave surrender its power and its pain.

When he moved away from her she woke. Not yet! She could feel his body humming with need, though they weren't even touching under the blanket any more. His need was her duty. Miriam's hand moved again, to tug at his fly.)

Charles snuffled to cover his groan and the muffled rasp of his zipper. The tips of those inquisitive little fingers were easing their way inside his jeans. He turned back toward her, eyes closed, then let his lids part a secret sliver. Miriam's face was serene, her eyes softly closed, but there was the shadow of a grin at the corners of her mouth. The little bitch! He kept perfectly still, with a knot of anticipation in his belly.

Her fingers wrapped around his shaft. With a series of gentle tugs, she manoeuvred his stiffening flesh, drawing him out of his jeans. Charles lay still, letting delicate fingertips explore his length, while psychedelic red against sable black surged behind his closed lids.

The sensations were excruciatingly delicious. A finger and thumb ringed him, just below his helmet. They stroked up delicately, travelling perhaps a quarter of an inch, and back down, and up again, and ...

She had to know that he was feigning sleep. It was their conspiracy; a scheme that liberated them from the restraints of decent behaviour until they could escape it altogether and be alone. His balls tightened at the thought of their private union. Until then he was free to respond in kind, to fondle her under the blanket, or to cover her hand with his own and pump himself into the release his flesh craved. But that would be weakness, or worse. Almost, a betrayal. His part in the plot was to take what she offered as his due. Hers was to pleasure him beyond his powers of endurance.

His slitted eyes dropped to his lap. Miriam's hand's movements under the shielding blanket were too subtle to draw attention. Her grip tightened, relaxed and tightened again. Her stroke extended to about half an inch. It was torture. He loved it. Half, or more, of the exquisite pleasure came from the strain of maintaining his self-control. An orgasm was growing, drawing power from the rigour of his restraint.

The need to thrust was close to overwhelming but he resisted, again, and found himself separate from his body.

He observed his pleasure at the same time as he experienced it, so doubling it. Before he could think, What the hell? he was coming.

Miriam ducked her head beneath the blanket, swooping, lips parted. Charles erupted. The spasms continued for five, ten, fifteen seconds, pouring his seed into her mouth in what felt like an endless stream. He stared out of the window, jaw locked to keep from howling, eyes watering with the effort.

Miriam sat up without removing the blanket from its place. With an enigmatic smile on her lips and her eyes closed again, she tucked his manhood back into his briefs and silently zipped his fly. 'Gobbler,' she said with a satisfied nod.

They arrived at their Egyptian hotel in the wee small hours. Charles wondered if he should invite her to his room. After all, she'd done what she'd done and he hadn't reciprocated. The professor's wife had taught him that that was a sin. Problem was, the professor had taught him Puritan work ethics. He was here to find Cleopatra. If he let some student mess that up he'd impale himself on a silver sword – or something.

Miriam murmured, 'We're both very tired. Goodnight, Charles,' releasing him.

Come morning, when he phoned her room, he got a message that she'd meet him in the underground parking, any time after ten, at his convenience. He indulged in a full English breakfast, likely his last good meal for a while, and descended at 10.15.

Like him, she was dressed in khaki drill, but whereas his pants were long, hers were baggy-legged short shorts. She tossed a clipboard into the back of the Range Rover Sport the University had arranged. The roof rack was piled with securely strapped boxes and bundles.

'It's all there, Charles, the extra fuel and water and all the supplies you ordered, plus some little extras I thought of.'

Charles cleared his throat. 'You're very efficient, Miriam.'

She lowered incredibly long eyelashes. 'Thank you, Charles. I promise to do my very best to serve you.'

Charles swallowed. Behind his fly, he was unfurling. The minx was – incredible. Before his arousal could show, he jumped into the driver's seat and announced, 'Let's go!'

They pulled out of the parking. The sunlight was eye-scalding despite the Rover's tinted glass. Charles paused to blink and let his eyes adjust. Miriam took sunglasses from the glovebox and twisted back to retrieve a bush hat from the pile that filled the space behind them.

'You seem to have thought of everything.'

'Since the day you chose me, Charles, I've thought of nothing else.'

He grunted. What should have been pure pleasure wasn't. Not entirely. She made him want to grab her by the hair and drag her behind a sand dune and if he couldn't take her in that way it was like he didn't want her at all. Best just to drive.

It took an hour to get out of the city but then they were on a modern six-lane highway that headed west.

Miriam asked, 'Music?'

'Sure.' Music would make the silence between them natural. He'd imagined they'd talk about the dig, mutually excited by the scale of what they proposed to do. But he found himself mentally floundering, similar to their time on the plane, where he hadn't moved or spoken while she'd pleasured him. It was a fierce sense of ennui – another damned paradox – that defeated his powers of speech.

Miriam slipped a CD into the player. Maria Muldaur's sweet voice purred the lyrics of 'Midnight at the Oasis'. It wasn't until that tune was followed by Eartha Kitt's 'Arabian Song' that he realised that Miriam had burned the disc expressly to entice him. That did it!

He turned to her. 'OK,' he said, as if all along she'd been asking a question. He let the statement sit a moment. She waited, just like, he noted, a good girl should. 'You're ... what? Submissive?'

'Yes,' she breathed out in a sigh so deep her throat trembled.

His eyes were drawn from the trembling blue butterfly beneath her skin at the base of her throat to those Turkish-coffee eyes. Yes. Wet. Incredible. And the fact that he wanted to crush her throat with one hand while he sifted the fingers of the other through her hair? He'd deal with it later. 'So, tell me. Will you do anything I say?'

'Absolutely anything.'

'No matter how ...?'

'No matter "how".' She bit her lower lip. 'It's always excited me, Charles, to obey, but boys my age, they don't know how to give instructions, not that any I've met have been worthy of my ...'

'Compliance?'

She nodded. 'But a girl has to do something, while she waits, doesn't she?'

'You think you've been waiting for me?'

'Yes.' Her eyes widened. 'But not ... not like that ... not like love. Or, not like forever.'

'Maybe you've been waiting for this.' He waved at the harsh landscape.

'Yes, Charles. That's it. We're not alone on this trip. She's here too.'

It should have sounded crazy but for a man who'd learned everything he could about the powerful Pharaoh, the little kohl-eyed sensualist, it made perfect sense. 'You're right. We're going to find Cleopatra, Miriam.' A grin split his face. 'Goddam!' He slapped the steering wheel. 'Now, I want you to amuse me.'

'Thank you, Charles.' She twisted in her seat to check the non-existent traffic, then rested her palm on his knee.

'No.' He didn't look at her. Her hand shot away from his knee. 'You did me yesterday. Now you do you. Tonight I do you.'

'Yes, Charles.'

(She half-rolled to face him. Miriam set one booted foot up on the dashboard and extended the other leg. One hand hooked the crotch of her baggy shorts aside.

There was a hollow inside the top of her thigh. The skin there was paler and more translucent. A fingernail's point followed the line of a meandering vein to the plumpness of her sex.

Miriam cupped and squeezed herself hard enough to whiten her knuckles. 'Ouch,' she whispered, continuing to maul herself viciously, compressing and twisting her own delicate flesh.

'I like it when I'm a bit bruised,' she said. 'You know, swollen and dark with blood.'

Her hand moved aside to show him what she meant. The look on his face was almost scary. Clearly he found it as incredibly erotic as she did, though it seemed to be news to him.

Miriam toyed with her lips, almost tickling them, parting them to display the oyster pink inside. Her aroma filled the Rover. She could come in a second, which would be good but then he wouldn't be watching her, focused on her, and that's what she wanted, all of Charles, just for a little while.

The lyrics of 'In a Persian Market' gave way to those of 'Cleo and Meo'.

Miriam leaned forwards to turn the air conditioning to full-blast cold and adjust a vent to direct its stream of frigid air directly at and *into* her sex. Her engorged lips fluttered apart from the force. Her building climax ebbed even as the cold clawed its way into her tunnel. She shivered, slowed and started again.

For ninety minutes she played with herself. Sometimes she thrust her hand inside her shirt to squeeze and twist her nipples. She sucked her own juices from her fingers with an avidity that wasn't entirely for show. She brought herself to the peak again, and again, never once toppling over though the need was becoming horrendous. Better though than any orgasm was the look in his eyes when he glanced from the road to her and back, and back again. She felt like a princess of pleasure.

He told her, 'We're about ten minutes from the turn-off.'

'Thanks for the warning.' Her thighs strained apart. Three fingers stabbed urgently. The ball of her thumb rotated on her nub. One foot rose to cover the vent of the air conditioner. 'It hurts,' she mumbled, which wasn't exactly true. 'Maybe I waited too long?' The orgasm that had so generously offered itself over and over again now dallied, suspicious, no longer willing, after so many false starts, to be easy.

'Nonsense. Show me how you come.'

Oh God, his voice, his eyes. She humped up into her own hand, driving her fingers deep, mashing her clit with an artlessness that could only achieve success because it was her practised hand squashing and squeezing and slapping her clit. 'Shigh,' she grunted. She'd been about to say 'shit' but she changed it in case she wasn't to swear. Her boot pressed on the bars of the vent. Her head banged back against the headrest. The orgasm roared to life and tore through her, seizing what she'd baited it with for so long. 'Shigh!' The first paroxysm almost hurt; so did the second. The third launched the ripple effect that washed over her again and again until she was limp.)

* * *

They left the highway and headed south on a single lane of crushed white stone. Abu D'bara had been a thriving little market town in Cleopatra's time. When they reached it, it comprised three crumbling walls of baked mud and a service station that had been built from rusty Coca-Cola signs.

Miriam topped up the fuel. Charles bought two icy bottles of Coke and two oranges from a toothless old man with a raisin for a face.

From there, it was due west until they came to a dry gully, which they drove in as far as an oxbow bend. Charles turned south again. After a jolting hour they came to a ruddy sandstone cliff, which they followed until it was cleft. The gap was two feet wider than their Rover. If they hadn't been looking for it, they'd have passed it. It was invisible from twenty metres away.

The narrow slot rose and fell, twisted and rose and fell again, for another hour of tortuous driving, until they topped a rise and there it was, spread out below them, an oasis – *the* oasis.

'That's it!' Miriam gasped. 'You were right. I knew you would be.'

'That's more than I knew,' Charles confessed. 'It's bigger than I expected but it has to be the one.'

The pool was about a hundred metres long and varied from ten to twenty metres wide. On their side, there was a beach but the other shore lapped against a modest cliff's face. There were at least fifty nodding date palms. The ground cover was scrubby bushes and patches of coarse grass.

They parked and got out. The air was winey with rotting dates.

'Here!' Miriam handed Charles a steel probe. 'I can set up camp if you want to make a preliminary exploration.'

Charles looked at the sky. He only had about half an hour before sunset, so he nodded and set off.

Thirty unproductive minutes later, he returned. There was a two-and-a-half metre canvas cube set up next to the Rover. Steaks were sizzling on a hibachi. A card table was set for two, with canvas chairs close by. Miriam passed him a Bloody Caesar in a beaded glass.

'Magic?' he asked.

'We've a dozen more Cryovac steaks and two hampers, from Harrods and from Fortnum and Mason. After that, we've some dehydrated supplies if we need them. There's a solar panel on the Rover's roof to charge its battery, so we can run our small fridge all the time and the air conditioning for about an hour a day if we need it.'

'You're incredible.'

She bobbed a curtsy. 'I've just got time to rinse my shorts out before the steaks are done.'

'I'll keep an eye on the food.'

He'd turned the meat twice when Miriam returned, swinging her sopping shorts. Her safari jacket was long but she'd neither buttoned nor belted it. Miriam looked down at her beautiful breasts and shrugged. 'It's cooler like this.'

Charles almost told her that she didn't need flirtatious tricks but he swallowed his words. She didn't *need* them, but it was another of her games, like 'Pretend you're asleep while I fondle you', that were making Charles's life – he had no better word – 'exquisite'.

Still, something was missing. He couldn't think what it was, but there was a void inside him, even in this paradise, even with this houri avid to do his bidding. It was irritating, really, this constant shadow-companion of wanting.

They ate quickly and without conversation, eager as newly-weds. Charles bathed in the lukewarm pool and hurried back with a towel about his hips. He didn't care, in fact was rather proud of, the way his towel jutted ahead of him.

There was a dimmed LED lamp hanging inside their tent. Miriam had zippered two sleeping bags together and spread them over a foam pad. Their sleep would be comfortable, if they got any. She was stretched out on their makeshift bed, naked, propped up on one elbow, peeling an orange.

She extended a segment. 'Dessert?'

'No thanks.'

'Sure?' Her fingers folded the pulpy crescent over her left nipple. Tiny sacs of juice burst and splattered her coffee-tinted peak.

'You're very persuasive, Miriam.' Charles dropped beside her, losing his towel, and suckled on her sweet sticky nipple.

'Harder?' she asked. 'Please, Charles, bite me!'

His eyes were level with her throat, where that enticing vein showed blue through her skin. His teeth closed gently, then clamped, indenting her tender nipple flesh. Any harder and he'd be breaking her skin, drawing blood. Perhaps that was what she wanted. In fact, he felt sure that she wanted his teeth to wound her. Charles wasn't ready for that, not yet...

As if she sensed his inner turmoil, Miriam crushed another slice of orange, over her right nipple. Charles sucked from one nipple to the other and she responded by arching against him, but there was no doubt, the more his teeth threatened her, the harder she writhed.

Miriam plucked another segment from her orange. She trailed it down her skin, between her young breasts, over her lithe torso and gently curved tummy, to her mound. Her thighs spread wide. The fingers of one hand parted her nether lips. The fingers of the other pushed the segment between them.

'I'll do that,' Charles said. He took the piece of orange into the curve of his middle finger and probed, then drew back, caressing Miriam from that special place behind her pubic bone, up and across the straining nub of her clitoris. He increased pressure with each stroke. Little sacs burst. Juice coated Miriam's flesh.

Charles shimmied down. He tongued orange in and out of her sex, until the mangled remains disappeared down his throat. An inch from his eyes, her inner lips were delicate, and scarlet. Beneath her skin, a vein pulsed so strongly he could count her heartbeats. He sucked one tender lip into his mouth. With it held between the lips of his mouth, he could *feel* the throb of her blood as it pulsed.

It was *so* tempting . . . He let his incisors sink into the flesh, just a tad, still divided by a thin sensitive film of flesh. She groaned, so he did it again and then released her pussy from his mouth like a beast of prey dropping its catch.

'I could eat you, little bird,' he said. He propped himself on his elbows and stretched his body the length of hers. 'And I might. But not tonight.'

'Tonight is all we have, Charles,' she whispered.

'I still need you,' he whispered back.

He entered her then, roughly, in one hard thrust that travelled deep inside her tight tunnel. Six hard strokes and he'd had enough of it. Too soft, this tunnel, too yielding.

He pulled out, flipped her over, yanked her to all fours and was in her bum before she could take another ragged breath.

He'd done it once, with the professor's wife, but the surety with which he slicked her hole with a careless swipe of spit and poked his raging hard-on at the centre of the puckered hole was that of a man learned in the ravaging of back passages. As if he'd done it many times, taken even his own gender in this way, making them serve.

The rougher he got, the louder she got. He wound his fist in her hair and tugged her head back. Her mouth dropped open and she was shrieking, which made him laugh. He couldn't see the pulse in her throat but it didn't matter any more, he could hear it, or was it his own pulse, his own heartbeat recklessly, wildly *fuelling* the monster between his legs.

His hand dropped from her waist, where he'd held her still so he could pull all the way out and thus re-pierce with every thrust. He grabbed a fistful of her pubis and held her tight enough to *touch* her climax with his fingers while he fired a half-dozen shots deep into her pit.

Their voices mingled and travelled the breeze of the desert night, rising to the stars.

(Does he dream as I do? The face of a boy, really, in repose. A scholar. Miriam dragged herself out from beneath him. Was that why it sometimes seemed she sensed more of the mystery than he? All her fanciful daydreams while he'd studied on and on? Was she dreaming now? No, only he slept.

There wasn't even all that much blood. A couple of drops where her aching sex was, well, empurpled. 'The colour of royalty.'

She curled up next to him, utterly sated. His arm dragged her in tight, moulding her to him. Miriam. Queen for a night.)

He woke with cold water splattering on his face. Charles looked up, up the full length of Miriam's naked dewy body. She wore a knife in a rubber sheath that was strapped to her thigh and nothing else. She looked as if she'd stepped out of some X-rated action film.

'I've found something, I think,' she announced.

'Found something?'

'A cave, it might be, or a tunnel, or it might be nothing at all.' She unhooked the lantern from overhead and slid it into an oversized Ziploc bag.

'Explain?' he asked. Was this the same girl he'd buggered

like a banshee last night? He shook his head, forget last night. Focus.

'I went for an early swim. Over by the cliff, I dived deep, down to where it's damned cold. There's a slab of rock down there – looks like it fell off the cliff – propped against it. I tried to look in but it was too dark to tell much, but I'm sure there's something there.'

Charles writhed to his feet. 'Let's go!'

Miriam pressed the ON switch of the lamp, through clear plastic.

'Clever girl!' he told her. He followed her, naked, across the pool and dived when she dived, following the bright light she held. For a moment, the light disappeared. Charles eeled behind the slab of rock and saw it again, dimmer, a couple of metres into a tunnel that was too square to be natural. Then it disappeared again, leaving him in the darkness. He accelerated with one hand extended. Part of the tunnel had collapsed sometime, leaving a gap a metre wide and half that high. Charles dragged himself through, scraping his back, before he realised that there wasn't enough air left in his lungs for him to turn around and swim back.

Dead end? Either there'd be air at the end of the tunnel or not. No point in panicking. The pressure in his lungs became incandescent. The urge to inhale was as powerful as the one to climax had been the night before, when he came to a part where the water shimmered above him. He arrowed straight up. Charles head burst into air. He sucked in so hard his throat rasped.

They'd emerged in a small pool in a chamber. Miriam gasped. 'I didn't think I was going to make it.'

'Me neither.'

'What?' Miriam laughed. 'It never occurred to me that *you* were in danger. You're – powerful. Indestructible, Charles.'

'Let's see what we've found, shall we?'

Miriam lifted her lamp. There was a rock shelf about waist height above the stone floor. A golden diadem with an emerald-eyed three-headed snake glittered.

'Her symbol,' Charles confirmed. 'We're in the right place.' Their eyes met. Even in the gloom, both pairs glittered with glee.

Further along the shelf was a cedar-lined lapis-lazuli chest. Now how did he know it was cedar lined? Had he read about it somewhere? Not a lot was known about Cleopatra's jewellery. Yet now he clearly visualised there being a dagger with a silver blade and the feline form of Bast, in gold, for a haft, inside.

Miriam stood and raised her lamp high. Charles climbed out of the water. He flipped open the chest and there, on top, the dagger. There was something amusingly erotic about the weapon, though he couldn't think what it was exactly.

In the middle of the grim chamber there was a crude stone sarcophagus.

'Her!' Miriam gasped.

'Yes, her,' Charles agreed.

They held their breaths and stepped lightly as they approached the coffin of Cleopatra, though surely no sound could penetrate the thick stone.

'What do we do, Charles?'

When a impossible dream is realised, it can be paralysing. Charles felt numb. 'A team should take it from here,' he said.

'I guess we've done our part?' Miriam said.

'Yes, a team should take it from here,' he repeated. 'Representatives of the Egyptian Government of course.' He took the three steps that put him beside the knee-high stone box.

'We shouldn't touch anything,' Miriam reminded him.

'Exactly.' Charles's fingers hooked under the stone lip. He

lifted and pushed. Miriam lifted and pulled. With a deafening shriek, the slab slid, then crashed to the floor and shattered.

Charles and Miriam stared at each other over the open sarcophagus. Until they looked into it, all things were possible. He nodded. They peered down.

And there she was!

Cleopatra hadn't been mummified. Nor had she decayed. Her pure-white linen *kalasiris* had turned to the colour of scorched papyrus but her divine face, her perfect form, were exactly as Charles remembered.

Charles remembered.

A kaleidoscope of blurred images tumbled through his bewildered mind. He saw ... He glimpsed ... Not much of it was coherent and what was made no sense at all. He shook his head. Perhaps he was hallucinating? And how could it be, if it made no sense at all, that it answered everything?

Miriam reached down. When her fingertips touched Cleopatra's dress, it crumbled to dust and fell away, leaving her naked.

'She sleeps,' Miriam said.

'For over two thousand years.'

'We will wake her.'

(Miriam drew her knife from its sheath and sliced it clean across the base of her thumb. She leaned over the painted porcelain face to let her bright blood flow between the Queen of the Nile's slightly parted lips.

The flow slowed to a trickle. Charles reached for Miriam's knife.

'No,' she said. 'Not your blood. Not yet.'

'How do you know?' Charles grabbed her wounded hand. He lifted it to his mouth.

'I just do. Don't you?' Miriam tugged her hand free of his

217

and stepped back, out of the lamplight and into the gloom of the cavern.)

Cleopatra's kohl-rimmed eyes opened. She smiled, a small weak smile, and inhaled. 'You've become human,' she said to Charles in Macedonian Greek.

The memories, the images, coalesced. 'Yes, my darling, my punishment for helping you. I have died and been reborn many times.'

'Human.' The great Queen languorously lifted an arm to brush the hair from his eyes. She laughed a rusty low laugh. 'And me the vampire. It's funny, don't you think?'

'As I once set you free from death, now it will be in your power to grant me the same.' Charles grinned. 'We will be unstoppable.'

Cleopatra sighed his name, 'Imenand Khaldun.'

Miriam repeated it, in English, 'Hidden Immortal.'

Charles stretched and flexed, as if he too had been encased in stone for centuries. Hidden from all, even himself, for an eternity.

'Miriam?' The Queen beckoned her servant forwards.

'She has served you well in this incarnation,' he said.

Miriam dipped her head in silent thanks.

'I . . . I need . . .' Cleopatra's voice, though still lilting as a harp, was faint.

'I know,' Miriam and the man who had been Charles Lomax said in unison.

He stepped into the sarcophagus and knelt astride his queen's shoulders. Miriam reached down to wrap her cool fingers around his shaft. Finally, all the erotic sensations that he hadn't known since the last time he'd made love to Cleopatra returned. There was lust, in plenty, but there was also adoration, and compassion and wonder and magic or something darker than that, darker even than death. *'I love you; I feed you, from my body.'*

Miriam stroked him reverently.

Cleopatra waited, red lips parted.

Imenand Khaldun said, 'I give you life,' and climaxed.

Madeline Moore is the author of the Black Lace novels *Wild Card* and *Amanda's Young Men*.

Left Hand Man
Mathilde Madden

I'm really not in the vampire business.

I kill werewolves. And that's the way I like it. Lycans are simple. You take 'em down – a fatal wound with a silver weapon – and the motherfuckers stay fucking down.

Not like vamps. No one makes a career out of killing vamps. Vamps are already dead.

But I wrecked my arm hunting lycs. My boss didn't want to buy the magic to fix me up. He didn't like me working the field. Wanted me chained to a desk. Me busting up my arm was just the excuse he needed.

But there was no way I was settling for that. Look like some useless over-the-hill pen-pusher in front of the wife that'd just left me for a great hulk of werewolf superman-beast. So I went looking for the only person I knew with enough power to fix it for me. Lilith.

Obviously, I wouldn't normally go to a witch for help. Even in a situation like this. Witches like to flay people for the bad manners to ask for favours. But Lilith, well, she kind of likes me. Likes me enough to let me get away with things.

Which was how I ended up in bed with her. Not that that was a hardship, she's a great-looking woman. A lot of witches are pure smoking hot. Because they can be. Because they can be anything they want. But Lilith doesn't play those games. Lilith is a grandmaster.

Grandmistress? No, that sounds weird.

She has that special spark about her that makes my dick pulse just to think of her. She always wears these suits, pencil skirts, peplums, seamed stockings. Bundle all that together with a slightly too long, too big nose and a jawline that's a couple of clicks too far into masculine, and you have hotter than the hell she could send me to just by thinking it.

And she likes me too. She likes me because I know what she likes. And I've known her long enough that, unlike most men who know how powerful she is (trust me, she could make the earth stop turning) I'm willing to do what she wants without being scared about my life suddenly becoming a *Hellraiser*-ish blur of blood and ripping pain.

Lilith likes to get tied up. And, yeah, I get a kick out of tying up a witch. I carry handcuffs around with me anyway for all kinds of reasons.

So I don't take much persuading when she strips out of her suit, throwing tweedy fabric to the floor, and climbs onto the bed in just her gloss-nude stockings with black seams (God I loved those stockings) and a pair of shoes that only a witch could walk in. I fasten her wrists to the headboard and when the locks snick shut she sighs like she's really restricted.

I go down on her first. I know I can't give her the due pounding she would've enjoyed with a busted arm. But I still show her something, holding her legs apart with my body and using my mouth on her hot witch's cunt until she's writhing, pulling against the cuffs on her wrists. When I think she's on the brink, I stop.

'Damnit, Blake, finish the job,' she snarls and she lifts her hips, bucking her frustrated pussy up closer to my face.

'Fix my arm,' I say, bold as hell. 'Fix my arm up and I'll fix you.'

'Fuck you, Blake.' Something in her don't-make-me-angry expression makes me think of thunder, of sudden storms and of lightning straight through my heart.

I hold steady. 'Well, sure, but where's the fun in that?'

Lilith is panting, twisting at the cuffs, angry and aroused. 'You don't get magic like that for free. Or for a fuck. Maybe we can do a deal, but if you want me to even think about that get that tongue, no, actually, get that cock busy and fuck me.'

'I don't know if I can.' I lift my slinged-up arm and then regret it as it twinges.

Lilith rolls her eyes. 'Oh God, forget that for a second.'

And then the twinge is gone and all the pain is gone. A little witch's miracle. I pull my arm easily out of the sling and shift up, bracing myself on the bed with both – both – arms as I slip into her prewetted shallows. Oh God, you know, I love my faithless wife. Always will. And I do tell her I've never cheated except with a witch – and it doesn't count with a witch – but, oh, no one, no one feels like Lilith. Nothing feels like a witch's sex desperate for your cock inside it.

'Harder now, baby,' Lilith moans. She tugs at her handcuffs, but still makes out as if she can't free herself, even though she's just done some stunning magic on me without so much as a nose twitch.

'You want it harder?' I say, my voice rough with a snarl.

'God, yes.'

'Then say "please".' Lilith moans. She's aroused and annoyed. 'Cause, you know, she never says please. No one asks a witch to say please.

'Fuck you.'

I draw back. I just leave the tip of my dick inside her. Her sex pulses begs like the hungry maw of a baby bird. 'Say "please". Say "Please, Blake, fuck me."'

'I could rip your fucking arms off.'

'You could say "Please, Blake, fuck me."' I slide my cock up the ravine of her sex and swirl the head on her swollen clit.

She meets my eye. 'Please, Blake, fuck me.'

Down I go. Down and in.

'Please, Blake, harder. Hard.'

I do as she asks. It feels amazing. I don't know if it is the ecstasy of my painless working right arm, the way it feels bearing my weight. But God. God!

'Please, Blake. More, harder. Fuck me harder, please. Please!'

I fuck her and fuck her and each thrust seems to make her yell out for more and make me harder inside her.

When I crest, she's there too. She brings it. Crying out in chains and stockings. Her sex pulses, slick, clenching around me.

'So –' I roll over and look at Lilith who has already freed herself from the handcuffs while I was still lying dazed beside her '– thanks for the spell on my arm.'

'The spell?'

'Yeah.' I lift my right arm and wiggle my fingers in the air.

'Oh baby.' Lilith looks kind of indulgent for a moment. 'I can't make exceptions for you – it's like I said, you want that kind of magic, you have to pay like everyone else.'

'What, but you've already fixed my . . .' I catch the look in her eye. 'Oh no! Oh . . .' I stop talking as my arm dissolves into pain.

Lilith leans over and takes my suddenly useless right arm and folds it neatly back into its sling, making me yell out some more.

In disbelief I turn away from her and pull a pill bottle from the pocket of my white coat on the floor. The drugs I've been using to control the pain of my compound, paranormally complicated fracture are strong. I've got a lot of good contacts here and there. If you want to wake up, or go to sleep, or just not feel it any more, there's often a pill if you know where to go. I take two without looking back at her.

'Come on, Blake. You know how the system works.'

There are tears prickling my eyes. More about frustration than the sudden return of pain. 'You witches charge a fortune for medical. How can I get that amount of money?'

'If I were you, I'd try someone like the unArmageddoners.'

And that's not such a bad idea. I do have some marketable skills, after all. OK, with my right arm in a sling I'm not the best prospect of a paranormal bounty hunter – but I'm sure I can still find at least one suitable job for a man of my talents. Lilith quotes me a price. I nod. 'And you'll fix it for that.'

Lilith smiles. 'As soon as you earn the money, I'll fix your arm.'

So I put an ad on this site I know. It's kind of like Craig's List but for freaks. Well, I mean real freaks. Well, I mean people like me. Me and the unArmageddon Society.

The unArmageddoners exist because every minute, every day, stuff is happening that could bring about the end of the world. Freaky-deaky supernatural stuff that could cause the seas to boil or the sun to turn inside out.

The unAs spend their time scouring ancient texts, looking for possible Armageddons and stopping them happening. It's a huge money-sucker of a project. But they're pretty well funded. Trust me, no one hates the idea of the world ending like the super rich. They don't want to get all set up with their yachts and their diamond-studded breakfast cereal just to discover someone has called time on the universe.

The people that contact me first offering me work are almost certainly unAs, although they never say that.

They arrange to meet in a pub. Two fey-looking men and an older woman called Mira. I don't want them to know about my busted arm so I leave my sling behind and hope they don't notice it limp in the sleeve of the white doctor's coat I like to wear.

Mira's all business as she pulls out a large file and drops it on the table between us. I take my spectacles from the top pocket of my coat with an awkward left hand.

'This,' says Mira, lifting out some papers from the top of the box, 'is something we've been monitoring closely. It's about a –'

'Vampire.' I squint at the squiggles, translating. 'Oh God – a fertile vampire. How did that happen?'

Mira sighs. 'A human woman and a greedy man. She was, what do you call it, a concubine, a courtesan . . .'

'A whore?'

'Well, yes, a favourite whore of this very rich man. And he knew of a prophecy that told how his most desired companion would be taken by the night owls.'

'Vamps?'

'Yep.'

'So, as he was very rich, he bought some magic to stop that happening.'

'He bought protection?'

'Well, sadly, no. Rich men don't get rich splashing their money on full vampire protection. What this man wanted most in the world was to marry this whore and have a family. Well, that was maybe just a silly dream or something to keep her sweet and her legs open. Who knows? But what he ended up buying from witches was a protection of her fertility.'

'And that was cheaper than vampire protection?'

'Way, way cheaper. And way stupider, considering how she was predoomed. Vamps got her, of course. Bit her. Turned her. And that's where the problems start, cause she's . . .'

'A fertile vamp.'

'Could have been a lot worse. The time she was turned was pretty much around the time of the vampires' withdrawal from interaction with humans. In fact, she was one of the last humans to be turned. So it's not really a problem, unless . . .'

'Unless she has sex with a human.'

'Yes.'

'And if she does?'

'If she does. And gets pregnant . . .' Mira makes a face.

'A dead-alive hybrids is one of those things that would probably reboot the universe?' I say. 'The end.' Under the table one of the fey-looking men is rubbing my upper thigh. I'd push his hand away but it's my right thigh and I don't have the workable limbs there. So I ignore it. 'But that isn't going to happen because vampires never fraternise with humans.'

'Things are breaking down. The order is changing. And now the Black Emerald clan is gone and Darius Cole is back. And he's known for "fraternising" with human women.' Mira could hardly hide her look of utter disgust. Not surprisingly really. Vamps = gross.

'So what exactly do you want me to do?'

'Find this fertile vampire. Constance.'

'And then?'

'Kill her.'

'Isn't she already dead?' Under the table the hand on my thigh moves higher, then cups my crotch. Oh God.

Mira looked flustered for a second then says, 'Put a stake in her. We'll do the rest.'

'So, to be clear: the money is for the stake. Stake this vamp – Constance – and I get paid, right?'

'Right,' she says and she holds out her right hand to shake.

I look at it a moment. 'Oh, I don't think there's any need for a handshake,' I say weakly.

Mira eyes me. 'Oh, you'd rather seal the deal with Puck?' She throws a glance at the guy who's feeling me up.

I nod. I don't have a choice.

So somehow, just because I don't want them to find out I'm damaged goods, I end up in the alley behind the pub with Puck on his knees in front of me, swallowing my cock, to cement the deal, while Mira and her other unA lackey look on at me gasping and tensing as I buck in his excellent mouth.

Which is how I got here: shooting at mirrors. Mirrors are usually a werewolf thing. There are clear parallels symbolically with the moon. And, as we all know, those lycans love their moon mistress. Also, and this is just a theory mind, I think lycs like using mirrors just 'cause vamps can't. No reflection and all that. 'Cause lycs hate vamps.

But there is one thing vamps do use mirrors for, and that's for being fucking tight wads.

I said that lycs hate vamps, right. And they do. But vamps don't really hate lycs. Vamps couldn't really give a shit about lycs. The fact is, vamps really hate witches. That one's mutual. Vamps hate witches. Witches hate vamps. And that's where the mirrors come in.

Vampires keep away from humans these days. 'Cause even though vampires are evil hard-to-kill fucks, they have one obvious weakness. Daylight. Pretty damn crippling that is – can you imagine a cheaper more easily available weapon than that? OK, it doesn't technically kill them, but it is very painful and totally debilitating. So killing vamps might be a mug's game but trapping them is easy meat seeing as how they can't go out in direct sunlight. Find the castle they're sheltering in and start smashing it up with a wrecking ball at dawn and they soon see sense. And as for being hard if not impossible to kill on account of already being dead, well, that can suddenly look like a distinct downside when the people who have captured you don't so much want to snuff you out as see you suffer.

There used to be a lot of money in recreational vampire torture. A sort of extreme sport for sick fucks. Course there was an element of risk. But if you starve the vamps of blood for long enough they get pretty weak. Now I can't get too sanctimonious here like I've never tortured a werewolf in my time, but I always did it for information not fun. Although that's not to say I didn't enjoy it. And not to say that if I got my hand on that filthy hound my wife's fallen in love with I might suddenly remember some vital information in the war against wolves that he might be withholding.

But that's enough about my domestic troubles. Basically scrapping between humans and vampires was one of those horrible stalematey things where no one wins, lots of people get hurt and lots of money gets spent on achieving precisely nothing. One of the most obvious ways in which vampires are so much smarter than humans is the way that they said, 'Fuck this,' and just quit. Over a hundred years ago vampires just said bye-bye humans. Hid themselves away. Cut all the ties. And now, apart from people who make it their business to know about the paranormal world, humans have more or less forgotten vampires were ever real.

But hiding's not all that easy. Especially in a densely populated country like this one. Not a lot of isolated lonely castles where no one ever goes in and no one ever comes out stay unnoticed for that long. That's why vamps needed proper cloaking spells. And the only people who can make proper cloaking spells are witches.

So the vamps had to go crawling to the witches for the spells and the witches charged them a fortune. Now, vamps are all aeons old, which makes them mostly unimaginably rich. That's inflation for you. Wise investments. Playing the long game. As they can. But they still hated paying money over to witches. So they scrimped as hard as they could. They cut corners. They extended the cloaking spells with mirrors.

So that's where my gun comes in. Mira knew Constance was with the Blue Cusp vamp clan. The info on where the Blues are based was easily bought. There are people on the internet who track where all kinds of spooky-ookies live. Think of it as a kind of Google Middle Earth. So I know what I'm doing here. And all I have to do to make a hole in their cloaking is find one of their damn cheapskate mirrors.

So that's why right now I'm doing what no live fucker ought to do and shooting up into the trees round where I strongly suspect a vampire clan castle to be. I'm safe from human interference – I got a little cloaking of my own – but this is slow work. So far I've missed every time. It's hard to hit invisible things with my right arm in a sling and only my far less helpful left arm available for shooting.

Five or six more bullets wasted and then there's a sound somewhere between a crash and a tinkle, and shards of mirrored glass rain down onto the ground. I look up at the now visible shattered mirror hanging up in the trees and beyond that to the stone castle in the distance.

Bloody fucking hell. Quite literally.

Tugging the huge bell pull by the castle's imposing front door has no obvious effect. I look up at the impressively tall smooth walls of the castle. It did look somewhat impregnable. That's kind of the point of castles, isn't it?

Scaling castle walls with only one working arm and no particular skills in cat burglary isn't really something I'd ever consider a good plan. Luckily, I have skills that are far more use than athleticism and dual upper limbs. I pull a bunch of lock picks from my pocket and set to work on the imposing door. Despite having to curse through the job cack-handed, it's creaking open for me in less than a minute. Typical. You see this all the time. They put all their effort into making the walls a hundred feet high and too smooth to climb, the door unbreakably sturdy, a foot thick with ironwork the breadth of a man's arm and then the lock is the tinniest easy-picker. Some people just don't get security. Lucky for me.

I just need one last thing before I skip merrily to my doom. It's just a theory, but I hope to God it works. I take a pair of mirrored sunglasses from the top pocket of my white coat – I do like to wear a white coat, it gives one an air of authority – and put them on.

In the huge entrance hall of the castle of the Blue Cusp vampire clan I peer through the dark lenses of my sunglasses. There are still many hours of daylight left and there's no sign of life. Safer, sure, but there's little I relish less than the thought of rousing some of these bloodsucking beasts from their daytime pits. But as I walk through the castle it seems almost that bit too deserted.

Then, finally, from behind a door, I hear some very distinctive noises. The door's ajar and I nudge it further open so I can see inside. It's dark in the bedroom beyond – darker still through my tinted lenses – lit only by a single candle on the nightstand and with the curtains drawn tight. There's a naked male vampire on the bed kissing a woman (possibly also a vamp) underneath him.

The guy is very pale with dark spiky hair. He's tall and thin and his veins are blue contours beneath his skin.

Vamps are usually pretty clued in to people watching them, but these two are uncharacteristically oblivious. As the male starts to move around to nuzzle the female's neck, I see her twisted rope of red-gold hair, her pale spider-lashed eyes, her kiss-swollen mouth. She's very pretty and, yes, a vamp too. The male's movements are alien-insect jerky. I didn't think vamps moved like that. Maybe it's just him.

I can see the female's tits now. She's as pale as he is and her breasts sit on her chest like two perfect scoops of vanilla ice cream. They probably feel just as deathly cold. But a treacherous part of my brain can't help thinking that her incandescent beauty would keep me warm. And when I say 'brain' there, I ought to say 'erection'.

So I decide it's time to move (that or whip my dick out and really enjoy the show).

I shoulder the door and leap through it, shouting, 'Freeze,' and pulling the gun from my sling.

The male vamp lifts his head and shows his fangs. He looks truly monstrous. I take a single step back. My fucking gun is shaking.

Fucking, motherfucking left hand!

'Is that a gun?' The vamp says, amused. 'Are you pointing a *gun* at me?'

Very quietly I hear the woman say, 'Oh, fuck.' She's a perceptive one.

'It is a gun,' I say. 'But the bullets are wooden and I'm not pointing it at you. This is aimed right at your girlfriend's heart so stick your hands up.'

The male vamp turns to face me, raising his hands. 'So what do you want?' He says it with a weary drawl like he wishes I would just piss off and leave him to his fun. Like I'm fooled. Like there's any way both of us are leaving this room alive.

I keep the gun on the female. I try to sound bored too. Like I'm here about the plumbing or something. 'I'm looking for someone. Vamp called Constance. You heard of her?

'Don't know who you're talking about.'

I can see his stupid vamp facial expression through the sunglasses. I think he's trying to psych me, but the lenses are weakening it for now. Stalemate. There's really only one possible move.

I spring and leap, covering the distance between me and the male vamp before he can react. I hit his stomach with both feet and down he goes. That's my wife's move. She's such a dirty fighter. Oh God. I fucking miss her.

I ram my gun into the male vamp's mouth and look up at the female. She's watching me like she's at the cinema and rubbing her fingers in a wound at her neck then licking the blood from them – which is probably the vamp equivalent of munching popcorn. 'So, sweetheart, how about I talk to you instead?'

'Sure. What do you want with Constance?'

'I'm here to kill her.'

'Oh, really?' The female vamp's eyes sparkle. 'Well, in that case what do you want to know?'

Underneath my gun male vamp makes a guttural sort of protest. So I pull a stake out of my sling and do it.

Staking a vamp is surprisingly easy. I always thought it would be tough. Stakes are kind of blunt and you'd think it'd need a lot of pressure. But I was reckoning without the crumbling undead chest. It's like pushing a stick into sand.

And then I'm on top of a dead-dead vamp body. But I don't really even notice how totally gross this is because as I stash my stake back in my sling I nudge my injured arm a bit and, goddamn, I instantly wish I'd been more careful. Suddenly my right arm is alive with pain.

I pull the bottle out of the inside pocket of my lab coat and pop two pills. Then I pause a sec, and neck one more.

'Diminishing returns?' I look back at the female vamp on

the bed. I hate the way I find her so hot. She's got this face that's seen it all – had a million cocks in that mouth of hers. And God, I really do hope to fuck that she's really up for helping me take out Constance – up for it enough to not, say, decide to kill me instead while I'm distracted by my useless sodding arm. But she's smiling. She's probably one of those vamps that likes humans in pain. Which not all of them do, but enough of them get off on it that they deserve their reputation as sadistic bastards. Mind you, I've been called that myself. And not without justification. Which is another reason why I'm single right now.

But instead of fantasising about how fucking great she'd look with that smirk taken off her face by a light box in her face and one of those crucifix-studded ball gags that those vampire tormentors Charles and Erin Cobalt like to use, I shrug at her.

'You want something better?' She holds up a very dirty glass bottle. 'It's an opiate, kind of like laudanum.'

I stroll over to the bed and take the bottle. 'Any thoughts on dosage?'

She looks at me, sort of confused. 'Too much love'll kill you,' is all she says. So I drink half the bottle.

As I set it down one of her bony dead arms comes up, fast and furious and curls around my neck. She draws me to her. She smells sickly sweet. Her lips are by my ear. 'You interrupted something.'

The stuff I just drank is rushing through my brain. 'Huh?'

'You killed my fuck.' She tumbles me over as she kisses me and I land on the bed, sinking down in the mess of stained linen and lace that cover it. The single candle gutters in the draught and we're in the dark.

It's all feelings then. Feelings and the idea of her and her soft sweet dead scent. The buttons of my lab coat ping away as she rips it open, still kissing me. She gets my jeans undone and her hand is on my cock then. Her cool, cool skin breath-taking against my hot and wanting flesh.

That makes my mind even sludgier, slowing to a deathly drift. I put my left hand over hers, meaning to rip it away, but in the end I just freeze there, holding it still. 'I'm not sure I have time for this. Plus my wife just left me. I'm feeling rather emotionally delicate as it is.'

'Blood,' she whispers. 'People think vampires don't get a lot of fun out of sex with humans. Not without biting them, but they don't see it how I see it. We're vampires. We live – such as we do live – for blood.' Her fist tightens around my hard cock. 'And what better combination of sex and blood than this. Why would anyone not think that a vampire would find this wooden stake – this stake of blood-wood, this sex and death and food *thing* that human males carry around – anything other than delicious?'

Her mouth is cold. She takes me right inside in one swallow. I'm right down her throat, bucking up on the bed in the pitch dark. Oh God. My hot hard dick in her cool slick mouth. It's like fucking tight freezing fog, liquid nitrogen; like my dick might shatter.

I fuck her cold throat, lifting my hips in easy flickers. She sucks me so hard and tight. Her hands are on my balls. Slick and wet and cool. She strokes me and coaxes me. And just when I'm close to coming she pulls her mouth away. My hips keep pumping in the air.

She laughs and shifts. Then her lips are on mine and she is setting herself down on my cock. She's good. It feels like she's engulfing me. For all she's cool, I feel like I'm burning up behind my sunglasses in the dark.

Less than an hour in a vampire castle and I'm fucking an undead bitch. What the hell is wrong with me? Sure I'm missing my faithless vow-breaking wife, but it's not like this is going to help. Course I shouldn't be here. I don't do vamps. But I'm full of drugs, right? It's the drugs made me do this. I'm panting. She puts her hands on my chest, sliding under my sling and stroking my nipples hard. Her sex works my cock like nothing I've ever felt and it's then that I get an unexpected flash of clarity. She is way, way too good at this. Vampires don't fuck like humans do. Don't fuck like this. She said so herself. They bite each other. So how did this one learn to fuck human men this well. I think of her mouth – the way I'd felt like she must have sucked a million cocks . . .

There used to be a thing of vamps biting whores way back in the day. They were out alone at night. Easier. Weaker. Friend-lier. People care less about them. Makes sense. Same reason serial killers often pick on them as a victim of choice. So now a lot of the female vamps you meet these days were whores when they were human. (So they have mouths for sucking twice over.) But even so, if I was ever getting fucked by a woman who was once a rich man's favourite whore, a woman whose sex he'd pay witches to protect . . .

'Oh God,' I say, 'it's you.' She clenches around me hard enough to stop me thinking anything for a second.

Shit. Shit. I can't fight the way she's making my cock feel and the pills and her drug – whatever the fuck that actually was. God, why do I have this strange weakness to take unknown substances when I'm in pain?

She's the fertile vamp. I can't, won't, mustn't go over edge. But the wind is so strong . . .

'I know who you are.'

She laughs and her sex tightens again, drawing me still closer to doom.

I try to scramble away, get my dick free at least, but her arms come down on my shoulders, vicious strong. My prone position and my ruined arm lose the battle for me. I can't move.

She clenches. It's too late. I'm over the edge. I'm coming.

I wake up tied to an altar, which is never good.

I guess I must've lost consciousness. Hard to say. Whether it was the truly fucked-up nature of finding myself bollock-deep in the woman I was meant to be topping before any human man got his seed inside her, or whether it was simply the drug cocktail, something turned my lights out as I peaked.

My three working limbs are lashed down to the corners of this fucking Satan-worshipping table or whatever the fuck it is. I'm wearing nothing but my shirt, still hanging open the way it was when I passed out. They haven't even removed my shades. The room is dark, lit by yet more sodding candles even though there is no reason at all for vamps not to use electricity. Fuck, even lycans can cope with switches.

There are four horribly familiar faces surrounding me, one of them is Constance. And the other three are the supposed unAs who hired me, except they're clearly not unAs. They're not even human. They've removed whatever fucking glamour they were using so I can see now that they are fucking vamps too.

Oh God, was I really this naive? 'You fucking tricked me. You didn't want me to kill her. You'd figured out what she was and you *wanted* a human male to impregnate her. Fuck ...'

Mira is the boss here again. 'Fuck, indeed. Humans are so weak. So easy to play.'

'Guess so, although I'm not sure why you didn't just invite me back for coffee. Your plan resulted in that poor bastard in the bedroom getting staked.'

'Oh,' says Mira, 'not to worry. He'll be fine. We can reanimate him with the correct spellwork.'

'What about me?' I say, my voice sounding suddenly dustier. 'Am I going to be fine? I don't suppose you tie people to altars just to say thank you, do you?'

'We need to keep you,' says Mira, 'in case your seed didn't take. You're not Superman. It might take a few more couplings.'

I recoil in horror and my arm jolts with pain again. My drugs are wearing off. And with the return of the pain comes a little more mental clarity. There's got to be a way out of being kept here as stud to their vampiric brood mare, especially as fucking Puck's looking at me like he's going to be my personal fluffer every time I'm forced to fuck the dead bitch.

Got to be a way ... I let my mind turn over what Lilith said to me again. Then I look at Constance. 'Do you have any more of your magical opiate?'

'Huh?'

'Please. My arm hurts so much.' And God, all I can hope is that my mirror shades really do stop vamps reading my mind in any great detail and all she sees is an injured man tied firmly to an altar.

Constance reaches inside a pocket of her lacy confection of a dress and pulls out the dirty bottle. She moves forwards and brings it to my lips.

I drink. The drug slows my brain, but it dulls my pain too. I feel my right arm getting lighter and lighter. The pain becomes more of a tingle than a fire. Inside the sling, I try not to wince as I force the fingers of my right hand to close around the stake that's stashed in there.

Lilith said that as soon as I earned the money she'd fix my arm. Mira said that I earned the money for staking Constance. All I can hope for is some pure literalism.

Every ragged, frayed-edged nerve in my arms screams as I make it move. I yank the stake out of the sling with my right hand and aim it at Constance's chest. Sure, staking a vamp doesn't take a lot of force, but I feel like I'm going to vomit it hurts so much. And then, oh God, as Constance begins to scream her terror, I feel Lilith's magic uncoil. I knew it. As she'd already spelled my arm better once, she'd have just masked that magic rather than do a recast. The magic to fix me was right there all along.

'That's right.' And as Constance falls to the ground, extra dead, Lilith is right there behind her.

'What are you doing?' I try to sit up but I'm still tied down. Plus I'm a little distracted by the way Mira and her vampy boys are screaming and poised to kill me to death. I'm blinded by fangs for a sec and then ...

Nothing.

Confused I pull the ropes away from my left hand and sit up. The other three vamps are splayed on the floor and there, grinning, is Lilith.

'You just killed them all?'

'Well, kind of. Really, though, they were already dead. I just made them the less noisy kind of dead. They were pretty tiresome. Sorry, you look upset?'

'What are you even doing here?'

'Some magic has a pull. Like a reverse kickback. When your spell activated it brought me here. Sorry. Did I spoil something?'

'Oh God, well, you know, here I am making superhuman efforts just to get out of here alive. I was going to fight my way out. Or die trying. Praying that staking the freak would fix me enough that I'd stand a chance, and then you turn up and *kapow* them all. I know you can't really understand this, but hanging out with a witch can make a person feel kind of impotent.'

'Impotent?' Lilith smiles. 'Well now, that would have made things far simpler.'

* * *

Blake Tabernacle and Lilith also appear in Mathilde Madden's Silver Werewolf Trilogy: *The Silver Collar*, *The Silver Crown* and *The Silver Cage*. A novella in this world is also included in the Black Lace collection *Possession*. She is also the author of the Black Lace novels *Peep Show*, *Mad About the Boy* and *Equal Opportunities*.

Flashback

A. D. R Forte

Someone was watching her. The hair on her arms and the back of her neck stood up like an angry feline's, and under the beat of hot noonday sun she felt as cold as if she stood in deep shadow. She looked right and left, gaze picking apart the lunchtime crowd crossing the square, then spun to look behind her. Nerves prickling raw.

All she found were lawyers and brokers in suits. Tech geeks in button-down shirts, bums, a few thugs. A girl with spiky pink hair. A couple of old men ogling the busty blonde chatting a mile a minute on her phone. The guy in the bad suit, slack-jawed and leering at the blonde. People, lots of people, all absorbed in themselves. Not in her.

But she'd felt the weight of that gaze, like a touch, like an icy hand on her back. She shook her head. *There's nobody watching you.* So either she was losing her mind or she was on the verge of a coronary. She needed to get more sleep, maybe a massage. They did free massages on Tuesdays. Mental note to get one. Sit down, eat your sandwich, relax.

But her very nice latte tasted like cardboard, and the minute she'd planted herself on a patch of free wall next to two broker types eating tofu and talking stocks, she jumped up again. That untraceable, inescapable prickle again: watching her, sizing her up. Placing its claim on her. Latte spilled on her wrist and she looked down at her trembling hand.

Nice. Completely fucking nuts.

In her other hand, the plastic-wrapped sandwich had been crushed into a gooey lump. She gave the milling, oblivious crowd one last look, sipped the tasteless latte one more time for the sake of normalcy, just in case anybody *else* might be watching and making up their minds she was a complete flake. Then she took a deep breath and turned for the safety of her office, for her desk behind security access cards and metal doors and glass. Walking as fast as her loafers would carry her with anything like decorum.

But not running away from nothing. Oh no. Definitely not. She wasn't that crazy ... yet.

All afternoon her mind strayed. Words and numbers blurred when she tried to read them and hid their meanings. She found herself looking out of the window often, at the sun-baked street outside.

She wasn't the kind that panicked easily.

When she'd been nine the neighbour's pit bull had slipped his leash and come chasing after her. She'd stood perfectly still, hands at her sides, in the middle of the lane and the dog had skittered to a halt and barked. Then, to her shock, it lay down and put its head on its paws, growling slightly until the neighbour came running out to leash it. No, she didn't spook easily ...

'... are you OK?'

Her heart leaped painfully and she swallowed the tangle of nerves in her throat; looked up to see a woman standing beside her chair. She knew this woman, saw her every day. What was her *name*?

No matter. She gave the woman a smile. 'I'm fine.'

'You sure?' The woman's brow furrowed. 'You look really flushed. This bug that's been going around ... my kids have it and it's rough.'

Was she flushed? Why? The vent above her head was purring, softly blowing streams of cool air across the desk. She shook her head. 'I'm OK ... Really. I don't feel sick.'

Janine. That was it. How could she forget? She'd known Janine, worked with her, for five years.

'Well, I ...' Janine began and then trailed off as they were interrupted.

'Afternoon, ladies. How are you?' He smiled at them, a dimple breaking the smooth mahogany perfection of his skin for an instant. Marc? No, Marcus. She knew *his* name, even though she'd first met him a brief month and a half before when he joined their little hive world on the twenty-seventh floor.

Janine looked briefly at him; turned back with a frown.

'I think Kat's getting the flu but she claims she's fine.'

A frown mirroring Janine's replaced the charm of the smile. 'Are you sure?' he said, turning to face her. His gaze seemed to be picking her apart. 'We can cancel this afternoon's meeting if you're not up to it.'

Dammit! She was fine! To prove it, she stood and smoothed down her skirt. Forced a smile onto her face. No need to let them know her head had begun to ache with gusto the moment she got to her feet. Or that she did feel stupidly hot after all.

'I can meet this afternoon, it's not a problem. And I ... I'll leave early after that, OK?'

She looked from one to the other. Did they see? Did they sense her unravelling like a ball of yarn dropped on the floor?

Marcus smiled, but the expression never reached his eyes. Hawklike and golden brown, they watched her. At odds with the easy baritone of his voice.

'OK. Don't want you working yourself to death on me now, Kat.' He gave her arm a quick double pat, nodded at Janine and strode off – movements so smooth he might have been gliding not walking. Or else she had too, too much caffeine in her system.

The moment he'd disappeared from sight, Janine grinned. 'Must be nice to have *him* wrapped around your little finger.'

'Is he? Why?' Absently, she reached for the remains of the latte. It would taste even worse now, having sat ignored for two hours on her desk, but she needed liquid. Her throat had turned to sandpaper.

'Oh, come on. That man is definitely easy on the eyes.'

She shrugged. True, Marcus was beautiful by any standards, dashing in his suit and his vigour and his intelligence. But she thought of the look he'd given her not two minutes before and the latte spilled again.

It wasn't often that beautiful men talked to her with possessive intent, as he had from the very first day. And she wondered why.

She pondered it looking at her reflection in the mirror in the mornings, but that gave her few useful answers. Reflections just showed simple things like eyes and teeth and naked skin. All the other things, the hidden things other people picked up on without even knowing they did, the things *she* didn't even know: those stayed veiled.

In fact, she liked it better when the shower misted up the glass and her image turned smoky like quartz. A pale mist shadow in a whole roomful of hazy mist-shadow world. Fading into it.

She didn't talk during the meeting and finally Marcus sent her home, telling her she needed rest. But she didn't need rest; she was on edge. All the way home she fidgeted like a dog, alert to each and every sound and movement, tensing at them all, but there was nothing. Nothing but a city full of the ordinary dangers cities boast of – and she wasn't even sure what she felt could be called fear.

She had no idea what to call it.

The bus dropped her off. Her street lay quiet in the afternoon sun, the air heavy with the scent of magnolia. A bum shuffled down the sidewalk, head bent, fingers clutching a plastic bag that rustled in the breeze. Odd seeing a homeless guy here. They tended to stay away from the nice areas with the nice brick-front houses because the cops usually shooed them off.

But what did it matter? Nothing made any sense today.

She walked down the street, digging in her purse for a dollar. Not that she should encourage it, but so what if he bought booze with it and . . .

Movement at the corner of her vision drew her gaze. The plastic bag, caught by wind and spiralling away. She watched it tumble along the pavement. Empty.

Just part of his disguise. So that he could blend into the crowd, could follow without being noticed. Could watch without being seen. She stopped walking.

He raised the brim of the ragged hat and straightened up to his full height. Worn sneakers soundless on the sidewalk, walking towards her. Not the shambling gait of a bum now. He had the stride of a soldier . . . a warrior.

Towering over her, his eyes flashed golden, jade green and golden again – colour shifting like a kaleidoscope, light against the darkness of his skin. They mesmerised her. And the gaze was familiar. Had seared through her composure at lunchtime, and had haunted her mind ever since.

She felt him pulling at her, teasing her, promising, filling her with sense memories – heat and sun and the scent of water, the green smell of trees in the desert, blue water under scorching sun.

Shaking her head, she took half a step back. A sharp canine yip grated on her hearing. A woman with a small boy had just turned the corner, an even smaller dog skipped ahead of them, barking. A stream of noisy sound drifting down the sidewalk. How did she know that when she hadn't taken her gaze from his?

He smiled and reached for the crumpled bill in her hand. His fingers brushed hers. Heat raced through them, riling her to awareness, making her blood dance. She bit her lip so she wouldn't cry out, because if she did, it would have sounded a lot like passion.

Crazy.

Because before her was only a bum, head down, rummaging in his plastic bag, clutching a five-dollar bill. He stepped off the sidewalk and crossed the street, shuffling his way down to the corner while the little boy called to the dog. She saw the dog in the flesh now, tail pointed and pulling on its leash as it barked. At her.

She turned and looked behind her. Empty street. *Nobody's there.*

The boy yelled something, yanked at the leash, and finally the dog's tail dropped. It gave her a final yip, turned, ran back to its master. Peace reigned again.

Tired as if she'd been running for hours, she found her house with the flagstones on the walkway, the frosted glass panels on the front door. Something familiar. She made her way up the steps, unlocked the door. Her heart banged against her ribs. Shivering, she stepped over the threshold, shut the door and jumped as her phone shrieked into the silent house. Pain that had flagged into a faint ache flared again as her head bumped against the door frame.

Wincing she looked at the phone, silent now but urgently blinking blue. Marcus. Why? She answered, knowing her voice trembled with lack of breath.

'I wanted to check on you,' he said.

'You didn't have to.'

'What's wrong?' His voice sounded deeper. Resonating like ... like the snarl of a great cat. 'What's happened?'

She closed her eyes; she didn't want to answer him and

yet she did. Her head seemed to be on fire, and her skin. Maybe she *was* coming down with something after all ...

'I don't know,' she said, not sure he could hear her. Speaking more to herself than him. 'I have no idea what's happening any more.'

'Wait for me.' *Wait. Just wait.*

The line clicked dead and she stared at the phone in her hand. Frowning, she looked around the cool shaded room. Why had she left work so early? What had she been doing there before she did? Someone had told her to come home.

She remembered Janine asking if she had the flu and something else ... someone ... She'd taken the bus and that kid had been walking a noisy dog. So damn hot out there.

Stumbling a little, she made it to the couch and sank into the welcome softness of cushions. Her clothes chafed but she had no energy to take them off. No energy to do anything but wrap her arms around a throw pillow and close her eyes. She'd wait.

She woke up to darkness. Lethargy weighted her down, pressed her into the sticky hot darkness of the cushions. She was stifling in her clothes. Groggy, she pushed herself upright and used the fluorescent glow of street lights filtering through the shades and curtains to undress by. Shiver, shiver, shiver. So hot. Hotter than she should be.

Light made her head hurt, but the cold water of the shower felt so heavenly. Ice on her skin rinsing away heat and confusion. By the time she stepped out of the shower, she felt almost lucid. She could do simple normal tasks now without her thoughts wandering like disoriented cows.

The doorbell chimed. She stood in the murky hallway and stared at it. Who – at this late hour? Or rather, what hour was it? She hadn't thought to look at a clock since waking, or if she had, the information had fizzed away. If she craned her neck just right she could see the green microwave display. A minute past midnight. The doorbell chimed again and she bit her lip.

Foolishness. What on earth was there to be afraid of but sunshine and pollution? Statistically, her chances of death from heart disease only narrowly beat out her chances of a fatal car wreck or an armed robbery. Unseen, phantom threats were the least of her worries.

Yes. But it wasn't any phantom she feared. It was the truth that waited for her. The truth she'd been trying to ignore.

Was the air conditioning in the place even working? She walked through waves of heat to the door and reached for the handle expecting it to burn her skin, but the metal stayed cold under her hand. She opened it, looked into the empty night. Sniffed the air, sweet damp with the scent of night flowers and humidity. She heard the purr of his car engine.

Marcus leaned against the passenger door, phone in his hand. He looked up at her from under his brows and uncrossed his arms. She started down the flagstones still warm from the day's heat. Towards him.

You're barefoot and in pjs, idiot. But what did it matter? What did anything matter?

The phone disappeared into a pocket. He'd taken off his jacket and in the street lights his shirt burned white like the middle of a fire.

'Come with me,' Marcus told her when she stood before him. So close she could see his brown eyes flashing impatience he didn't bother to hide.

She flushed. 'Why? Why are you here this late anyway?'

But even as the rebellious words left her, he moved, pushing away from the door with catlike ease. Inhuman really to move like that. She looked up at him and her heart stepped up its rhythm.

His fingers brushed the line of her jaw.

'Perfect.' His fingers were too warm – no, they were hot. They burned along the arch of her neck, heating up the blood pulsing beneath his caress. She took a deep breath with effort. That feeling again. Trapped, but trapped so deliciously she didn't want to make the effort to break free.

His thumb stroked the skin beneath the collar of her top and sent ripples of feeling cascading between her thighs, each intensifying into desire. She was breathing between parted lips. At some point she reached out to steady herself and looked down to see she'd caught hold of a handful of his shirt. She twisted her fingers in the starched material as a protest, and she saw him smile. A sharp, dazzling smile. It made her cold and hot. It added to the raging need that she would have satisfied if only she could move. If only she could force him down on the concrete sidewalk, she'd get revenge for this.

Marcus laughed. He released her. Panting, she stumbled backwards and he caught her before her legs gave out. She was burning up again, worse than before. Shivering with unsatisfied lust.

She could smell the hint of spice and wind that hovered beneath the coolness of his cologne, feel the heat from his hands on her waist. So much like . . . like something else she couldn't recall

'Now. Will you come with me?'

And she nodded.

From the window of his loft, she looked out over the city glowing under a veneer of electric light reflected from the clouds. She hadn't said a word all the drive here. He'd gone too fast for her to speak, top down on the car so that her damp hair streamed back from her head and dried in wild tangles. She hadn't asked where he was taking her, just as she didn't turn around now when she sensed his heat again, the bulk of his body behind her. His hands closed over her shoulders.

'It's you, Marcus. What are you doing to me?' she demanded, forcing the words out between fighting the fever in her blood and the buzzing in her head.

He pulled her closer to him, his lips silken and hot on the curve of her ear.

'Nothing,' he whispered, and despite herself, despite everything that fought to stay alert, she felt herself slipping. Falling. 'Nothing but seducing you.' Laughter. 'And you will be mine.'

She closed her eyes. The beat of blood had risen to a furious cacophony in her ears; perspiration trickled down her spine. She unbuttoned the first button of her top, then the second, but it gave her no relief from the heat.

Strands of her hair clung to her neck and his hot fingers brushed them away. Caressing her neck like he'd done earlier. She felt moisture soaking into her pyjama bottoms as Marcus dropped one hand between her legs. As his fingers rubbed the wet cotton, the seam of the pants against her flesh, rising pleasure pulsed in her clit.

Purple clouds stretched across a darkening sky she didn't recognise. Sultry wind brushed her skin. He caressed her, seduced her and her blood longed for his touch.

Give in.

Yeah. Give in sounded like a good idea. Except . . . that afternoon there had been another burning touch, another sweet tug at her mind promising unthinkable pleasure. She had to capture the thought before it spun away, even if Marcus's fingers were swirling faster and faster over her aroused clit and her head was spinning.

Think. Remember . . .

From the steps leading up to the open terrace in the here and now, a voice carried to them, honey soft and as sharp as a dagger.

'Not so fast, Marcus,' he said.

This time she heard a real snarl against her ear as Marcus drew her back to his chest, one arm curled like an iron band around her. A nice, safe, protective gesture that was anything but safe. The snarl hadn't been a sound any human throat could produce, or any animal throat either. It made her think of the sound effects from sci-fi movies. Only real.

And in any other time and place, it would have scared her shitless. Tonight, caught between these two unearthly rivals for her attention – *for her* – fear was purely academic.

The other walked towards them, wind tugging at the edges of his jacket. So much for the bum disguise. The elegantly cut suit made him taller than ever, his shoulders broader than she remembered. Between them both, with her head barely reaching Marcus's chin, she felt tiny and toylike and crushable. A spark of adrenaline travelled through her muscles, tensing them. Her nipples pushed at the cotton of her top.

'Damar.' Marcus's voice rumbled through his chest and into her back. 'You have no place here . . . General.'

She heard the derision in Marcus's voice, saw the subtle shift in Damar's stance. He arched an eyebrow; a corner of his mouth tilted upwards.

'Don't I?'

He looked down at her and this time his lips curved into a full smile. She thought of the hot street, the wrinkled bill between their fingers, his skin on hers. She felt her body respond, urging her to move towards him.

Something clicked on the floor. A plastic button from her shirt. She looked down at the cut thread hanging loose from where the button had been, at the long, curving nails pressed against the flesh of her breast. She looked up at Damar again. In the glow of filtered light from the city his eyes held no colour, but she could see their glitter.

Older, wiser. No less feral. No less dangerous.

She shivered.

'I think it's up to her to make that decision, isn't it?' His voice was wind across an empty stretch of sand, soft for the moment until it turned deadly. She saw his lips curl back, saw the fangs catch light, even as a whisper of pain told her Marcus's nails had broken her skin. She smelled their hunger, their need.

'So Katherine. Tell us. Which of us will you have?'

Think about this in logical terms. Vampires do not exist. At the core of that argument lay the solution to everything. Her presence, their presence, the humid night folded around them, the noise of traffic in the city far below: all of it must not exist. And if it didn't ... if it didn't, then her choice had no consequence, did it?

That meant she could choose whatever she wanted. *Whatever* she wanted.

She put her hand over Marcus's. Did her touch feel as hot to him as his did on her naked flesh? Did she burn him the way he burned her as she moved his hand downwards? She felt the tug of his thumbnail severing more thread. More buttons clicked away into the darkness.

She felt the whisper of air on her shoulders as he helped her slip the top off. Damar watched. Silent. For half a breath she was afraid he would misunderstand and turn to go, but his gaze didn't waver. She held her breath and reached for the waist of the pants. They fell down easily enough.

Naked, she felt braver. She stood in an island of space between them, feeling the male, hard presence of their bodies before and behind her. Her blood tingled and warmed; it caressed her limbs. In her mind's eye she could trace its pattern: up and out from her heart to her arms, to her fingertips; down through her torso, behind her ribs, through her chest, her stomach ... surging between her legs.

She bit down into her lower lip. Bit it hard. The blood was pulsing between her legs, in a hungry little mouth pulling at her self-control. It responded to the tentative fingers she brushed across her breasts with sharp, sweet twinges. It demanded she caress her nipples, and it sucked greedily at the jolts of pleasure when skin touched skin.

Images tugged at the edges of her concentration. Inside her somewhere lay memories that roused and stirred now with each pulse of blood. If she wanted to, she could have closed her eyes and pictured the open stone arches of a palace in the dark. The moisture in the air could have been from the river twisting through the night.

Maybe they came from picture books or movies. Maybe they were no more than imaginary. But the palace stone didn't shine like a movie set, gold chipped from a faded painting. The river smelled of green algae. Vivid, like memories.

She didn't try to remember any more; she reached for Damar and ran her fingers along the lapels of his suit: rough linen instead of the silk her touch remembered. She smiled and pulled him closer as she backed up a step; stumbled into Marcus. She laughed as they both reached to steady her. Marcus's hands closed around her hips.

Damar caught her arms. Laughing aloud, she tilted her head back and offered her throat to him while Marcus's hands moved over her naked belly, fingers pressing into her flesh, pulling her ass to his groin. She arched. Male hands caressed her, nails sharp on her skin, brushing the bare peaks of her nipples. She clenched her stomach against the rush of need between her legs. Somewhere in the fragments of memories, wheels spun, raising clouds of dust. White dust on white columns.

Damar's lips travelled down the column of her throat, tongue wet on her skin. His mouth closed over the tip of one nipple and she cried out. She needed to be filled. She needed them both. Damar's mouth moved, and pain blossomed where his tongue touched the skin torn by Marcus's nails. She writhed, but Marcus held her in place, his mouth hot at the crux of neck and shoulder while Damar's tongue hurt her, drove her, made her sex ache exquisitely.

He lifted his head, looked over her shoulder, past her. She couldn't read the expression in those pale glittering eyes, but she felt the beat of preternatural hearts, faster than any human heart could ever keep pace with, vibrating through her naked flesh. Meeting in her.

Damar looked away.

The muscles in Marcus's legs shifted; one hand released her hips, going to his crotch. She closed her eyes, clutched at Damar's arms and he steadied her. He held her as she felt the weight of Marcus's body press against her with new purpose, as she felt him lift her body so that her toes, pointed, just barely kept purchase on the floor.

God. But this had nothing to do with God. Or at least, not what she'd learned of God all her life. This was far far older. Far more powerful.

Marcus's erect cock pressed into her, into folds wet with her own hunger, and she looked up again at Damar. At how his face transformed with desire to see her impaled. Drinking in her agony and her pleasure as Marcus pushed deeper. Hands on her hips, Marcus rocked her back, back. Pulled away only to thrust into her harder. Wetness trickled down her thighs as her sex clenched and clenched again. She sucked in air, struggling against a flood of broken pictures in her head.

They moved too fast: places, people, exotic and yet ordinary. Her head hurt, overloaded, bursting with too much. She whimpered, closed her eyes. Too much, too much.

Searing pain eased the weight.

Teeth, sharp teeth, sank through skin and tissue at the base of her neck. Her heart skipped, thudded, blood rushed helter-skelter through her veins. But the flood of memories receded, falling into place like pictures in an album. Chalky blue sky behind the whitewashed columns. Dark-blue ocean beyond the cliff. Morning sun rising over the orchard dark green and bursting with springtime foliage.

Part of her mind kept her hands gripping Damar's arms, but the rest of her consciousness slipped, like falling into sleep. Only a fraction of her left in reality knew Damar moved, pulling free, stepping back. And that part of her panicked. She knew her fingers flexed, fighting to maintain contact with his before he stepped back into shadow.

She'd chosen. Not one, but both.

He resisted and her head swam, but her desire held on to him. Seduced him.

I want you.

His lips burned on her wrist. At the base of her palm, his tongue swirled across the veins. Her clit fluttered. Light-headed, weak. She ought to pass out, but she hadn't. She could feel skin, silky but rough with stubble, under her drugged fingertips.

The world went still. Marcus still held her, deep inside her, but motionless. She felt the trickle of liquid down her shoulder where his mouth had been a moment before. In the stillness she caught the scent of the city: exhaust and hot asphalt. A whisper of lighter air, of trees and night flowers.

She trembled. *I need you.*

It hurt; the pressure of both cocks driven into her aching sex. She swayed, losing balance. She'd lost all perception of space, but they held her, their bodies as solid as stone. They anchored her. They made her cry with pleasure.

Closer. Impossibly, her heart sped up. Blood raced faster through her veins, flooded her belly with heat. The familiar feeling of being in an elevator in free fall. The need to cry out. Finally her muscles contracting, over and over. The spasms in her clit and her sex that always left her shaking and bemused. Only a dozen times harder than ever.

Shining coloured spots clung to darkness blotting out her vision. She felt the sharp, puncturing pain at her wrist, renewed pain at her neck. If she had breath, she'd have cried.

Twilight and sand. Blood and sex and pain. Then, as now.

Male hands, male bodies. She saw them both. Together. Lovers. Dark skin against darker, slippery with oil and sweat and kisses. The trappings of war lay discarded on a tent floor: armour, tunics, weapons, cloaks dyed the colour of blood. Ignored in the heat of passion.

Not her memories, but their memories. Fragments of mortal lifetimes they'd forgotten and pain they'd long buried under the weight of immortal years. Somewhere in her soul were the pieces they had lost to magic and time. She'd held the tiny broken shards together. Tonight she'd bound them with her body and her blood.

The light bulb came on. It explained everything: their rivalry, their desire for her. It explained the veiled pain in Damar's eyes and Marcus's anger. She smiled because she understood: she had always been the key. Then her tired mortal body gave up.

Dammit. For the first time in her life, she was going to pass out.

But at least she wasn't a flake after all. And she wasn't coming down with the flu either.

Always a good thing.

Feasting
Kelly Maher

Waves of heat shimmered up from the pitch-black pavement before her. The oven of summer in New England baked Etta's fair skin so that it turned the tender pink of freshly butchered lamb. Dark lenses protected her eyes as she scanned the horizon for the turn-off noted in the invitation packet.

She hadn't seen another car since passing through the small hamlet about ten miles back and began to wonder if she wanted to work in such an out-of-the-way location. The image of Randall fucking their realtor on *her* kitchen counter seared in her memory, reminding her why the offer of auditioning for the position of chef of the bed and breakfast's attached restaurant drew her like a bee to nectar. Also, it wasn't as if the restaurant was a complete hole in the wall. Jeffrey Steingarten had reviewed it when it first opened. If one of the most feared judges on *Iron Chef* enjoyed the food enough to recommend it, foodies flocked.

Rat-bastard Randall. She'd been gearing up for the perfect life with him in the new apartment and the beginnings of their own restaurant. It wasn't like either of them hadn't slept with others before, but they, or at least she, had always been up front about it before the encounter if it was outside of the party scene. To go behind her back like that ...

From behind an elderly maple tree, the sign for the turn-off appeared as if from the ether. She pulled the ancient Sebring to the side of the road and admired the eye-catching sign. Carved into the local granite was script proclaiming The Cavern's establishment in 1796 with what looked like birds spewing forth from the mouth of a cave. A cloud passed over the sun, providing a short cooling respite from the intense light of late afternoon.

Etta smiled up at the sky. 'Is that a good or bad omen?'

Shaking off the chill settling on her skin from the first atmospheric shade of the day, she resumed her trek to her potential new workspace. As she turned off the road, it felt like she was leaving the modern world behind.

The Bavarian chalet-inspired outbuildings made their first appearance about a mile away from the main road. Set among the forest of maple and pine trees, they made her feel a little like Gretel or Little Red Riding Hood entering the forbidden forest. Glimpses of white trimmed with dark wood peeped out on the road ahead between rolling curves.

A flash of brown and white exploded out of the forest feet ahead of her and she slammed on the brakes. The deer's white rump disappeared into the greenery on the other side of the road as she fought to control the fishtail motion. Through grit and memories of her dad teaching her how to drive in Midwest winters, she stopped the car inches from crashing into a disturbingly solid tree. Air shuddered in and out of her lungs and her heart fluttered like the wings of a hummingbird.

Closing her eyes, she focused on easing her system down from the adrenaline rush. When she finally felt reasonably in control, she manoeuvred the car back onto the road and stopped almost immediately. The promise of the outbuildings was more than fulfilled by the edifice gracing the clearing. Gingerbread trim emphasised the pristine whiteness of the wattle and daub walls. The sun glinted off of the mullioned windows. Etta lost a tiny bit of her heart.

The packet had indicated that she park in the visitor lot when she arrived, and she followed the signs to what looked like an old estate's cobbled stable yard, except for the orderly white lines created by white stones on the south end.

The musical tinkling of water burbling over rocks filled the air, and she saw the stream hidden from view by the picket fencing when she stepped from the car.

'Henrietta Johannsen?'

Etta jumped, turning to where the velvety dark voice sounded from just behind her. Her jaw dropped. He held his hand out to her.

'I'm David James, manager of The Cavern.'

'Uh, yes, nice to meet you. Please call me Etta.' She shook the proffered hand, trying not to let the firm muscled grip send her into a quivering paroxysm. Firmly reminding herself that jumping your potential boss and fucking his brains out was not a good thing to do during the first five minutes of an interview, Etta stepped back to grab her purse from the passenger seat.

Rebound sex always left a bad taste in her mouth, but boy, did David James tempt her into breaking her first rule of being dumped.

'I was pleased to hear your acceptance of our invitation. Randall struck me as being very proprietary about his star chefs. Does he know you're here?'

Etta felt the muscles in her hand twitching for the feel of her best paring knife. 'Randall chose to focus his energies down other avenues and we've parted ways.' In fact, the invitation had arrived in the mail the day after she caught Randall showing the cartoonishly nubile realtor a twist on how to *tenderise the meat*.

His smile was almost as blinding as the noonday sun. 'I wish I could say I was sorry for circumstances, but his loss is most definitely our gain.' He gestured towards the trunk of the car. 'May I take your bags?'

Pulling the latch to release the trunk, she shook her head. 'No need, I carry my own load.'

'Ah, but I insist. Mr Schwarz would be greatly displeased to have a female guest inconvenienced in such a way.'

'Mr Schwarz?'

David pulled both of her suitcases out of the trunk with what looked like minimal effort. Etta knew darn well they both would have exceeded the airline's weight limit had she flown. She took her knife case; she didn't entrust them to anyone.

'The owner of The Cavern. Actually, his family has owned it since it first opened.'

'Isn't Schwarz a German name?' The clatter of her heels against the cobbles echoed in the back courtyard. It was remarkably quiet for the summer season. Maybe their high season was the fall and winter. She could easily see leaf watchers and ski bunnies taking advantage of the romantic atmosphere.

'Yes, his great-great-whatever was one of the Hessian soldiers you read about in your history classes in school.'

'Interesting, I hadn't thought they came this far north.'

Again the grin. 'Apparently he was a deserter and had no intention of returning to Germany, providing he even survived the war.'

They stepped through the low doorway and Etta was blinded by the dark interior. Slipping her sunglasses to the crown of her head, she blinked, trying to make the lingering burn of the sun on her retinas fade. Faint shapes sharpened into view with every movement of her eyelids. A kitchen fitted out in the style of every culinary student's wet dreams filled her vision.

Clapping a hand over her mouth so as not to let the moan escape, she dropped her purse on the floor. She ran her fingers along the stainless steel of the cooling unit, the chilled marble pastry station, roughened cast-iron pots hanging against the wall next to fine copper saucepans.

'Does it meet your specifications?'

Sniffing the air, she followed her nose to a small alcove where she discovered a small herb greenhouse. Stunned, she twirled around on the tips of her toes, feeling as giddy as a little girl handed the keys to Cinderella's castle. 'Never in my wildest dreams could I have imagined a kitchen like this. I'm almost afraid to look at a space, thinking what should be there really won't be, but I'm blown away to find out it is.'

David leaned back against the heavy oak butcher-block island and placed his hands on it, next to his hips. Her eyes followed the movement, noting how trim he was built. And the bulge developing behind the fly of his jeans. A very nicely shaped bulge.

Etta blinked and glanced back up at his face. His lips curved up at the edges, and she swore a heated invitation gleamed in his eyes. Heat gathered in her core, preparing her. Only because she kept her eyes on his face, she noticed the flaring of his nostrils.

Licking her lips, Etta shifted her gaze to David's broad shoulders. Everything about this man turned her on, and she couldn't afford to screw this opportunity up. 'When does my interview start?'

'What makes you think it hasn't?'

Catching the sardonic tone in his voice, she looked up and saw one eyebrow had winged up. 'The packet mentioned I would have to prepare a meal. Are there any guests in residence tonight?'

'All the guest rooms, except for yours, are vacant. You are to prepare three dishes of four servings each. They must be ready by nine tonight. Once you have completed the dishes, leave them here on the counter and the wait staff will serve them to Mr Schwarz and his guests. You'll be notified in the morning if you have successfully completed your interview or not.'

Etta schooled her expression into one of impassivity, not allowing her dismay at not being present for her evaluation to show. 'Does Mr Schwarz or any of his guests suffer from allergies?'

'No, no food allergies. However, proteins are preferred as raw as possible.'

Now she frowned. 'For health reasons, I must fully cook all proteins.'

David reached out and stroked his fingers across her forehead, down her cheek, following the line of her jaw before resting against the side of her throat. 'I'm sure you'll find some creative way to abide by Mr Schwarz's wishes.'

Her senses jumped and demanded she comply with his every wish, submit to his rule. She caught herself leaning in, inhaling the light scent of pine overlying a muskier unknown scent on his body. He pulled back, but the spell lingered.

Gathering her fractured thoughts together, she moved to the refrigerator and opened it to inventory exactly which proteins were available to her. 'I . . . I'll certainly do my best.'

'The phone's on the wall to your left. All you have to dial is 1 to get a hold of me if you need anything.'

She nodded. 'Thank you, I will. Shall I call you when I've completed the dishes?'

'No. Only finish by nine. When you're done, head up to your room. You're on the second floor, room 213. I'll take your luggage up now.'

'Thank you.'

For such a large man, he made no noise as he deftly lifted her suitcases and headed up the staircase across the hall from the kitchen entrance. Etta shook off the observation and glanced at the industrial clock on the far wall. Just past five. Blowing air up at her bangs she rubbed her hands together. 'It's showtime.'

* * *

Etta scraped her sleeve against her forehead, and placed three thin stems of chive in the last mould of garlic-mashed turnips. With a final look at the clock, she saw she had one minute left. She drizzled juice from the pork loin over the slices of meat and set the sauce pot down. Wiping down the plates one last time, she flung the towel towards the sink and left the kitchen as instructed.

The stairs squeaked as she rushed up them to the next level. Shining brass numbers indicated room 200 at the head of the stairs. Following the dimly lit corridor to her left, she found the room assigned to her halfway down the hallway.

'Shoot.' David hadn't given her any kind of room key. Crossing her fingers, she gripped the curved bar of the handle and twisted. The door opened with nary a squeak. She peeked in, flipping on the light switch just inside the entrance. No one was there and her suitcases lay on a king-sized bed, unopened.

She shut the door behind her and flipped the lock. She wasn't sure if she was grateful or not for the lack of guests. On the one hand, she wouldn't have to deal with anyone besides the management and staff while interviewing. On the other, there was no one around to distract her from her thoughts. A knock sounded through the room. Her heart stuttered.

She clasped a hand over it. 'Sweet baby Jesus.'

Crossing back to the door, she looked through the peephole and saw her mouth-wateringly delicious potential boss standing on the other side, his shirt temptingly unbuttoned at the collar. Etta undid the lock and opened the door. 'Hi, David. Is everything OK?'

'As far as I know. Would you like to go outside for a walk? The grounds are gorgeous this time of year.'

She smiled. 'I'd love to. Let me grab a sweater from my bag.'

His eyes twinkled. 'Don't worry about it, it's still pretty warm out, and I can guarantee you won't catch a chill.'

'At least let me freshen up. I only got up here a few minutes ago.' She tugged at the hem of her shorts, feeling grungy from the marathon in the kitchen.

'Is ten minutes enough time?'

Etta bit back the initial retort that sprang to her lips. 'More than.'

'Great, I can wait out here for you. I need to check on one of the rooms for a damage report anyway.'

'Thanks. Ten minutes.' And she shut the door on him.

Moonlight edged the tips of the trees silver as they followed a walking path through the back lawn to the forest behind. With every step, Etta felt as if they were crossing into a simpler time. One where anything she did would be free of the consequences of the real world.

The rustling of animals and the scrape of leaves on the ground filled the forest as they walked down the trail. David rested an arm across her shoulders, pulling her close into his body as the path narrowed. Etta snuggled closer, letting the warmth of his body and the scent of his freshly laundered shirt seep into her body.

'This is a gorgeous area.'

'It's definitely a perk of working here. You should know by the time we get back if Schwarz wants to hire you.'

Etta laughed and tilted her head to the side so she could look at him. 'So you're tempting me with the beauty of the forest at night in case I have thoughts about turning down an offer if I get one?'

'I doubt you'll turn down any offer made to you. Why else would you have come all the way up here if you weren't willing to change your whole way of life?'

She pursed her lips and bobbed her head. Why else indeed. She felt as if there was some unseen force guiding her to what she truly wanted and needed. And she was ready to give herself over to it. 'Insightful, as well as cute. Tell me, what are the other benefits of the job?'

He dropped his arm from her shoulders, but kept hold of one hand as they entered into a grassy clearing. 'Three weeks' vacation, three weeks' sick days, a generous retirement plan and . . .' He stopped, raised his other hand and stroked her jaw, fingers trailing along the tender skin at the meeting of her underjaw and neck.

She swallowed, clearing her throat, as the tension in the air invaded her muscles. 'And what?'

'Me, fucking you any time you want.'

Thick air choked her lungs as his eyes bored into hers. 'That's . . . That's one hell of an incentive. What if I wanted to take advantage of it now?'

'I could do nothing but oblige you.'

Turning her, David ran his fingers down the back of her neck, tracing random circles and causing the fine hairs on her body to rise. He shifted her hair over one shoulder, exposing her neck to his lips. She moaned and sank back into his embrace. The edge of his teeth scraped against the tendon of her neck. Shivers raced through her system and her nipples pebbled against her T-shirt.

One of his hands moved to her front and cupped her breast, thumb and finger tweaking and twisting the nipple.

'Your body is incredibly responsive. I want to fuck you.'

As his rich voice whispered in her ear, her inner muscles clenched. 'Yes.'

'Here in the dusk of the day, before the moon comes, I'll make you mine.'

Etta dragged the hand cupping her breast down to where she needed it most. His fingers delved beneath the hemlines of her shorts and panties and plunged into her. Her eyes flared and her breath caught in her throat. Bright lights flickered in her peripheral vision, and she prayed she'd stay coherent long enough for him to claim her.

David spun her around, and stripped her so she stood naked as a jaybird in the middle of the forest clearing. His hands cupped her face and her eyes met the endless night of his gaze.

'I claim you before all who stand here as mine.' His mouth ravaged hers.

She submitted and gloried in the dominance behind his possession. Reaching down, she cupped his sac and massaged his balls. His hips pumped against her. Needing to give him the explosive pleasure she'd already experienced, she slid to her knees. The fingers of her free hand traced the veins prominently decorating his cock.

David threaded his finger through her hair and stroked, then pulled her face closer to where she wanted to be. Poking her tongue out, she flicked it against the tip of the deep-purple head. It bobbed before her as if signalling approval of the technique. She responded with a lick from root to tip, swirling the flat of her tongue against the little opening and gathering the pre-cum.

'Yes, like that.'

Circling her fingers and thumb around the base of his cock, she repeated the move again and again. Looking up through her eyelashes, she saw how desire sharpened the planes of his face, almost transforming him. She ran her tongue around her lips, revelling in the power she held over him.

'Do it. Now.'

Obeying, she took him inside her. One inch. Two. Until she had half of his cock in her mouth and down her throat. She milked the remaining length with her hand, building a rhythm.

He braced one hand on the back of her head and pumped his

hips, meeting then changing the beat to one of his pleasure. The moment she felt the tightening of muscles at the base of his cock and his balls drawing up close to his body, he pulled out.

He flipped her over, positioned her, head touching the ground with her arse in the air, open to him. His hands stroked up and down her spine, lulling her into submission. One hand paused at the base of her spine as the other moved back to her neck, holding her down.

'You accept me, my Viking English rose.' His roughened voice crackled through the crisp night air.

'Yes.' She dug her fingers into the ground, bracing.

The tip of his cock penetrated her, his length following in a measured pace. Once he was fully seated within her, he curved his front around her back and set his teeth to her neck.

Pumping in and out, he moved a hand to her front and plucked at her clitoris.

Etta groaned and shoved back against him. He pulled the orgasm from her, and sank his fangs deep into her neck.

Etta blinked. The scent of burned sage scraped at her nostrils. Wrinkling her nose, she lifted a hand to her sore neck. David must have left one heck of a hickey. Wetness met the graze of her fingertips.

She held her fingers up and, in the dim light, she could make out the red viscous fluid staining her fingers. Blood. Her blood. *Not a hickey*.

'Mmmm. Our little dove awakens. What did you call her, David? A Viking English rose? Very appropriate description.'

'Thank you, my lord.'

Etta turned her head to the German-accented voice. Candle and firelight gilded sharp planes of bone and muscle. Whipcord lean, the man lounged naked in a wingback chair, David kneeling at his feet, both hands occupied with cock.

'Who are you? Where am I?'

'So coherent. Even after being marked a mere hour ago. I am Anton Schwarz. You are in my den. More questions?'

He steepled his fingers below his chin, the erect curvature of his penis the only indication of his body's reaction to David's ministrations.

She felt as if she were swimming in gelatin, her senses fogged to all but the erotic tableau before her. 'What are you?'

'Nosferatu.'

He pronounced it as if she should know the term. 'I don't know what that means.'

'Max Schreck? Bram Stoker? Dracula?'

'Vampires?' Etta scrambled back against the wall, her eyes darting around the room, searching for an escape. She had to be dreaming. Vampires weren't real. David hadn't taken her out into the middle of the forest, fucked her blind and then bitten her. She had to have been exhausted from her cooking session and Mr Schwarz was a kindly old man currently enjoying the feast she prepared in the dining room downstairs. Right?

Schwarz waved his hand and figures stepped out of the shadows, ringing the room. All were naked tautly muscled bodies gleaming in the firelight as if oiled. The men's erections jutted from nests of hair of all different shades and textures. The women also crossed the range of colouring and race. At each corner of every mouth a graceful white fang edged over the lower lip. They closed in, forming a corridor, focusing her attention on Schwarz.

He reached over and poured something powdery into the brazier on the table beside him. Tendrils of smoke wafted in the air to her, filling her nostrils with the scent of spiciness and heat. Something aniselike underscored the scent, but she couldn't place the dominant smell. After a minute of breathing in the air though, her body began to relax, even prepare itself for Schwarz, David, any of them. The natural fear of these predatory creatures floated away on the air like the smoke, leaving her nipples puckered, her mouth watering and cream sliding down her inner thighs.

'You are greatly honoured. Entrance into my harem is very restricted. David here was not allowed in until he was in my employ for almost ten years.'

The rich voice wove a spell over her, stilling that final tiny something deep within her soul protesting the unnaturalness of them. She felt as docile as an ignorant lamb being led to slaughter. Not even the vision of David swallowing the monster's cock and working it as she had teased and manipulated his earlier could break the trance. All she wanted was to be claimed by him, become a part of him as he became a part of her.

'As my faithful minion's bride, you are now also mine. Come.'

To deny the command would be to deny breathing. She rose from her crouch and crossed through the gauntlet. Hands reached out and stroked her hips, breasts, arms, back, buttocks.

Schwarz's fingers wove through David's hair before yanking David's head away from his still engorged cock. Two lines of blood trailed down on either side. Cupping her chin with his free hand, Schwarz bent down, his black gaze staring into her eyes. Etta's heart fluttered, heat suffused her body and something wet pooled between her thighs.

'So David staked his claim to you in the woods, I claim you before the harem. Submit to him, to me.'

'Yes.'

His lips crashed down on hers. She first felt the sandpaper roughness of his tongue and then the lethal sharpness of his teeth scrape against her tender skin. Gasping, she opened to herself to his assault.

He thrust his tongue into her mouth, short bursts of male muscle, stroking in and out. He clasped her head and pulled her forwards. She collapsed against his thigh, her breasts pillowed on rock-hard muscle. Scrabbling for purchase and balance on the slick marble floor, her eyes flared at the penetration of a cock into her aching pussy.

Schwarz's gaze held her enthralled as she submitted to the fucking. Desperately, she tried to push back to increase the friction to send her over that final precipice, but Schwarz clasped her body still. Sharp fast thrusts preceded the climax of the person reaming her. Mere seconds separated the moment when the softening cock slid from her body and was replaced with the next one.

Etta moaned as the fatter one slid home. Her inner muscles rippled, caressing the new invader. Schwarz broke the kiss, but kept his firm grip on her head and shoulders. His lips caressed her ear long moments before his breath slid over her.

'Tell me, how does it feel give the ultimate pleasure without being able to take yours?'

He nipped her ear lobe and lava erupted into her veins. She strained, but her climax teased, just out of reach.

'Tell me.'

'I want to come.' Her fingers dug into his thigh.

'You will, little dove, when you have earned the right.'

Tears leaked out of the corners of her eyes, and she whimpered. One whisper of a touch on her clit, her breasts, her lips and she would come, but all she got was the pleasurable pounding of cock into her pussy. As soon as one finished, another took his place.

She lost count after the fifth man entered her, her nerves raw with bombarding sensations. Only when her quim was empty of anything but thick cream did she finally return to awareness.

Soft hands stroked her back, her arms, her sides, avoiding any trigger points, soothing away the numbness. They lifted her limp body and carried her to a padded platform. Stretching her limbs out, fur-lined manacles clamped around her wrists and ankles. Schwarz climbed up between her legs and, gripping her hips, he pulled them up. A silk pillow slid underneath, canting her up and open to his every whim.

Her gaze remained focused on the cock spearing out from the centre of his body. In the dim light, she couldn't make out the coloration, but if her eyes were in tune with her body, he would be the largest man to merge with her tonight.

His head swivelled around, his hand pumping up and down his cock. 'Tonight our harem is complete. The one we have waited for joins us. Through her turning, we are bound and all bow before her.'

'Hail, hail, hail.' The shouts reverberated through her body. Tremors racked her system and all she could think of was the need for Schwarz to fuck her, claim her, turn her. She undulated her hips, her inner thighs stroking up and down the hair on his outer thighs.

He looked down at her and snarled. She bared her teeth back at him and he threw his head back and laughed.

'Fuck me.'

He bent down and turned her head to one side, baring her neck to him. 'My pleasure, little dove.'

His cock drove into her as his fangs stabbed into her body. The climax just out of reach the entire night now washed over her, yanking her down into a tidal wave of lust, blood, power and life.

Visit the Black Lace website at
www.black-lace-books.com

LOOK OUT FOR THE ALL-NEW BLACK LACE BOOKS – AVAILABLE NOW!

All books priced £7.99 in the UK. Please note publication dates apply to the UK only. For other territories, please contact your retailer.

To be published in November 2008

THE NINETY DAYS OF GENEVIEVE
Lucinda Carrington

ISBN 978 0 352 34201 0

A ninety-day sex contract wasn't exactly what Genevieve Loften had in mind when she began business negotiations with the arrogant and attractive James Sinclair. As a career move she wanted to go along with it; the pay-off was potentially huge. However, she didn't imagine that he would make her the star performer in a series of increasingly kinky and exotic fantasies. Thrown into a world of sexual misadventure, Genevieve learns how to balance her high-pressure career with the twilight world of fetishism and debauchery.

THE NEW RAKES
Nikki Magennis
ISBN 978 0 352 34503 5

Fuelled by Kara's sexy performances, The New Rakes are poised for rock & roll stardom. And when Mike Greene, the charismatic head of a record company, offers the band a deal, it seems their dreams are about to come true. But Kara and Mike have history and this time he wants more than a professional relationship. Already in the thick of a love-hate relationship with her guitarist Tam, Kara's tempestuous affairs with both men threaten to spoil everything. Tangled in a web of sex, power and deceit, she finally has to choose between the limelight and true love.

To be published in December 2008

THE GIFT OF SHAME
Sarah Hope-Walker
ISBN 978 0 352 34202 7

Sad, sultry Helen flies between London, Paris and the Caribbean chasing whatever physical pleasures she can get to tear her mind from a deep, deep loss. Her glamorous life-style and charged sensual escapades belie a widow's grief. When she meets handsome, rich Jeffrey she is shocked and yet intrigued by his masterful, domineering behaviour. Soon, Helen is forced to confront the forbidden desires hiding within herself – and forced to undergo a startling metamorphosis from a meek and modest lady into a bristling, voracious wanton.

TO SEEK A MASTER
Monica Belle

ISBN 978 0 352 34507 3

Sexy daydreams are shy Laura's only escape from the dull routines of her life. But with the arrival of an email ordering her to dress provocatively, she wonders if her secret fantasies about her colleagues are about to become true. Unable to resist the new and more daring instructions that arrive by email, she begins to slip deeper into dangerous water with several men. But when her controller finally reveals himself, she's in for a shock and a far greater involvement in his illicit games.

ALSO LOOK OUT FOR

THE NEW BLACK LACE BOOK OF WOMEN'S SEXUAL FANTASIES
Edited and compiled by Mitzi Szereto

ISBN 978 0 352 34172 3

The second anthology of detailed sexual fantasies contributed by women from all over the world. The book is a result of a year's research by an expert on erotic writing and gives a fascinating insight into the rich diversity of the female sexual imagination.

Black Lace Booklist

Information is correct at time of printing. To avoid disappointment, check availability before ordering. Go to www.black-lace-books.com.
All books are priced £7.99 unless another price is given.

BLACK LACE BOOKS WITH A CONTEMPORARY SETTING

- [ ] THE ANGELS' SHARE Maya Hess — ISBN 978 0 352 34043 6
- [ ] ASKING FOR TROUBLE Kristina Lloyd — ISBN 978 0 352 33362 9
- [ ] BLACK LIPSTICK KISSES Monica Belle — ISBN 978 0 352 33885 3   £6.99
- [ ] THE BLUE GUIDE Carrie Williams — ISBN 978 0 352 34132 7
- [ ] THE BOSS Monica Belle — ISBN 978 0 352 34088 7
- [ ] BOUND IN BLUE Monica Belle — ISBN 978 0 352 34012 2
- [ ] CAMPAIGN HEAT Gabrielle Marcola — ISBN 978 0 352 33941 6
- [ ] CAT SCRATCH FEVER Sophie Mouette — ISBN 978 0 352 34021 4
- [ ] CIRCUS EXCITE Nikki Magennis — ISBN 978 0 352 34033 7
- [ ] CLUB CRÈME Primula Bond — ISBN 978 0 352 33907 2   £6.99
- [ ] CONFESSIONAL Judith Roycroft — ISBN 978 0 352 33421 3
- [ ] CONTINUUM Portia Da Costa — ISBN 978 0 352 33120 5
- [ ] DANGEROUS CONSEQUENCES Pamela Rochford — ISBN 978 0 352 33185 4
- [ ] DARK DESIGNS Madelynne Ellis — ISBN 978 0 352 34075 7
- [ ] THE DEVIL INSIDE Portia Da Costa — ISBN 978 0 352 32993 6
- [ ] EQUAL OPPORTUNITIES Mathilde Madden — ISBN 978 0 352 34070 2
- [ ] FIRE AND ICE Laura Hamilton — ISBN 978 0 352 33486 2
- [ ] GONE WILD Maria Eppie — ISBN 978 0 352 33670 5
- [ ] HOTBED Portia Da Costa — ISBN 978 0 352 33614 9
- [ ] IN PURSUIT OF ANNA Natasha Rostova — ISBN 978 0 352 34060 3
- [ ] IN THE FLESH Emma Holly — ISBN 978 0 352 34117 4
- [ ] LEARNING TO LOVE IT Alison Tyler — ISBN 978 0 352 33535 7
- [ ] MAD ABOUT THE BOY Mathilde Madden — ISBN 978 0 352 34001 6
- [ ] MAKE YOU A MAN Anna Clare — ISBN 978 0 352 34006 1
- [ ] MAN HUNT Cathleen Ross — ISBN 978 0 352 33583 8
- [ ] THE MASTER OF SHILDEN Lucinda Carrington — ISBN 978 0 352 33140 3
- [ ] MIXED DOUBLES Zoe le Verdier — ISBN 978 0 352 33312 4   £6.99
- [ ] MIXED SIGNALS Anna Clare — ISBN 978 0 352 33889 1   £6.99
- [ ] MS BEHAVIOUR Mini Lee — ISBN 978 0 352 33962 1

❏ PACKING HEAT Karina Moore   ISBN 978 0 352 33356 8   £6.99
❏ PAGAN HEAT Monica Belle   ISBN 978 0 352 33974 4
❏ PEEP SHOW Mathilde Madden   ISBN 978 0 352 33924 9
❏ THE POWER GAME Carrera Devonshire ISBN 978 0 352 33990 4
❏ THE PRIVATE UNDOING OF A PUBLIC SERVANT   ISBN 978 0 352 34066 5
   Leonie Martel
❏ RUDE AWAKENING Pamela Kyle   ISBN 978 0 352 33036 9
❏ SAUCE FOR THE GOOSE Mary Rose Maxwell ISBN 978 0 352 33492 3
❏ SPLIT Kristina Lloyd   ISBN 978 0 352 34154 9
❏ STELLA DOES HOLLYWOOD Stella Black ISBN 978 0 352 33588 3
❏ THE STRANGER Portia Da Costa   ISBN 978 0 352 33211 0
❏ SUITE SEVENTEEN Portia Da Costa   ISBN 978 0 352 34109 9
❏ TONGUE IN CHEEK Tabitha Flyte   ISBN 978 0 352 33484 8
❏ THE TOP OF HER GAME Emma Holly   ISBN 978 0 352 34116 7
❏ UNNATURAL SELECTION Alaine Hood   ISBN 978 0 352 33963 8
❏ VELVET GLOVE Emma Holly   ISBN 978 0 352 34115 0
❏ VILLAGE OF SECRETS Mercedes Kelly ISBN 978 0 352 33344 5
❏ WILD BY NATURE Monica Belle   ISBN 978 0 352 33915 7   £6.99
❏ WILD CARD Madeline Moore   ISBN 978 0 352 34038 2
❏ WING OF MADNESS Mae Nixon   ISBN 978 0 352 34099 3

BLACK LACE BOOKS WITH AN HISTORICAL SETTING

❏ THE BARBARIAN GEISHA Charlotte Royal   ISBN 978 0 352 33267 7
❏ BARBARIAN PRIZE Deanna Ashford   ISBN 978 0 352 34017 7
❏ THE CAPTIVATION Natasha Rostova   ISBN 978 0 352 33234 9
❏ DARKER THAN LOVE Kristina Lloyd   ISBN 978 0 352 33279 0
❏ WILD KINGDOM Deanna Ashford   ISBN 978 0 352 33549 4
❏ DIVINE TORMENT Janine Ashbless   ISBN 978 0 352 33719 1
❏ FRENCH MANNERS Olivia Christie   ISBN 978 0 352 33214 1
❏ LORD WRAXALL'S FANCY Anna Lieff Saxby ISBN 978 0 352 33080 2
❏ NICOLE'S REVENGE Lisette Allen   ISBN 978 0 352 32984 4
❏ THE SENSES BEJEWELLED Cleo Cordell ISBN 978 0 352 32904 2   £6.99
❏ THE SOCIETY OF SIN Sian Lacey Taylder ISBN 978 0 352 34080 1
❏ TEMPLAR PRIZE Deanna Ashford   ISBN 978 0 352 34137 2
❏ UNDRESSING THE DEVIL Angel Strand ISBN 978 0 352 33938 6

BLACK LACE BOOKS WITH A PARANORMAL THEME

☐ BRIGHT FIRE Maya Hess   ISBN 978 0 352 34104 4

☐ BURNING BRIGHT Janine Ashbless   ISBN 978 0 352 34085 6

☐ CRUEL ENCHANTMENT Janine Ashbless   ISBN 978 0 352 33483 1

☐ FLOOD Anna Clare   ISBN 978 0 352 34094 8

☐ GOTHIC BLUE Portia Da Costa   ISBN 978 0 352 33075 8

☐ THE PRIDE Edie Bingham   ISBN 978 0 352 33997 3

☐ THE SILVER COLLAR Mathilde Madden   ISBN 978 0 352 34141 9

☐ THE TEN VISIONS Olivia Knight   ISBN 978 0 352 34119 8

BLACK LACE ANTHOLOGIES

☐ BLACK LACE QUICKIES 1 Various   ISBN 978 0 352 34126 6   £2.99

☐ BLACK LACE QUICKIES 2 Various   ISBN 978 0 352 34127 3   £2.99

☐ BLACK LACE QUICKIES 3 Various   ISBN 978 0 352 34128 0   £2.99

☐ BLACK LACE QUICKIES 4 Various   ISBN 978 0 352 34129 7   £2.99

☐ BLACK LACE QUICKIES 5 Various   ISBN 978 0 352 34130 3   £2.99

☐ BLACK LACE QUICKIES 6 Various   ISBN 978 0 352 34133 4   £2.99

☐ BLACK LACE QUICKIES 7 Various   ISBN 978 0 352 34146 4   £2.99

☐ BLACK LACE QUICKIES 8 Various   ISBN 978 0 352 34147 1   £2.99

☐ BLACK LACE QUICKIES 9 Various   ISBN 978 0 352 34155 6   £2.99

☐ MORE WICKED WORDS Various   ISBN 978 0 352 33487 9   £6.99

☐ WICKED WORDS 3 Various   ISBN 978 0 352 33522 7   £6.99

☐ WICKED WORDS 4 Various   ISBN 978 0 352 33603 3   £6.99

☐ WICKED WORDS 5 Various   ISBN 978 0 352 33642 2   £6.99

☐ WICKED WORDS 6 Various   ISBN 978 0 352 33690 3   £6.99

☐ WICKED WORDS 7 Various   ISBN 978 0 352 33743 6   £6.99

☐ WICKED WORDS 8 Various   ISBN 978 0 352 33787 0   £6.99

☐ WICKED WORDS 9 Various   ISBN 978 0 352 33860 0

☐ WICKED WORDS 10 Various   ISBN 978 0 352 33893 8

☐ THE BEST OF BLACK LACE 2 Various   ISBN 978 0 352 33718 4

☐ WICKED WORDS: SEX IN THE OFFICE Various   ISBN 978 0 352 33944 7

☐ WICKED WORDS: SEX AT THE SPORTS CLUB Various   ISBN 978 0 352 33991 1

☐ WICKED WORDS: SEX ON HOLIDAY Various   ISBN 978 0 352 33961 4

☐ WICKED WORDS: SEX IN UNIFORM Various   ISBN 978 0 352 34002 3

☐ WICKED WORDS: SEX IN THE KITCHEN Various   ISBN 978 0 352 34018 4

☐ WICKED WORDS: SEX ON THE MOVE Various   ISBN 978 0 352 34034 4

☐ WICKED WORDS: SEX AND MUSIC Various   ISBN 978 0 352 34061 0

To find out the latest information about Black Lace titles, check out the website: www.black-lace-books.com or send for a booklist with complete synopses by writing to:

Black Lace Booklist, Virgin Books Ltd
Virgin Books
Random House
20 Vauxhall Bridge Road,
London SW1V 2SA

Please include an SAE of decent size. Please note only British stamps are valid.

Our privacy policy
We will not disclose information you supply us to any other parties. We will not disclose any information which identifies you personally to any person without your express consent.

From time to time we may send out information about Black Lace books and special offers. Please tick here if you do <u>not</u> wish to receive Black Lace information. ❑

Please send me the books I have ticked above.

Name ....

Address ....

....

....

....

Post Code ....

Send to: Virgin Books Cash Sales, Random House,
20 Vauxhall Bridge Road, London SW1V 2SA.

US customers: for prices and details of how to order
books for delivery by mail, call 888-330-8477.

Please enclose a cheque or postal order, made payable
to Virgin Books Ltd, to the value of the books you have
ordered plus postage and packing costs as follows:

UK and BFPO – £1.00 for the first book, 50p for each
subsequent book.

Overseas (including Republic of Ireland) – £2.00 for
the first book, £1.00 for each subsequent book.

If you would prefer to pay by VISA, ACCESS/MASTERCARD,
DINERS CLUB, AMEX or SWITCH, please write your card
number and expiry date here: ....

....

Signature ....

Please allow up to 28 days for delivery.